SON *of* A GUN

ALSO BY RANDYE LORDON

Brotherly Love
Sister's Keeper
Father Forgive Me
Mother May I
Say Uncle
East of Niece

RANDYE LORDON

SON *of* A GUN

ST. MARTIN'S MINOTAUR 🐟 NEW YORK

www.minotaurbooks.com

Library of Congress Cataloging-in-Publication Data
Lordon, Randye.
    Son of a gun / Randye Lordon.
        p. cm.
    ISBN 0-312-29131-0
    EAN 978-0312-29131-0
    1. Sloane, Sydney (Fictitious character)—Fiction. 2. Women private investigators—New York (State)—New York—Fiction. 3. Police—Violence against—Fiction. 4. Illegitimate children—Fiction. 5. New York (N.Y.)—Fiction. 6. Birthfathers—Fiction. 7. Lesbians—Fiction. I. Title

PS3562.O7524 S+
813'.54—dc22   **3 1813 00296 2982**   2004051415

First Edition: February 2005

10   9   8   7   6   5   4   3   2   1

This book is dedicated to safe havens past and present.

The Italian Countessa, friend and mentor.
I hope to see you again, here or there, wherever you are.

Jude and Annie's mom, compassionate, courageous, and clever, a light at the end of any number of tunnels.

Thank you. Thank you. Thank you.

And
finally
Brutus.

ACKNOWLEDGMENTS

Son of a Gun could not have been written without the help of numerous very special people, some of whom I knew, others whom I have come to know, and still others whom I have yet to meet but who nonetheless offered their time and information as if they were old friends.

Dean Speir and Jason Frank are many things to many people, but these gentlemen and scholars repeatedly set me back on the right path whenever I veered too far off and hollered for help.

Stacy Rabinowitz is one of New York's Finest. She has helped me in the past and stepped up at bat again this time, answering my E-mails and phone calls, as if she really had time for all this. From what I understand, her associate Frank Torres fielded a number of questions, not unlike the Great Oz behind the curtain. Thank you, Frank.

Thanks also to Louise Berenson, Timothy Smith (senior biostatician in the Bureau of Biometrics), and Wenhui Aoi at the New York State Department of Health; Detective Walter Burnes and Officer Sullivan at the Office of the Deputy Commissioner of Public Information; and a nice guy named Tyrone at the Parks Department.

As always, my friends have been enormously helpful. Susan Genis, Dr. Jay Solnick, Joanne Spina, Sarah "B" Segal, Dr. Tina Hayward, Arlene Cruella McCoy, Whitney Leigh Wallace Griffith,

Shan Wilson, Dr. Shawn Cannon, and Susan Rose. I thank you all for your intelligence, your generosity, and your patience.

There are those who offered not only information and inspiration but also the basics—shelter, friendship, shoulders, and love: Pearl Wolf, Shellie Goldstein, Colette Roy, Christa, Mark, Lizzie, Frankly, Butch, Suzanne, Denise, Stacy, and the melodic Linda Calder . . . hard times, new friends. Thank you.

And last, but not least, Carol Edwards. Thank you.

SON *of* A GUN

ONE

"*I don't know why you* couldn't call a handyman," I grumbled to my elderly aunt Minnie as I replaced the washer on her kitchen tap.

"It's too simple for them. I'd look like an idiot," she said, puffing on a cigarette by the window in her Park Avenue kitchen and indulging my dog, Auggie, with treats of last night's porterhouse.

"Notice how I don't comment on the fact that you *are* an idiot."

"That was nice. Thanks."

"In the future, if you would kindly remember that I am a private detective and not a handy gal, we will live out the rest of your life in relative peace."

"Yes, but it was my handy gal who fixed the faucet," she said slyly.

"Shut up."

"Besides, we'll all get enough peace when I die. Might as well stir things up now. And what are you complaining about? A washer is nothing. In return, you get homemade popovers. I slave for you, and this is the thanks I get."

"Thank you Aunt Minnie," I said as I tossed out the old washer and nuzzled Auggie, who was pushing her seventy-pound bundle of soft fur and love at me. Half Samoyed and half golden retriever, she sighed with an almost contagious contentment.

"Why are you so grumpy? It's a beautiful morning. Don't tell me you miss your girlfriend already." She was referring to my partner,

Leslie, who was at that very moment en route to Kennedy Airport for a flight to California, where she was to meet with Christa Maiwald, a renowned artist looking for a new interior decorator.

"No," I said too quickly.

"Okay, what's up?" she asked as she pulled the popovers from the oven. "And don't say 'nothing,' because I'm too old to play emotional hide-and-seek. Remember, we're playing Beat the Clock with my lifeline."

"Oh shush, you're going to outlive all of us," I said, pouring another cup of coffee.

"Enough with my longevity. Could we please talk about your relationship?"

I didn't say a word. It had been a difficult morning.

"What?" she asked, pausing as she placed the warm popovers into a lined basket.

"Nothing."

"Bullshit." She set out strawberry, almond, and plain butter, along with a plate of soft cheese and a smaller basket of baguettes. "You might as well tell me now and get it over with, because you know I'll make your life a misery until you do."

"We didn't part on the best of terms, and that always bothers me, especially when one of us is flying."

"Why? What happened?"

I shook my head and tightened my jaw.

"Just spit it out."

"I learned last night that she tried to hire Miguel without my knowing it," I explained, referring to one of the operatives at Cabe Sloane Investigations, the business I own with my longtime friend and associate, Max Cabe.

"To do what?" She lifted a brow as she motioned for me to sit.

"She wanted him to get background information on Harold." After nearly a dozen years of widowhood and two months in a whirlwind romance, Leslie's mother, Dorothy, was going to tie the knot with her seventy-four-year-old Romeo, a man her children barely knew. This disturbed them enough to want to look into his background.

2

"Dot's beau?" Minnie asked.

"Yup." I slathered strawberry butter onto a steaming popover.

"What's that about? The wedding is in a few weeks."

"I know. This is a potential nightmare. I mean, I like Harold. He's a little too country club and John Waynish for me, but hey, I'm not about to marry him." As far as I was concerned, Dorothy was happy for the first time since I had met her years earlier, when I'd learned things about her that no one else in her family knew. I'd respected that confidence for all these years, but that information only made this situation harder for me. Dorothy and her husband, Jesse (Leslie's father), had not been intimate with one another for many years before his passing. Now, in her seventies, Dorothy had rediscovered herself as a sexual being. Who the hell was I to aid and abet in taking that away from her?

"Is it just Leslie, or her siblings, too? Minnie asked.

"Everybody. Actually, more Marcia and Paul than Leslie, but she's the one who tried to hire Miguel."

"I don't get it. Why didn't she just ask you?"

"She didn't think I would want to get involved because of Lloyd," I said, referring to my past experiences with her brother.

"Well, she's got a point there," Minnie said, handing off a piece of baguette to Auggie.

"Don't feed her from the table, Min."

"Technically, this isn't a table," she said, because we were, in fact, sitting at a counter. "Why did she wait until now?"

"She actually talked to Miguel a few days ago, but naturally he wouldn't take it on unless it was sanctioned by Max and me. And Leslie was reticent to tell me, because from the beginning, when everyone got up in arms about Dorothy getting married, I suggested that they all seemed more concerned about their own interests than their mother's happiness. I assumed that what they all feared, while not voicing it, was what would happen to their inheritance if this *interloper*, as Marcia constantly refers to him, married their mom and got his mitts on her bank account, which is, as you know, flush."

"You have such a winning way with people, don't you, dear?"

"People don't like it when you speak your mind." I polished off a popover and tried not to meet her gaze, which I knew was leveled directly at me. I continued in my own defense. "The thing is, Leslie *assumed* how I would respond and chose not to tell me because of that."

"But she did tell you."

"Relationships are about communication, and if you don't communicate, then you have no relationship," I mumbled.

"Oh my God, could you be any more judgmental? Of course you two have a relationship, and a damned good one, you idiot. She was afraid to talk to you, she finally did, and when she did, you responded in the very way she thought you would—which is what kept her quiet in the first place. What's wrong with you?"

"There is nothing wrong with me, and why are you rushing in to defend Leslie when I—"

"When you're acting holier-than-thou? I don't know."

I grabbed a piece of baguette and slathered on some cheese, neither of which I wanted but which I brought to my mouth as a means of keeping quiet. It was a delicious distraction.

"All I'm saying, sweetheart, is that while I understand how hurt you were by her not talking to you first, you still have to acknowledge that she *did* open up—and that is communication."

I shifted uneasily in my seat. I knew that Minnie was right, just as Leslie had been right to assume that I wouldn't have wanted my office involved in anything related to the Washburns, if only because of the history and the fact that her siblings have always seemed uncomfortable with me. Being that both her sister, Marcia, and her brother Paul are passive-aggressive, it's always been something unspoken, but just because something is ignored doesn't mean it doesn't exist.

"Okay," I finally said.

"Okay what?"

"Okay, I'll call and apologize."

"Don't do it for me," she said, feigning innocence. "Do it for Auggie." She sounded as if she were talking to a baby as she rubbed the expectant furry face between her veined hands.

At that moment, my cell phone rang. I was certain it was Leslie calling to tell me how much she loved me.

I wish it had been.

"Hey," I said as I moved out of the kitchen for privacy.

It took a second before I realized that the voice on the other end of the line wasn't Leslie's but, rather, that of my good friend Peggy Dexter-Cannady. I waited as she tried to stop crying long enough to tell me her husband, John, a police officer, had been shot and which hospital he had been taken to. It was surreal—watching Auggie lazily eat breakfast, while on the other end of the phone my old friend's world was unraveling.

It's amazing how much information a person can process in a nanosecond. As soon as I recognized Peggy's voice, I knew something hideous had happened. I understood her panic, and I realized that, despite my own fear, I had to keep a level head. I stood there white-knuckling the telephone receiver and promised I would meet her at the hospital.

Dogs, though the most perfect creatures on the planet, require attention, and I knew that without Leslie I would be in a bind, because Auggie was just at the point of having to cross her hind legs.

"Min, I have to go. Can you take care of Auggie for a little while?"

"Sure, what's up?"

"John Cannady was shot. I have to go to the hospital."

"Oh my God. Is it bad?"

"I don't know, but it can't be good. I'll have Kerry pick up Auggie later, okay?" My secretary, Kerry Norman, is always happy to have Auggie to play with.

"Call me. Let me know what happens."

"I will." I left without kissing her good-bye, without reminding her that I loved her, without thanking her for the popovers or the dog-sitting.

In the back of the taxi, I tried to call Leslie, but her phone was already off. I simply left a message that I loved her.

* * *

5

By the time I arrived at the hospital, the members of the media were already gathering. This was only to be expected, since John was a cop, and a captain, at that. There was also a group of officers gathering outside to lend Peggy whatever support she might need.

I found her in a room that had probably been an office before, since it was small and one wall had wire-mesh windows that looked out into the hallway, but now it was modestly furnished with orange plastic chairs and a framed print of a forest in the snow. With her was a uniformed officer, a good friend of theirs, Hank Yarberg, who had known John since high school. Black mascara had streaked down and dried on Peggy's gaunt cheeks. Her eyes were swollen and bloodshot, and her hair, which was now short and red, with dark roots, seemed to have been charged with static electricity, which made her look like a long, slender chipmunk on speed. She wore a gray Donna Karan suit with a white silk blouse, both of which were stained with blood. She had been staring blindly at the floor, chewing on a nail before, she saw me. As soon as I entered the room, she stopped. Her lower lip quivered as she reached out for me. Hank looked relieved when he saw me.

In another lifetime, I was a cop, and though I'd been a private investigator for a long time, I still had a lot of friends who were on the force, friends like John. Fortunately, I'd had very little experience with such situations.

Hank stood awkwardly to the side as Peggy and I embraced. He kept his big hands thrust deep into his pockets, while his sad brown eyes stayed glued to a spot just beyond us.

I acknowledged him with a look as I rocked Peggy in my arms.

The sergeant nodded and squeezed his lips together.

The muffled sounds of the hospital ER filtered past the closed door and the thick glass. I knew that outside on the street news crews were converging, ready to record the events as they unfolded, as reporters always put it.

When Peggy showed signs of loosening her grasp on me, I asked Hank if he would hunt down a bottle of water for Peggy. I knew how hard it was to sit in a room with someone while waiting for life or death news. Asking Hank to find bottled water gave

Peggy and me privacy, while at the same time giving him something to do.

"What happened?" I asked once she'd let go and started pacing the small room. I sat on an orange plastic chair, my back to the windows. As I waited for her to find the words, I studied the poster on the wall. In the foreground, a branch of a tree was covered with ice, and beneath the photograph was the title: CHANGE. Just under that was written "*There is nothing permanent except change.*" I wondered who had picked out this particular artwork for the hospital and if they'd purchased it in the hopes that the sentiment would be somehow comforting or inspirational. You figure if you're in an emergency room waiting area, you are in the midst of change and hardly need a reminder.

Finally, she said, "I don't know what happened." She brought her thumb to her mouth and started scraping her teeth against the nail. "It was like every other morning. I got Lucy ready for camp and then John walked her there. While he was out, I made our breakfast protein shakes and put the toast in the toaster. I was excited because I had found this health bread that he likes and I was going to surprise him with it. Silly, isn't it, the things we can get jazzed up about?" She stopped and pressed her palm against her mouth. When she could catch her breath, she whispered, "It's so easy to take everyday things for granted. And then you don't even know what happened, but suddenly everything is wrong. I was listening to NPR, but I had it on in the living room and I had turned up the volume for 'Morning Edition.' He took a long time getting back, and I was getting peeved, because he knew I had an important meeting this morning." Her voice inched up a register as she fought tears. "I thought if he'd gotten stuck talking to our neighbor Mrs. Murphy, he'd need help getting free. She's lonely and, well, as nice as she is, it can sometimes be hard to disengage with her. Anyway, about halfway down the hallway, I saw that the front door was open. Then I noticed what I thought was a foot and a leg, but it didn't make sense, because the toe was pointing to the ceiling, like whoever was attached to it was lying down." Peggy sank onto a chair at the far end of the room, as if she needed to keep her distance.

"I realized that it was John's shoe. I remember screaming his name. He was lying on the floor, his palms up, his eyes closed, his head propped against the baseboard, and the newspaper was opened at his side." She stopped and clutched her stomach. "Oh God, Sydney."

When I got up and touched her shoulder, her arms flayed, as if fending me off, and I knew that in a way she was fending me off because the last thing she wanted at that very second was comfort. I understood that, as faulty as her reasoning might be, Peggy felt responsible for not having been able to help John. It is that basic element of love, the instinct to protect, which can either produce miracles or make us crazy.

My heart was breaking for my friend, but there was nothing I could do other than keep my distance and wait for her to find her own way.

"When I knelt down beside him, I saw the hole in his shirt and the blood. I mean, I knew he had been shot, but I hadn't heard anything." She spoke softly to her hands. "I hadn't seen anyone." She brought her fingertips to her forehead and started rubbing. "I started screaming, but I don't remember much else. The next thing I knew, John was on a gurney and they were telling me I couldn't ride with him in the ambulance. By this point, there were police everywhere. One of the neighbors must have called and said a cop had been shot. Hank was there, and he drove me over here. God, the whole thing is just so horrible."

I knelt in front of her and asked, "Where's Lucy?"

"At camp. But I called Marcy and asked if she'd pick her up and take care of her until I could find out what was happening. I have to call the camp and let them know that it's okay for Marcy to pick her up." Marcy was not only a close friend and a police officer but also the wife of my business partner, Max Cabe. Peggy suddenly grasped my hand. "Oh my God. Do you think Lucy's in danger?" She squeezed my fingers until they started to feel numb.

"No. Absolutely not. And you know she's safe with Marcy. She's a cop, so don't even worry about that."

Just then, the door opened behind me. I twisted around and

saw Hank filling the doorway. He cradled a large brown bag in his arms and said, "Peg, I just heard that the mayor's on his way over."

"I don't want to see anyone," she whimpered.

Hank and I shared a helpless glance. Finally, I said, "He wants to offer his support, Peg, whether you voted for him or not." I waited to see if this would bring about even the hint of a smile. It didn't, so I added, "Look, I believe in the ripple effect of love. Maybe it can't move mountains, but it *can* make a difference. And let's face it, we could use all the help we can get right now."

TWO

By three o'clock that afternoon, the news was good: John had survived surgery, and though the recovery process was going to be difficult, at least he was going to live. The hollow-point bullet had entered at a lateral angle, damaging his right ventricle and lung but stopping at the shoulder blade. All things considered, John was a lucky man.

It wasn't until 9:00 P.M. that Peggy and I left the hospital. When we got back to her building, there were several plainclothes police officers stationed on the block. One of the officers, a handsome young man with a scruffy goatee, stopped Peggy and asked how John was. After she told him that he seemed to be out of danger, I asked if they had had any luck with the investigation during the day.

He shook his head as he rubbed the back of his neck. "From what I know, not yet. But this is New York, and John is a popular man. It's just a matter of time before we find the putz who did it. Within minutes after the shooting, this block and several others were shut down as tight as a drum and our people were all over it. Officers are working overtime to do what they can to help, because . . . well, because it's John."

We thanked the officer, then talked to the doorman for a minute. He was able to tell us that the police had taken the tapes from the security video cameras in the building. We already knew that the men and women directly involved in the investigation had moved quickly and thoroughly and, out of deference to five-year-old Lucy, ordered that the crime scene be untaped.

By the time we made it up to the apartment, we found Marcy and Lucy asleep on Lucy's bed, a dog-eared copy of A.A. Milne's *Winnie-the-Pooh* open between them.

Peggy tucked Lucy in for the second time and then went to take a hot bath, while Marcy opened a bottle of Chianti and I threw together a spinach salad, despite Peggy's protests. She hadn't eaten all day, and I was starved. Besides, feeding people, especially someone in Peggy's situation, always helps me feel as if I'm doing something useful.

In the kitchen, I gave Marcy the medical update and she told me about her day with Lucy.

"Look, she may be five, but she's a cop's daughter, and I think they're a different breed. At first, she was so excited to see me and go to the zoo that she didn't even ask what was up. It wasn't until we got to the penguin house that she asked where her folks were."

"What did you say?"

Marcy looked helpless and shrugged. "I didn't know what to say. I mean, I knew it was coming and I *thought* I was ready—hell, I'd even talked to a friend who's a therapist—but as soon as I saw her, I realized that I wasn't prepared. First, I didn't know if Peggy would want me telling Lucy anything, or if that was something she would want to do. That made me hesitate, but I realized that I had to tell her something. And you know I can't lie."

"You told her he was shot?" I froze in disbelief.

"No, of course not. But I did say, 'You know your daddy's a police officer, and how much he loves his job, right?' Naturally she said yes, so I said, as if it were no big deal, that her daddy had been hurt at work but that he was going to be absolutely fine."

"That's it?"

"That's it. Then I just waited for her to ask questions. My therapist friend told me that sometimes kids don't want to know anything and adults wind up giving them more information than they can handle. I think the rule of thumb is to wait for the questions

12

and then answer only in general terms. If they want to know more, they'll ask."

"Did she ask?"

Marcy took a sip of wine and nodded. "Yes. She wanted to know where Peggy was, and I told her that her mom was with her daddy. That was it. Now, I admit I kept the poor kid so busy that she didn't have time to think, but she was obviously concerned. When we got home and Peggy wasn't here, Lucy asked if her mom and dad were coming home. I promised her that her mom would be here when she woke up."

"Fortunately, you are a woman who keeps her word."

"You betcha."

Neither of us knew what was happening with the actual investigation, other than the fact that there were a zillion theories floating around—everything from it being a revenge shooting to a botched robbery—but nothing substantial. All we knew from peripheral sources was that no one in Peggy and John's apartment building had seen or heard anything unusual before Peggy had started screaming.

My cell phone rang just as Marcy was speculating that because there was no obvious sign of struggle, there was the likelihood that John knew the shooter. The caller was my friend and secretary, Kerry Norman, who had picked up Auggie from Aunt Minnie.

"Hey, how are you guys?" she asked without preamble.

"Well, it looks like he's going to make it."

"Yeah, it's all over the news."

"How's Auggie?"

"Good. How's Peggy?"

"Hanging in there. Did Leslie call the office?" I asked, disturbed that I hadn't heard from her, though surely she must have arrived in California long ago.

"No. Does she know about John?"

"It's not the sort of thing you leave on a voice mail. I just left a message for her to call."

Before we got much further, my call waiting kicked in. Thinking it was Leslie, I ended the conversation with Kerry. I was wrong.

It was Miguel Leigh, who will someday be a partner in the firm.

"Yo, Sydney," he shouted over the voices raised in the background. I knew Miguel was at his mother's apartment, where family—young and old—gathered nightly. It was a struggle to hear him over the din.

"How's the capt'n? Is he okay?" he asked, referring to John.

"He will be." I gave him a brief update.

"It's weird to know the guy they're talking about on the news," he told me when I was through.

"Yeah. Listen, tomorrow I want you to start a background check on Harold Hardy."

"Mrs. W.'s beau."

"That's right. Meet me at the office at nine and then we'll go over everything, okay?" I had decided at some point during the day that if Leslie, who was in an uncomfortable-enough situation with her siblings, had asked for a background check on Hardy, and I had the resources, it was no big deal to do it. The thought that I might in some way be jeopardizing my friendship with Dorothy was a bridge I would have to cross when I got there. As Leslie always says, we all make mistakes. I didn't know if this would be another one in my life, but I was committed.

"You got it. You guys need anything?"

I told him no, but my rhetorical list of possible answers was growing.

Marcy left just before Peggy and I sat down to dinner, and Peggy seemed grateful to have the continuing saga of my extended family as a distraction from her own reality—until the phone rang, that is.

THREE

It was just after 11:00 P.M. when Peggy answered the phone. She'd nearly jumped out of her skin when it rang, thinking that it was the hospital with bad news. I noticed her hands were shaking as she clutched what Lucy called "the walk-around phone." After a couple of minutes, she left the kitchen. I tried to listen, wondering if it was the hospital calling, but I heard only a door closing at the other end of the apartment.

We had agreed that I would spend the night with Peggy and Lucy, because it would make me feel better. Ever since college, Peggy'd been good about letting me have my way. With Kerry looking after Auggie, I wasn't restricted to a pup schedule and had the freedom to stay with Peggy as long as she needed.

By the time she returned from her call, I was sipping a cup of Tension Tamer tea in the living room while watching the Sci-Fi Channel, because the last thing I wanted to deal with was the eleven o'clock news.

"I made you a cup of tea." I motioned to the mug on the coffee table.

Peggy looked ashen as she silently walked past me into the kitchen, then came out a moment later with a short glass half-filled with an amber liquid.

"What happened?" I asked, muting the sound on the TV.

"Nothing. The um, hospital . . . they just wanted me to know that John was resting comfortably."

"Really?" She looked like she had seen a ghost.

"What do you mean, 'really?' What, you're going to give me the third degree?"

I held up my hands to indicate a truce. I knew the day had to be hitting her hard and that there was no one better to take it out on than family. "You ever see this show?" I motioned to the television and turned the volume back on.

Peggy sank onto the sofa as she shook her head and stared blindly at the screen.

"Well, you see that good-looking guy with the pouty lips and the plastic hair? He's a channeler, not unlike my very own aunt Minnie, except that he gets paid *beaucoup* bucks to do it. Essentially, he brings people back from the dead, or at least messages from them, all for the fine art of entertainment. What do you think of *that*?" I brought the tea to my mouth just to shut myself up.

"I think . . . I think I'm in trouble, Sydney."

I turned off the television. "What's up?"

She didn't respond immediately, but I knew to be patient.

Finally, she said, "You know I never wanted children." She stole a glance at me, but I can't imagine I was anything more than a blur to her. I'd known Peggy since our college days at Columbia, and even back then she'd vowed that she never wanted children. When she met John, she fell head over heels in love, but he wanted children and she was dead set against it. She had never said why she'd changed her mind, but two years after they were married, they had Lucy. I always figured this was their business, so I never asked about it. I was just glad that they had worked it out, because there are some couples who are just meant to be together and raise great kids, couples like John and Peggy.

"I always told you that I thought a child would alter my lifestyle too much, but in truth, I was afraid." She sighed so heavily, I could practically feel her breath.

"Afraid of childbirth?" I prompted.

She shook her head. "No. Not that giving birth isn't a formidable

16

concept, but that's not what concerned me. I was . . . I was afraid that if I gave birth, my child would be evil." She laughed sadly before taking another swig of her drink.

"Go on," I said gently, trying to let her know with my tone that I was unfazed and solidly beside her, as I'd always been.

She opened and closed her mouth several times before blurting out, "I have always known that any child of mine would run the risk of being genetically impaired, that my family history would repeat itself.

"There's just so much you don't know, Sydney, things I've kept secret from both you *and* John, the only two people in this whole stinking world I've always known I could trust. But I never said anything. And if I didn't *have to*, I wouldn't be saying anything right now." She stood up and abruptly disappeared into the kitchen, where I found her refilling her glass from a bottle of cognac.

I walked up beside her, pulled a glass off the shelf, and helped myself to a brandy. "Nothing is so big or so bad that we can't find a way to manage it together. Come on," I said leading her to the kitchen table. "Tell me what's happened."

"What do you know about my family?" she asked when we were seated at the well-worn Parson's table.

I studied my old friend and wondered where she was headed with this. "I know that yours was not the closest of families. You had a falling-out with your brother when you were very young and you haven't talked to him since. Your dad died many years ago of cancer, but you never had much of a relationship with him, so the loss was something that didn't affect you much, or perhaps you just didn't talk about it. I also know that regardless of all that, you and your mom managed to have a very close friendship, especially toward the end of her life." I shrugged. "Is that what you mean?"

Her nod was barely perceptible. "My father's side of the family is twisted, and I think they always have been. I mean, my father was a very cruel man, Sydney. He never thought before he spoke and he never spoke before he hit. The only person he never touched was my mom. She had this amazing control over him, and I'm sure it was because of her that he took only one shot at me, when I was about three or four." She ran an elegant hand through her short hair and bit her lip. "It was my first day of nursery school and I was scared. I refused to go inside, and that made him livid. I don't remember the event, but as I understand it, he spanked me so hard that I couldn't sit down for several days.

"Anyway, Dad wasn't the only one in the family who had this psychotic mean streak. His mother was terrifying. She was evil incarnate and her face reflected precisely who she was, but everyone else would go on and on about 'What a beauty Sonya is.' Beauty," Peggy snorted. "Not only was there nothing real about this woman *physically*—because everything on her was tucked, nipped, lifted, or dyed—but she didn't have a genuine bone in her body. Only once did I ever see the real Sonya. I was about fifteen and we were getting ready to have a family barbecue. For the life of me, I can't remember what triggered it all off, but the next thing I knew, Sonya was screaming at my dad to hit me, to draw blood. That's exactly what she said. 'Hit her, Rick. Be sure you draw blood.'" Peggy's laugh could have easily been a sob, but her eyes remained dry.

"Anyway, mom walked in just as dad was about to hit me. It's kind of stunning when I think of the power she had. I mean, she merely stepped in on all this, and my father absolutely froze. His arm was still raised over his shoulder and his hand was curled into a tight fist, but he didn't move a muscle. And Sonya? Her face just kind of sucked into itself, as if her lips were disappearing into her head, so she couldn't even squeal like the pig that she was.

"Mom asked what was going on, but no one said anything. I was too afraid to talk, and, now that I think of it, I suppose they were, too, only for different reasons. Mom told me to go into the house. I don't really remember what happened after that. I suppose we had a lighthearted family gathering, us being the original cast of *Freaks*, all mulling about in our concrete backyard, a regular paradise." She took a sip of her drink and continued. "One of the things I had gathered over the years, from listening to the adults talking in hushed tones and asking questions that no one ever fully answered back then, was that at the turn of the century, my father's grandfather was hung for the cold-blooded murder of a pregnant woman, in whose house he had sought shelter from a passing storm." She stopped and studied my face to make sure this was all sinking in.

"So, we have my great-grandfather—the eldest in his family, and I think there were six or eight siblings there—who was a psycho and killed a pregnant woman. Then there is his daughter, Sonya. Now Sonya was also the eldest. I think her younger brother was either killed in a war or died from influenza. I have no idea which. Then there's my father, who was an only child. Since he had no siblings, my theory may be wrong, but bear with me. I think I have been right about this all along, which will explain an awful lot to you. Finally, there's my brother, Karl, whom I haven't told you much about. You simply have to trust me when I say he's a sick fuck—or at least he used to be. He was the kind of kid who thought it was fun to torture kittens. So. Do you see a pattern?" She took another sip of her cognac and watched me over the rim of the glass.

"Your brother, your father, his mother, and her father." I ticked off the cast of characters on my fingers and felt pretty clueless.

Peggy nodded like a *sensei* with her star pupil.

"My theory is that the *firstborn* children in my family are destined to have a predisposition toward psychosis."

"Peggy, you can't think for one second that Lucy—"

"No, God no, Sydney, not Lucy." She got up from the table and started pacing.

I tried to keep my feelings from showing.

"Lucy's not my first." She was standing across the room, her back pressed against the refrigerator, her body framed by several of Lucy's colorful artworks, which were held fast to the stainless doors with magnets.

I didn't know what to say. A quick check of my feelings revealed that I wasn't shocked or particularly upset that she had neglected to tell me this little bit of her history. No, I was . . . curious. The two of us had known each other since college. When on earth did she have the time to have a baby without my knowing it? I wondered.

"Well?" Her voice cut through my silence, demanding my response.

I opened my mouth to speak, but nothing came out right away. Finally, I asked, "When did you have the baby?"

She shook her head and turned toward the counter, as if she could will herself away from me.

"Hey," I said. "Don't turn away. I'm your friend and I love you. I feel bad that you thought you had to keep this a secret for so long, but you have to know that as far as I'm concerned, the Dexter legacy is not about you. You don't have an evil bone in your body," I reminded her.

In a matter of moments, her cheeks were drenched with her tears.

"I was raped my senior year in high school. I wanted to have an abortion—I had already found a way to arrange for it—but my mother found out and wouldn't let me." She took a deep breath as she walked to the sink, rinsed her face, and pulled a paper towel off the rack. She kept her back to me and hid her face in the towel.

I came up behind her, gently turned her around, and held her while she cried. I was hurting for Peggy, but there wasn't much I could do except hold her until she was spent. I was sure that I hadn't heard the end of this story.

"What a shitty day," I mumbled when her crying had subsided into faltering gasps for air. She pulled back and actually smiled at me. Her eyes were red and swollen, her face puffy and blotched, her lips dry, and her nose wet, but she still smiled.

"I'm scared," she whispered.

"Tell me why."

"I was always afraid the past would come back and haunt me. That phone call before? It wasn't the hospital. It was him."

"Who?"

"I didn't know until now if it was a boy or a girl. I didn't want to know. I was a kid. I really thought I could leave it all behind. But I can't. He's found me, Sydney. And he's going to kill me."

FOUR

One of Peggy's many skills was her amazing memory; it was not only photographic but audio, as well, which meant, for example, in college she had been able to remember entire lectures, or at least the salient points. So when she repeated her conversation with her son to me, I wouldn't have sworn that it was verbatim, but I knew it was pretty damned close. As far as I was concerned, even if it wasn't accurate, I wanted to know what Peggy thought she remembered and, perhaps more important, how she felt.

I tape-recorded what she said for Kerry to type up at the office the next morning.

I started by asking the question, "What happened during the course of your phone conversation this evening?"

"When I picked up the phone, a male voice said, 'Hello, is this Peggy Dexter?' I said, 'Yes.' Then he said, 'Hello, Mother.'

"I said, 'I beg your pardon?' And right away, he said, 'Well yes, I suppose you should. Tell me, how's Johnny doing?'

"Just the way he said 'Johnny' made my skin crawl. That's when I think I asked, 'Who is this?' and he said, 'Your progeny, your son, the little lad you left behind. You do remember you gave birth, don't you?'" She paused here and squinted, as if trying to see the conversation. She rubbed her forehead as she continued.

"I don't think I said anything. I didn't know what to say. Then he said, 'Sure you do. That would be a difficult thing to

21

forget, wouldn't it? Or did you? *Helloo*? Are you there, Mommy?'

"I was stunned. All I could think to ask was, 'What do you want?' because I knew he wanted something. Otherwise, he wouldn't have been calling, right? I don't think I expected a real answer, but by now I was beginning to panic and I didn't want him to know it." She was talking as if she was in a trance.

"He said, 'You know that hurts. I can hear the coldness in your voice, and instead of asking how I am after all these years, all you want to know is what it is I want.'

"Sydney, you know me. I'm normally a compassionate woman, but this creepy call comes in right after John's been shot, and just the way he asked about John made me sick. So I asked him, 'How did you know about John?' That's when he chuckled and said, 'Come on, Mom, my kith and kin are front-page news. I find that terribly exciting, don't you? Do they know yet who shot him?' " Peggy stopped and squinted at me. "I don't know if he was trying to taunt me or was simply curious, but why would he have called tonight of all nights? So I repeated, 'What do you want?'

"And very coolly he said, 'Well, I *had* hoped for a warm, loving family reunion, but from the sound of your voice, I suppose that's out of the question. I should have known that, though, and I guess I did. I mean, after studying you and your family for the last year, I could easily have predicted that you reserve your show of love for the inner circle only. What a lucky little girl Lucy is to know that her mommy wanted her and loves her. Not all children are so fortunate.'

"He knows about Lucy, Sydney. He's watched us for over a year. How creepy is that? What on earth am I going to do?" She shot out of the armchair and started pacing the room like a caged animal.

"Tell me what happened next," I said calmly.

"When I said, 'What do you want?' he said, 'Golly, Ma, you keep asking the same question. Gimme a break. I only learned that I was adopted five years ago, which, I don't mind telling you, came as quite a surprise. I mean, you spend your life living in a family, thinking that you are part of *that* heritage, and then, when it's too late to make any appreciable difference, you learn that things might have been very different if you had been wanted at birth. It took a long time to find you, and when I did, I was so excited that I almost rang your doorbell a dozen times to introduce myself. But then I realized that I wouldn't know what to say. And what if you had rejected me like you did when I was so vulnerable? I don't think I could have taken that. So I started to study you and your family, which is really *my* family, too, isn't it? And the more I watched you, the more I realized that you really fucked me over.' Then he went on to list things about me, as if he needed to prove to me that he had done his research." She held out her hands in an attempt to steady herself emotionally.

"I can tell you that at that point my heart was ready to pound right out of my chest. I didn't know what to do, but I didn't want him to know I was upset, so I asked, 'And what did you conclude?' He laughed and said, 'Oh, you're good, Mom. Asking what have I concluded is essentially asking again what I want. I have concluded that nothing can make up for the hell I have lived because of you. And so you must be punished. I think . . . I think *that's* what I've concluded. I think what I really want from you, Mommy, is for you to understand that life isn't all pearly white smiles and home-cooked meals. I want you to understand what it feels like to be alone and angry and frightened. I want you to understand what it means to be flinching constantly because you don't know when you're gonna get hit again. I want you to know that I am here, that I didn't die because you wouldn't love me. And I am about to make your life a living hell. I think I want you to die.' "

"What happened then?" I asked when I realized she had stopped talking.

Peggy hid her mouth behind her hands. She took a deep breath to control her crying and said, "He hung up. At that point, he had worked himself into a real lather." Peggy let out a mournful cry and sank back down onto the armchair. "Oh God, Sydney, what have I done? *What have I done?*"

"I'm not sure what you mean."

"If you could have heard the tone in his voice, his pain . . ."

"Oh no, no, don't even go there, Peg. You did the only thing you could have done. Don't forget you were a teenager, a teenager who had been raped. Christ, it was the sixties. Abortions were illegal, and yet you were willing to take that risk because the last thing you wanted was a child. It's easy to forget now, but unwed mothers were stigmatized no matter what the circumstances behind the pregnancy. You were young and wedged between shame and fear and you did the only thing that was sane and self-preserving."

"But maybe he was right. Maybe if I had kept him and loved him, his life would have been different. . . ."

"You bet if you had kept him his life would have been different, and so would yours. But do you really think you could have loved this child who was the end result of your being brutalized and whom you feared would be like your father and Sonya, two people you absolutely loathed? Look, I am not about to let you blame yourself for this, Peggy. Besides, for all you know, the kid *was* raised in a loving family. If your theory's right, and I believe it's one hundred percent valid, chances are that nothing in the world would have changed his path. *And* . . ." I held my hands out to her, as if offering a reasonable concept. "And no matter what, the kid threatened you, which means that he's potentially dangerous. So it doesn't matter what caused it; the important thing is to fix it. Do we agree?"

The flash of panic in her eyes was unmistakable.

"Sydney, no. Please. There's got to be another way. *You* look for him."

"Peggy. John is in the hospital with a gunshot wound. This kid might well be the gunman. The police—"

"And he might not!" She gathered the material of her shirt in her fists and tugged at it. "Please. *Please.* Think about it. If you were a police officer and got wind of this, wouldn't you come to the conclusion that this was the *only* place to focus your attention?"

"Absolutely not. Peggy, the NYPD is an amazing force."

"Jesus Christ, don't you think I know that!" She slapped her hand over her mouth when she heard how loud we were getting, then glanced in the direction of Lucy's room and moved back to the sofa, where I was sitting. She sank down next to me. "Sydney, we've known each other a long time. You have to know that I would never, ever ask you to compromise your integrity, but—"

I cut her off. "This isn't about integrity, Peg. This is about having all of the available resources working together to solve the problem. I can't solve this problem. And believe me, you are not doing anyone a bit of good if you think withholding this from the police will help matters. Listen to me," I said, taking her hands in mine. "There are endless possibilities. The man who called tonight may or may not be your son. He may or may not have shot John. He may or may not be a threat to you in the future. But there is one thing that is absolutely certain: He must be caught. Whoever he is, he's dangerous, even if his only intention is to taunt you. I really think we need to call the detective in charge of the case."

Peggy eased out of my hold, hid her face in her hands, and sobbed until there was nothing left in her but rasping breaths.

"Won't you please look for him?"

"Honey . . ."

"Please. I trust you and Max with all my heart. And this is just so . . ." Her voice trailed off. "Please, I'm begging you."

"Yes, of course we will. But you have to tell the police. This is just too big for CSI."

When she finally spoke, her voice was so thin that I could barely hear her. I asked her to repeat herself as I bent closer to her. "I will. Let me tell John first. I don't want him to hear it from a stranger or read it in the paper."

It was a request I couldn't refuse. I knew it was likely a mistake, but I gave in with the caveat that if he wasn't strong enough by the next day, she would have to tell the police anyway.

It was late and we were both wiped out, but I needed to get information about the past if I was going to start poking around in it. "When and where did you give birth?"

She exhaled. "Um, it was 1968. December. It was a weekend, in the middle of the month, either the fourteenth or the fifteenth.

I don't remember the exact date, but the hospital was in the Bronx."

"Good. Which one?"

She stared at me, her mouth slightly open. "Wait—it was, ah, the Bronx Regional Medical Center."

"And your doctor's name?"

A blank look washed over her. She shook her head.

"You don't remember?"

"No. Jesus, it's as if I've blocked out that whole phase of my life."

"It's okay." I threw a few more questions at her, but it was useless.

By this point, we were both exhausted, so the only sensible thing was to get some sleep. "Things always look better in the daylight," one of us murmured as I shuffled from one closet to another, locating sheets and pillows. Peggy was fully dressed and snoring soundly on top of her covers before I could find out where she kept the extra toothbrushes. In all the years that she had lived here, this was the first time I was going to spend the night. I turned out the light but found that sleep was still a long way off for me. In the darkness, all I could see was Peggy's face contorted with fear. This woman who had been and always would be like a sister to me was, for the first time since we had met, an enigma. It's silly to think that there is anyone in the universe who doesn't fume, fret, or carry the weight of their own unknown somewhere on their body, but Peggy had always been so strong, had always seemed to deal with her feelings openly and honestly. When her father died, she had handled the situation with strength and grace; she was able to be there for her mother, while at the same time avoiding the rest of her family. When her mother had a heart attack and died while the two of them were shopping for Easter hats, she asked John to arrange for her mother to be taken to the morgue and for the local precinct to contact Karl, all the while keeping herself removed from any contact with her brother, though she attended the funeral and honored her mother's memory by making a huge donation to the Heart Association. She cried, but she never seemed to wallow. I never saw her lie. I had never had cause to distrust her.

"You still don't," I reminded myself as I pushed my back against the sofa pillows and let the veil of sleep finally fall over me.

FIVE

I awoke to the smell of coffee brewing and the sound of Lucy's voice whining, "But why *can't* I wake her up?" I opened one eye and saw my five-year-old goddaughter lingering in the doorway between the kitchen and the living room. I imagined Lucy looked just like her mother had when she was that age: tall, slender, knobby-kneed, with big brown eyes and very straight sandy brown hair. I had asked time and again if, in fact, mother and daughter shared the same hair color, but all I ever got was a shrug. I figured the only people who had ever seen Peggy's natural hair color were all dead now.

Lucy caught me studying her.

"Hey, didja miss me?" I gave her my usual greeting.

She came racing over to greet me. "Yeaaaaaaaaah," she screamed as she flew through the air, headed directly at my bladder. I brought up my knees to protect myself and caught her as if she were a health ball.

"Hey, you." I tucked her between me and the back of the sofa and started tickling her.

"Lucy, stop screaming," Peggy called from the kitchen.

"Stop screaming," I said as I continued to torment the poor kid. I had her just under the armpits and was allowing the sadistic tickler in me free.

I finally gave in to her pleas for me to "Stop! Stop!" but only when I saw Peggy standing at the doorway with a spatula in hand.

"Come on, Lucy, I want you to eat your breakfast." Peggy took a deep breath and added, "Sydney, coffee's ready."

I gave Lucy a hug and kiss and told her I'd meet her at the "chuck wagon."

Bored by all things cowboy, my goddaughter rolled her eyes and suggested that I "get real."

I dragged myself off the sofa and wondered what was wrong with this child; how could a kid not love horses and saddles and chaps and boots? As I brushed my teeth, I realized that if I added spurs, leather gloves, and a quirt to the list, I'd have little Lucy attired for any number of bars along West Street.

I found Peggy and Lucy at the kitchen table, where Lucy was working on a plate of scrambled eggs with toast and Peggy was nursing a cup of coffee. I had seen my friend through finals, pregnancy, numerous hangovers, and oral surgery, and in all that time I had never seen her look so bad.

"What?"

I shrugged as I moved past the table to the counter, where a thermos filled with French roast awaited me, just like at a coffeehouse. "Nothing. You just look like I feel."

"Mommy?" Lucy asked, banging her feet against the legs of her chair.

"What, honey?"

"Where is Daddy? *Exactly?*" She examined her toast as she asked this.

"He's at the hospital, where the doctors are taking very good care of him."

"Is he coming home today?" She used her index finger to push the eggs around on her plate.

"No, sweetheart. Daddy won't be home for a little while, but you know what?"

"What?" She stared wide-eyed at her mother, her finger still making aimless circles on her plate.

"Maybe in another day or two you can visit him at the hospital. Would you like that?"

Lucy opened and closed her mouth but said nothing. She cast

an eye at me and then looked down at her plate. Finally, she nodded.

I gave Peggy the high sign, silently asking if she wanted me to leave them alone. She shook her head, got up, and moved her chair next to Lucy's. Lucy crawled into her mother's lap and Peggy wrapped her arms completely around Lucy. They looked like two little monkeys. For a moment, I was convinced that Peggy could protect Lucy forever just in the strength of her embrace.

I became momentarily invisible as I made toast for Peggy and me.

"So, what happened to Daddy? *Exactly?*" Lucy asked, again stressing her favorite new word. A week earlier, it had been *perfect*.

Peggy sighed and then said, "You know how we always tell you how dangerous guns are?"

Lucy must have nodded, but I was busy rummaging around in the refrigerator for butter and jam.

"Well, someone who shouldn't have had a gun did. The important thing is that Daddy's going to be just fine."

"Where was he shot?"

"In his chest."

"Is he gonna die?"

"Absolutely not."

"Promise?"

"I promise Daddy won't die anytime soon. Now, are you all ready for camp?"

"Yeah," she said, twisting the word into two syllables, as if contemplating an out, but Peggy was way ahead of her. Before Lucy could suggest not going to camp, Peggy got her jazzed up about "puppet day."

I volunteered to pick Lucy up from camp and take her home with me so that Peggy could spend time with John and still touch base at work.

"Will you bring Auggie?" Lucy asked when she and I were hurrying out the door to get her to her first activity on time.

"Auggie who?" I turned to Peggy and told her I would be right back.

The camp Lucy attended was just a few blocks from their

apartment, and we skipped and speed-walked the whole way. I gave her a kiss good-bye and stayed in the doorway, watching as she hooked arms with a friend. When she turned back to see if I was still there, she gave me a huge smile. I couldn't help but wonder if her half brother, nearly thirty years her senior, looked anything like her.

Walking back to Peggy's, taking what I assumed was the same route John had taken the day before, I speculated whether his attacker had followed him as he made his way back home, or if he had been waiting in the building, anticipating John's arrival. Was John the victim of a random act of violence or a deliberate target?

I felt my cell phone vibrating inside my pocket. Though I'd had one of these for awhile, I had to admit that cell phones placed me in a bad position philosophically: I liked the convenience but thought they bred bad social behavior, not to mention brain tumors. However, it was unquestionably easier to carry around my own phone, rather than having to seek out a public phone—which in New York City was a crap shoot, since 98 percent of the pay phones were either broken or gummed up with cooties from the zillions of people using them. Inconvenience or malignant tumors? You would think it's a no-brainer.

"Hello?" I moved toward the curb and stopped to listen.

"Hey, it's me." Mixed with my sense of relief at finally hearing from Leslie was the very distinct feeling of anger at her for not having called sooner.

"Did you get my message?" I asked.

Despite the din of traffic around me, her sigh was crystal clear.

"I did. But when Christa picked me up at the airport, we went directly to her new house in Malibu. It's amazing, Sydney. The house is separate from the studio, though they're both on the same property, and the sunlight is unbelievable. Anyway, by the time I got to the hotel, it was too late to call you." She added, "I'm sorry" as an afterthought.

"I was worried." I suddenly felt small and silly, exposed on the street.

"If it makes you feel any better, it's not yet six here and I'm calling you."

I tried to muster up enthusiasm I didn't feel and asked how she liked the artist Maiwald.

Leslie waxed poetic about her new client and her client's family before asking how things were at home.

That's when I told her about John. When I was finished, she asked if she should come home.

"No. There wouldn't be anything you could do here anyway. When do you think you'll be home, though?"

"I had planned four days here. But if you think I could be of any use there, I'll fly back today."

"No. Don't worry about it." Right at that moment, I was caught in the middle of a honking battle between a silver Ford Explorer and a red-and-purple 1965 Pontiac GTO, both of which were vying for a suddenly vacated parking spot next to where I was standing. When I couldn't hear her, I hit the red button and terminated the call. It was just as well, because as much as I wanted to connect with Leslie, I felt a wedge between us that I didn't want to think about. I just wanted to get back to Peggy.

I hurried back to the apartment, where I found her sitting in the living room with a man who seemed to fill the easy chair effortlessly. He was the kind of big that made you think he could toss a refrigerator across the room just for the hell of it. He wore a gray suit, a white shirt, and a half-knotted red tie.

"Sydney." Peggy tried to stand but faltered. "This is Detective Samuel Cooper."

The detective made no attempt to get up or offer his hand. He worked his flat cartoon lips into what could have either been a smile or a sneer and said, "So, this is Sydney Sloane."

I didn't know what he meant by that, so I chose to ignore it. "Detective Cooper." I offered up my best good-girl smile and perched myself on the arm of the sofa.

"As I was saying, I know that you spoke with Hank Yarberg at the hospital yesterday, Mrs. Cannady, and answered some preliminary questions then, but I was wondering if you would mind answering a few questions for me."

"Of course not." When she swallowed, her long neck seemed

to get even longer, like a swan preparing to dunk. Cooper didn't seem to notice because he was fighting to extract a small notebook from his breast pocket.

Despite the fact that I knew Peggy's myriad reasons for being uneasy, her movement disturbed me, like an itch that's just far enough under the skin to be completely elusive.

"Mrs. Cannady," Cooper began, his tone both respectful and cautious. "Could you please tell me exactly what happened yesterday morning—the moments prior to and just after the shooting?"

Peggy told Cooper precisely what she had told me the day before at the hospital. He listened attentively and interrupted only to get more specific details.

When she was done he asked, "Tell me, ma'am, have you noticed a change in, um, in your . . . in Captain Cannady's behavior or routine over the last few weeks?" He made it a point not to look at me.

"No. Nothing unusual. Why?"

When he didn't answer right away, Peggy said, "John's a very even-tempered man, someone who's almost predictable. He loves his work, his family, and his friends and he spends a great deal of time with all three."

"So there has been no notable change in his mood?"

"No. Why? Are you suggesting he should have been different?

Cooper held out his hands as a means of placating Peggy and exhaled a cross between a cough and a laugh. "Please, ma'am, that's not at all what I'm saying. It's just that in an investigation like this, where the victim is with the force and is an individual who is well-known and loved and respected by so many other officers, we don't want to leave any pebble unturned, if you know what I mean."

Peggy did understand and Detective Cooper continued his line of questioning, focusing essentially on John's recent routine and his life outside the force.

When he finished, I asked if he had any news he could share with us.

"I'm afraid nothing much," he said, leafing through his little notebook as if searching for something to jar his memory.

"Detective Cooper, surely you can tell me what the police learned yesterday," Peggy said in a way that defied refusal. "I haven't spoken with anyone. I haven't been told a thing from an official source."

"Oh, I'm sorry. I didn't realize that. For starters, you should feel a real good level of comfort, knowing that all of the top brass are involved in this one, Mrs. Cannady. There's no way whoever did this won't be found. Also, as soon as the word got out that it was the captain who'd been shot, we had a slew of officers coming in and volunteering their time. Because of that, we were able to return the crime scene to its previous state, so your daughter wouldn't be any more traumatized than she probably already has been."

"I appreciate that," Peggy whispered.

"Now, for what has been done so far in terms of the, you know, investigation. We immediately cordoned off an area that covered a three-block radius, though in actuality we made our sweep wider than that. Between checking plates and canvassing the area, we've already brought in half a dozen people for questioning."

"What have you learned?" Peggy asked.

"Nothing of any value—*yet*." He stressed the last word. "Keep in mind that we're still getting information from that sweep. We've also left a security detail here as a means of protection for you and your daughter. I'm sure you've noticed the uniformed officers out front and patrolling the area, but plainclothes officers are keeping an eye on the building, as well. Everyone is involved in this investigation, Mrs. Cannady, from the chief of detectives to me and my partner, Paul Doherty."

"Where is your partner now?" Peggy asked.

"He's interviewing one of the people from yesterday's sweep. Paul's a good guy, and more importantly, he's a great detective."

"What about Internal Affairs?" I asked, knowing that they had to be making inquiries into John's personal life, outside of Cooper's questioning of Peggy.

Detective Cooper took a deep breath and gave a halfhearted shrug. "It's all procedure; nothing to be concerned about," he said gently, brushing me off.

"Internal Affairs?" Peggy asked me.

"Whenever an officer is shot, IA has to look into it just to see if there was anything in the officer's personal life that might have been the root of the trouble."

"But this isn't something you have to worry about, Mrs. Cannady," Samuel Cooper said, then added quickly, "That aside, we employed the Canine Unit, whose search started out in a promising way, but ultimately they came up empty. The dog picked up a scent in the stairwell and she followed it to the laundry room, where it essentially dead-ended. The dog lost the scent, but as her handler was packing her up to leave, Chloe—that's the dog—led us to an apartment where an elderly woman lives alone. The old woman doesn't get a lot of visitors, so it was easy to get a list of the names of people who go to her apartment—her maid, the maintenance men, a nephew, and a young woman in the building who runs errands for her."

"What did you find in the laundry room?" I asked.

"Apart from the fact that the dog lost the scent?" he asked. "There was a woman in there doing her laundry from seven until eight-fifteen and she said that the only people she saw there were one of the maintenance men, who unlocked the room for her at seven, and a woman she's seen a few times before. She doesn't know what apartment this woman lives in, but that'll be easy enough to find out. The problem is, if the shooter was in that room, either before or after the shooting, she would have seen him, because the room doesn't open until seven."

"The other woman was there the whole time?"

"No. She came in looking for a sock she thought she'd left there the night before. We're looking for her. The only other thing I can tell you, Mrs. Cannady, is about the security cameras in your building. You know where they're located?"

She nodded. "The front lobby and the service entrance in the back."

"Right. Well, the camera at the service entrance captured thirty-eight different people between midnight and eight-thirty in the morning, which is when our people retrieved that tape. The front security video has a little glitch, which makes the image unclear for about ten seconds every twelve minutes or so. Ten seconds is, unfortunately, ample time for a visitor to pass into the building without being caught on-camera. We have our work cut out for us, but we've already ID'd a good number of the individuals caught on tape at the service entrance." He took a deep breath, scanned his notes, and then asked Peggy if there was anything specific she wanted to know.

She couldn't think of anything, but I asked if he had planned on having someone keep an eye on Lucy until they found the shooter.

Peggy shot a panicked look at me and then at Cooper.

"It's standard procedure," Cooper reassured her. "We have a security detail watching over John at the hospital, someone posted here, and then someone at your daughter's camp. I would think that must be comforting," he said, casting a hateful glance at me.

"It is. Thank you."

As Cooper was leaving, he solemnly promised Peggy that he would personally find the man or woman who had shot John, but I didn't buy it.

Who knew? Perhaps Sammy Cooper was a brilliant detective and would wrap up the case in a matter of hours. I admit that I am a woman who has been known to jump to unfair conclusions about people, so even though I doubted it, I would have loved to be proven wrong.

SIX

Inevitably, I was struck by the paradox of traveling *downtown* from Peggy's apartment to reach the Upper West Side, where I live and work. Peggy's apartment was in the most northern section of Manhattan, a once-dicey neighborhood known as Washington Heights–Inwood. Once upon a time, Washington Heights was so far north that people would complain of nosebleeds just getting there, but, like every other neighborhood on the isle of Manhattan, it was now going through an urban upgrade.

Reviews of these metro sprucing-ups have been somewhat mixed. For example, visitors love the new Times Square, but there are many, like myself, who feel that it's been reduced to amusement-park status, a twenty-four/seven homage dedicated to wasting energy. Neighborhoods that once had their own unique allure, like Alphabet City and TriBeCa, have become clones of one another, with their Starbucks, French Roasts, trendy Thai restaurants, and health clubs.

Moving uptown was initially a big challenge for Peg, who was accustomed to her lofty digs in artsy-fartsy SoHo, which was just a hop, skip, and a jump from her office in the Financial District. But when the police sergeant from Hell's Kitchen and the Wall Street whiz kid decided to combine forces, they realized that they would both have to make compromises. John suggested that they move to Washington Heights, where real estate was affordable and where they would both feel as if they were embarking on something new and different, aside from this being the first marriage for each of them. Peg's income was far more substantial than John's, but that didn't seem to get in the way. They both agreed that they would live a life where they each contributed the same amount to their monthly expenses. Anything extra was put into another account, slated for vacations, retirement, and, when Lucy came along, her college fund. Back when one feared for their physical safety north of Columbia University, we all teased them that at least John had a gun and could defend himself uptown, but the truth is that in the seven years since they had moved there, Washington Heights had become more and more desirable, and while it would probably never run the risk of being chic, I could see it teetering on the brink of hip. Not yet, but one day. At least it had gotten a start with a trendy new acronym—WaHI.

This is what I was thinking about during the twenty-minute subway ride to my office on Broadway in the Eighties. It was easier to think about real estate than about how Cooper would handle the investigation or how uneasy I was that Peggy hadn't mentioned the hostile newcomer in her life when talking to the detective. I had no idea whether Samuel Cooper was a kind man or a cold one, whether he was a competent investigator or a boob. I trusted, however, that he wanted to find the person who had shot John because he knew and genuinely cared for John. It seemed that a lot of people did. It was obvious from the outpouring of love and support that Peggy was receiving in calls and flowers, as well as offers for help with everything from baby-sitting to housecleaning and preparing meals, that she and John were deeply loved.

Seeing Cooper's admiration for John reminded me of the first time I'd met him. He was a sergeant back then, working on an investigation into the murder of a young waiter from a catering outfit. There was just something about John that made you know right away that he was a man you could trust. Hell, I liked him so much when I first met him that I introduced him to one of my single friends, Peggy.

By the time I reached the office, everyone was there: Max,

Kerry, Miguel, and my dog, Auggie. I was barely over the threshold when Auggie got a whiff of me. As angry as she was for my having abandoned her, she was excited to see me. Between the barking, the yowling, and the jumping, my arrival was effectively announced to the entire building. Fortunately, all of the other tenants knew Auggie and most of them—except for one crank on the top floor—loved her. Then again, I thought, what's not to love?

There is no better creature on the planet than the dog. Or should I say *my* dog? Auggie, a good-natured beauty, never seemed to carry a grudge, even when a cantankerous Chow named Ollie tried to take a piece out of her in the park.

"How's John?" Kerry asked as I tried to keep Auggie from knocking a bag of warm bagels out of my hand.

"I haven't heard anything since last night, but he *will* be fine," I said, knowing I would elaborate when we were all gathered. I put the bagels on her desk and gave Auggie a proper greeting. Auggie is a big dog with cream-colored fur and black lips, which are more often than not pulled up into a wide smile. She likes to jump on her hind legs and throw her full seventy pounds at me. Normally, I catch her paws and parrot her movements and together we wind up doing this crazy dance.

During this ritual, Max came out from his office, spied the bagel bag, and lifted it off Kerry's desk. Miguel appeared at my office door at the same time.

When they all started asking questions about John in chorus, I suggested that we go to my office, where I could update them all at once. Even as I put my bag on my desk, glanced at my phone messages, and listened as my cohorts divvied up the bagels, I wondered if I would tell them about Peggy's frightening late-night phone call. She had promised to tell John as soon as she saw him. In turn, I had promised Peggy that Max and I would do everything we could to help the police find this man. As long as I'd committed him to this, I knew I had to tell Max.

As it turned out, as far as the actual shooting was concerned, Max and Kerry and Miguel had all read accounts of it and the investigation in the paper, which I hadn't.

"What's the prognosis?" Max asked as he started eating a poppy-seed bagel with cream cheese.

"Good. Whatever that means. The doctors told Peggy to expect a full recovery, but it's going to be a long one. There was a lot of damage. First of all, the shooter used a hollow-point bullet," I said.

"Caliber?" Max asked.

"It's at ballistics."

"Shell casings?"

"I don't know. Cooper didn't say. I'll ask later. We do know, however, that the bullet entered John's body at a slightly upward angle, ripped through portions of his chest, and finally stopped against his right shoulder blade."

"So the shooter was shorter than John," Miguel said.

"Possibly," I replied, glad to know that he was thinking lucidly before noon, not always a given with Miguel.

"Or there might have been a struggle prior to the shooting and the gunman was on the ground when he opened fire," Max offered as he clicked his worn steel-toed boots together. "The angle of trajectory is what's important."

"Maybe the shooter was acting," said Kerry, whose background in theater always added another dimension to things. "It's possible," she added, defending herself as she looked at Miguel, whose response was a groan, his eyes cast to the heavens. "Hey, *you* think he was shot by a midget. All I'm saying is that the guy could have been pretending that he had, like, a heart attack, so he could attack John when he was vulnerable."

"I didn't say *midget*," Miguel snorted.

"Children, children." Max held out a hand. "If you don't behave, you're each going to have to take a time-out. Kerry has a good point, Miguel, which only illustrates how many different angles you have to be aware of when you're exploring something like this. You know as well as I do that scumballs prey on the good nature of people. Remember what happened to your aunt Ruby?"

Miguel mumbled something in Spanish, kissed the pendant hanging from the chain around his neck, and showed it to the proper saints above. Max then turned his deep brown eyes back to me and asked quietly how Lucy was taking it.

"Kids are amazingly resilient," I said.

"Marcy said she seemed to be taking it pretty well," he replied.

"Yeah, but they hold things in and let it frighten them in ways we never even think about, and the next thing you know, they're totally fucked-up, entering into loveless relationships just because they're afraid of being alone or unloved." Kerry said this from the sofa, apparently telling the coffee table, upon which she was resting her feet.

Miguel, Max, and I stared at her, wordlessly, before Miguel finally said, "Yo, girl, you got some problems on the home front?"

She turned her gaze to us and shook her head. "No," she said smugly as she smoothed out the fabric of the authentic bright yellow-and-red-and-black tartan kilt she had bought in Scotland with her fiancé, Patrick. "I'm an actor, which is a lot like being a psychologist. I've studied people my whole life, and believe me, I know what makes us tick."

Max nodded, Miguel slid lower into his seat, and I said, "Moving right along . . ."

"So do they think it's someone John arrested before?" asked Miguel, returning to the matter at hand.

I shrugged. "They haven't ruled out anything yet. They don't know."

"I read in the paper that Internal Affairs is investigating, too." Miguel pushed himself back up in his chair.

"That really pissed me off," Kerry said.

"Why?" Max asked, polishing off his coffee.

"That's like telling the world they think John got shot because he's crooked."

"No, it isn't," I said.

"It is, too," replied Miguel, who obviously agreed with Kerry.

"Don't be ridiculous," said Max, dismissing them as he stood up. "You two are professionals. IAB *has* to investigate. It doesn't mean that they're looking for their officer to be dirty."

Kerry pushed the corners of her mouth down as she toyed with a large papier-mâché earring of an ear dangling from her right lobe. She shrugged and glanced up at Max, who crumpled his empty coffee cup into a ball and tossed it into the wastebasket.

"It's simply protocol," Max said, speaking from the experience of his many years on the force.

"Max, you and Sydney come from law enforcement. I don't," Miguel said, gracefully avoiding the fact that he came from the other side of the law. "Because of that, I think I have what you could call a healthy suspicion of the police and how they work. To me, an Internal Affairs investigation means the hierarchy thinks the cop was into something bad."

"How does Peggy feel about that?" Kerry asked, wrapping the thin sporran strap of her kilt around her fingers.

"She understands that it's not a condemnation, just standard procedure." I didn't know this for a fact, but I assumed that because of the call the night before, her focus was elsewhere. I continued without pause. "Just for the record, Detective Cooper told us that IAB is just going through the paces."

I watched Max walk to the window and look out at the avenue below. The West Side took longer to develop than most areas in Manhattan, but as far as I'm concerned, it was well worth the wait. My office faces Broadway, which was originally known as Bloomingdale Road and then the Boulevard. Back then, the dirt road would have been dotted with shantytowns and swampy land, but now it would soon be hopping with local morning traffic, and at least half a dozen people would be headed uptown with Zabar's bags in hand. The Cinema II complex directly across the street wasn't open yet, but in less than an hour, seniors would be getting an early start on the new releases.

"You know, I was thinking that it might have been a robbery," Miguel said as he rubbed the insides of Auggie's ears. "I mean, we're talking Inwood, right?"

"You know what I was thinking?" Kerry asked. "I know this is horrible to say, but you know how much time John gives those kids after school? Maybe one of them went ballistic."

"Anything is possible," I said, mesmerized that Kerry was able to wear a frilly chartreuse silk blouse with her yellow kilt and red snakeskin cowboy boots and not look like a buffoon. "Do you know Samuel Cooper?" I asked Max, who was leaning on the windowsill. He looked positively ethereal with the sunlight pouring in behind him, rendering him all but invisible to me.

"No. I knew a George Cooper once, but he was with the coroner's office. Why?"

"Oh, *maaan*. I know you, Sydney," Miguel said excitedly. "We're getting involved in the investigation, aren't we?"

I leveled a gaze at him. "What do you mean by 'we'?" I asked.

He bobbed his head several times and mumbled something.

"Sorry, I didn't catch that." I sipped my apple juice and cocked an ear in his direction. Now Miguel, too, became engulfed by the halo of morning light coming in from the east.

"CSI," he said clearly.

"As we all know, the police frown on outside help when it comes to their ongoing investigations. Right now, I think it's best to watch how things unravel and try to keep as well informed as we can."

The phone rang.

Kerry jumped up to answer it and Max pushed away from the windows. I leaned over to Miguel and said, "I believe you and I have a date."

"CSI, can I help you?"

Max passed Miguel and said, "A date with Sydney? Man, I wouldn't want to be in your shoes." He looked at me and said, "I'll be in my office. We have loose ends."

"Here," Kerry said, holding the phone out to me.

"Who is it?" I asked.

"Leslie."

I glared at Miguel and mouthed to Kerry, "Is she on hold?"

"Yes," she mouthed back.

"Miguel, go to your office. We'll talk when I'm through." I took the receiver and waited for their exodus.

Auggie watched Max disappear into his office and Kerry and

Miguel exit into the other. She paced in a circle, uncertain as to whether she should follow Max, or Kerry and Miguel, or stay put. Not having opposable thumbs and thus unable to turn a door-knob, her choices were limited when the last door shut, so she pushed past my feet and made herself at home under my desk.

"Hey," I finally said into the mouthpiece.

"I didn't like the way our last call ended." She sounded so far away, and I was suddenly overwhelmed with missing her. "I can't stop thinking about John and Peggy and Lucy, and how we never know what can happen in a second that will change our lives for-ever. I love you, Sydney. I'm sorry I've caused so much tension be-tween us."

"I love you too, honey. It's just a strange time. And by the way, I am going to have Miguel check into Harold's past."

"You are?" She sounded genuinely surprised.

"Yeah. I figured if you're this concerned, it couldn't hurt to look."

When the call ended ten minutes later, I felt reconnected to Leslie in a way that calmed me from deep inside. As long as I live and as jaded as I am, I will always be fascinated and baffled by the impact of love, good or bad.

After hanging up the phone, I made a list of the things I had to deal with. I placed the items in two columns, one titled "PEGGY," the other "MIGUEL." Under Peg's name, I noted "Talk with Max" and "Have Kerry transcribe the tape from last night." I had trouble fo-cusing on Miguel's list because the priority of Peggy was so com-pelling.

I knew that I would entrust Miguel with investigating Hardy's past and try to relinquish my usually tightfisted control. Miguel was an excellent operative, if still a little green, but it was time to let him out of the nest and see if he could fly on his own.

I pushed away from the desk, walked to the door dividing Max's office from mine, and knocked before letting myself in.

SEVEN

"Sydney." Max looked up from a file he was reading, put it down on his cluttered desk, and leaned back into his seat as if to say he would put everything on hold to hear what I had to say.

But I knew that. That's why we were such good friends, why we'd worked together so well for so long. He knew I would do the same for him.

I walked over to the striped sofa just opposite the doorway I had entered and plopped myself down with a huff. Max's office, which was smaller and quieter than mine because it faced the street rather than the avenue, was a friendly, manly space filled with toys, dark wood, and sturdy furniture. Whereas the walls in my office were a wispy pastel, he had recently painted his off-white, with a bold burgundy trim. Flowing muslin drapes covered the windows in my office from floor to ceiling, but Max had wooden venetian blinds. A worn dartboard hung on the wall opposite his desk, next to the official office entrance. Normally, a different photograph was attached to the dartboard each week, though for the last month Bush the Younger had been smiling stupidly from his perch in Max's Hall of Infamy/Stupidity.

"You okay?" he asked.

I shrugged. "We have to talk."

"Okay."

I sat there for the longest time saying nothing. I didn't know how to begin. I felt pinched between two very different loyalties for the same person. On the one hand, I didn't want to expose Peggy because I wanted to protect her; yet on the other hand, there would be no protecting her until her she was exposed.

Struggling to find the right words, I warned Max about the sensitivity of what we were about to discuss. When I finished my preamble and had given him an overview of Peggy's background situation, I played him the tape I had recorded the night before. I figured that hearing the conversation from Peggy directly would sum things up far better than my stumbling to remember specifics.

It was just as difficult hearing it the morning after as it had been the night before.

"Wow," Max finally murmured.

"I don't think this bodes well," I said, pressing the rewind button.

"No. I don't, either." He took a deep breath and rubbed the back of his neck. "You think this guy is the shooter?"

"I don't know. Anything's possible. But the thing is, it's definitely a possibility, and that's what I was trying to explain to Peggy. I mean, I respect the fact that she doesn't want John to hear this news from anyone but her, but withholding something like this could hamper the investigation."

"Right. Which would only make *her* look suspect."

"Exactly."

Again we just sat there, keeping our thoughts to ourselves. The whirring of the rewinding tape and a truck hitting a pothole outside momentarily filled the space between us.

Finally, Max asked, "So what's the game plan?"

I shook my head. "How much can we do before she tells the police?"

"That depends, I suppose. When is she planning to do that?"

"I would hope before noon today, but I don't know. It all depends on how well John's doing."

"The man's been shot, Sydney. And from what you said, it's not a simple wound. How well do you think he'll be doing?"

"Not very. But you never know."

He made his thoughts very clear with a simple look.

"Okay, well, I think we need to compartmentalize here. You should know that I promised Peggy that we would find her long-lost—"

"You *what*?" Max exclaimed, cutting me off.

"Well, what was I supposed to do?" I responded defensively. I was mad at myself because I knew I had made a promise I might not be able to keep. That bothered me a whole lot more than it bothered him, and I told him so.

He ran his fingertips along the edge of his desk. "All right, listen. Here's bottom line: If *he* found *her*, we should be able to find him, right?"

"I would like to think so."

He pulled a pad of paper and a pen toward him and said, "Okay. When and where was he born?"

When I told him the name of the hospital, he put down his pen and stared blankly at me.

"What?" I asked.

"Remember maybe fifteen, twenty years ago there was a hospital fire that did so much structural damage, they had to raze the building? I think some slipshod construction company was doing work in the basement, and between stupidity and a sloppy cleanup, there was a fire. Do you remember that?"

I scratched the side of my face and knew that in the recesses of my mind this was sounding familiar. "Maybe," I said uncertainly.

"Guess which hospital that was."

"No."

"Yes."

"Were patients hurt?"

"No, but as I recall, the administration offices and records department were pretty much wiped out." He picked up his pen again, and I knew this time he was doodling on the clean pad of paper. "They tore down the building after that."

"Their files weren't computerized?" I asked.

"Maybe. We can hope so. If they did computerize the information, then it's just a matter of finding out where they decided to store the data. It has to be somewhere." He made a note on the legal pad.

"Well, look, you said it yourself: He found her, so we can find him," I said, standing up and walking over to retrieve the darts. I came back to his desk and faced the board. "How do the adopted trace their history to their birth?"

"Many of them hire idiots like us."

That's what I liked about Max; this was a man with a firm grasp for the obvious.

"Okay. Point well taken, but I've never had a case like this, have you?"

"Nope. My guess is that it makes things a whole lot easier if both parties want to be found," Max said from behind me.

"Yeah, well, that's good. We know she wants to find him, and you have to figure he wants to be found. He called her, didn't he?"

"And hung up without leaving a trace. Did you do one of those star numbers after his call?" he asked.

"Yes. The number was blocked. But maybe the police could get the records."

"Sure," he said, affecting an easy tone. "That's a piece of cake for them. They just have to *know* to do it." I kept my back to him and nodded. "In the meantime, if I'm not mistaken, phone companies offer a service where if a caller is using a blocked number, the call can't go through."

I landed a dart on Bush's arched brow, sighed, and deposited the remaining darts on Max's desk. "Wouldn't our objective be to *trace* the call, rather then block it?" I asked as I slid onto Max's visitor's chair.

"True."

We pushed a smile at each other and moved on.

"All right, from what you said, it seems that we're starting out at a disadvantage because Peggy—this woman with the photographic memory—has blocked out pertinent information, like the name of the obstetrician."

"That has nothing to do with photographic anything, Max." Even I was surprised by the harshness in my tone, but that didn't stop me. "Shall I remind you that as a teenager, in her senior year in high school, she was raped? It was 1968, she was seventeen years old, and she decided to get an abortion, which, if you recall, wasn't legal back then, not to mention incredibly dangerous, because who knew if you were getting a butcher or a legitimate doctor? And you know she would have gotten a butcher, because she was a kid and she was handling all of the arrangements by herself."

"Hey. Calm down. I'm on your side." He made eye contact before continuing. "I just want to know what we do and don't know, that's all. Now, does she remember the exact date of birth?"

"She knows it was in December, but she's not sure if it was the fourteenth or the fifteenth. She knows it was a weekend."

"Is she sure it was *that* weekend? Not the one before or after it? That'd be what—the seventh and eighth or the twenty-first and twenty-second? For that matter, is she positive that she gave birth on a weekend?"

"I don't know. I'll find out." I took a deep breath. "I just keep thinking how traumatic this was for her. I mean, I met her at Columbia right after all this happened, and I've never known about it. Not a word. Max, if you could have seen her last night. It was excruciating."

"I can imagine. And I hate to say this, but you know as well as I do that the longer she holds on to this piece of her past, the harder it will be to convince the police that she wasn't somehow involved in the shooting."

"Don't be ridiculous," I said, dismissing the very thought I had been avoiding. My face must have revealed my feelings, because instead of going head-to-head with me on it, Max asked me to tell him everything I knew about that time in Peggy's life.

"After the pregnancy or before?" I asked.

"Before. During. Right after. How much did she tell you last night? Tell me everything you know." He was looking for straws.

"I know that her mother found out about the pregnancy."

"How?"

"I don't know. You knew Rita. The two of them were really close. My guess is that she knew something was wrong with Peggy, put two and two together, or maybe made a guess, and before Peggy knew it, Rita was in control. She never would have let her daughter have an abortion, even if it was legal then, which it wasn't, at least in most states, if I remember correctly. Considering that she was such a religious woman, it would make sense that she would have arranged for Peggy to be helped by some sort of Christian charity. From what Peg said last night, the timing was such that she was supposed to be going off to college anyway, so her father never knew what was up. She said that part of the bitterness between them was because, as he saw it, she just up and disappeared during that period of time."

"Where did she go?"

"I don't know." I was surprised that I had neglected to ask that the night before, so I tossed in a guess or two. "Maybe she had an apartment. Or she could have gone to a shelter, I suppose. Did they have shelters like that then?"

"I would think so. In fact, now that I think of it, my mom's younger sister used to bring in girls like that all the time," Max said.

"What do you mean?"

"I remember she was always hiring these fat girls for short periods of time as either a mother's helper or a maid, but from what my cousins said, they were all pretty lame. In particular, my cousin Julie hated it because the girls were always throwing up. To this day, she has a phobia about vomiting."

"When was this?"

He shrugged. "I don't know. Sometime back in the sixties. This was out on Long Island."

"How did she get the pregnant girls to come and clean?"

"They didn't just come and clean; they actually *lived* with the family." He furrowed his brow and stared at a spot on his desk. "I think that maybe she arranged to get these girls through her church. I mean, I can't think of another way, unless there was a black market for pregnant cleaning women."

"It's amazing how much we don't know. It's not as if we weren't alive then. I think we have to assume that there were other services out there that helped young women in need."

"I don't know, Sydney. In a way, I doubt it. I mean, we're talking the sixties. Unwed pregnancy was like leprosy back then. The stigma attached to an unmarried pregnant woman was . . . Well, look at Peggy. Here we have a bright, liberated, strong woman who to this day can't talk about what happened to her back then."

"Maybe it's the rape she can't talk about," I suggested.

"Did she say who raped her?"

"No. But I didn't get the impression that she knew him. If Peggy knew who had raped her, she would have said 'Ed, a guy from down the street, raped me,' but she didn't. Instead, she said that she had been attacked, and that makes me think that she didn't know her attacker. Don't you think?"

"I think we have to ask her directly. Or rather, you do."

"Right."

"Does she have any idea who adopted the baby?" Max asked.

"Max, she didn't even know the *gender* of the baby until last night."

"Did Rita know?"

I shrugged, unable to answer and feeling as if it was futile to speculate at this point.

"So, all we know for sure is that she gave birth to a boy sometime in December 1968 at a hospital that no longer exists."

"Yes."

"There are no names of attending physicians, adoption agency, or legal advisers?"

"No."

"Well then," he said, as if we had already successfully wrapped up another case. There was even a quirky smile attached to his handsome face. "I would say we're totally screwed. But"—he punctuated his thought with a finger pointed to the ceiling—"I am confident that we can find him, though you realize it's likely that his adopted parents gave him all the pertinent information about Peggy."

"I'm not so sure about that. I don't know if that information was available to adopting parents back then. Remember, he told her he only learned five years ago that he was adopted, and that he had been following her for the last year. Christ. Do you think that means it took him four years to find her?"

"I hope not. We don't have that kind of time." Max took a deep breath.

"You want to know something? I'll be much happier when the police are in on this, but until then, I'll do some research and find out what other resources, if any, were available for unwed mothers. For all I know, Planned Parenthood was helping women back then."

Max shrugged. "I don't know." He proceeded to pop every knuckle on his two hands.

"Listen, you should know that just because *I* promised her we'd find him doesn't mean—"

"Don't even go there. The objective is to keep John and Peggy and Lucy safe. Who knows, finding this guy might be one way to do that. I am definitely in."

"Thanks." I left through the door that led from his office to the outer office, where I asked Miguel to wait for me in my office. The office is situated in such a way that the seven various doors have always made me think of the farces by Feydeau.

I handed off the tape to Kerry, briefly explaining the situation to her, certain that she would get it done quickly and efficiently, without the need to ask for her discretion. It's nice to be able to work with people in whom you can place such confidence. Rare, but nice.

EIGHT

"Okay, so now I want you to run a background check on Harold Hardy." I was behind my desk and Miguel was lounging in a chair across from me, Auggie at his side.

He nodded as he rubbed Auggie's right ear. She leaned into his hand with total trust.

"Did you start anything on it?" I asked casually.

"Huh? Not really," he said, drawing out the words long enough to make me believe he had. Had I been in his position, I know I would have, if only for practice.

"Right. What do you have?" I asked.

"Okay." He straightened up in his chair, stopped petting the pup, took out a small spiral notebook, and started to leaf through the pages. He exhaled as he got comfortable in his seat. "Harold Hardy is a seventy-four-year-old white male, originally from Altoona, which is in Pennsylvania, in case you didn't know."

I did.

"He served in the army in Korea. Nothing real exciting there. When he got out of the service, he came to New York. You figure it had to be more exciting than Altoona, right? Besides, there was this girl. Looks like with this guy there's always a girl. This man is what you call a real Lolarrio," he said, stressing his Spanish accent so that it sounded like *Low-laahdio.*

"Lothario," I said, correcting him.

Auggie barked once at him, demanding more attention, which she wasn't about to get, since I could see he was already jazzed about what he was sharing with me.

"Whatever. He likes the women. You know he's been married?"

"I know he has an ex-wife. And if I'm not mistaken, he has several children, right?"

Miguel nodded. "Three. Joey is forty-six and an investment banker; Gina is forty-three and is a hand model, and Troy is forty and lives somewhere in Idaho. It doesn't look like they have much contact with that one. All three kids came from his first wife, Paula."

"First wife?"

"Oh yeah. Harold's got quite a past."

"I'm glad to see you didn't start researching this yet," I told him. By now, Auggie had changed strategy and was moving toward me.

Miguel smiled brightly and continued. "Listen here." He leaned forward and rested his elbows on his knees. My associate was a handsome young Latino with soulful dark eyes and appendages that might as well have been made of rubber. "Paula Bell was his first wife. They got married in 1951 and divorced fifteen years later. He married wife number two, Cissy, in 1970. That lasted for something like five years. She died in Madrid."

"How?"

"Apparently, the hotel food didn't agree with her."

"There was an investigation?"

"There was a death certificate. Cause of death: food poisoning."

"Did they have children?"

"Nope."

"Go on," I prompted as Auggie rested her chin on my knee. I gently rubbed her behind the ears and listened.

"Number three was a woman named Maggie. He married her in 1978. Now, she was five years *younger* than Harold, which was a switch from number two, who was six years *older* than him." He leafed through another page. "Maggie died on her way home from a night of disco in 1983. This time, a heart attack was recorded as the cause of death, but from what little I was able to learn so far,

Harold and Maggie lived in the fast lane, going to places like Plato's Retreat, the discos, and I would guess they were doing a lot of drugs." He paused and looked at me. "I mean, can you see going to a sex club without doing drugs?"

I assumed this was a hypothetical question, and so I responded with my own question. "Was he with her when she died?"

Miguel shook his head. "Nope. She had just gotten out of a taxi in front of their apartment building. She hit the bricks before she reached the front door. A couple of people on the street saw it happen. Her doorman was the one who called the police."

"And drugs weren't connected to the cause of death?"

"Nope. At least not on paper. But I haven't talked to no one about it yet."

"Anyone," I said as I scribbled "Maggie—poppers?" on a piece of paper. "Do they know where Harold was when Maggie died?"

"At a coffee shop in Sheridan Square, having breakfast with a woman named . . ." He flipped through several pages before he found what he was looking for. "Zelda. Zelda Hershowitz. She still lives in Manhattan." He gave me a quick glance, but it was enough for me to see how proud he was with the work he had done. "But wait—there's more." He looked up. "Wife number four, who was named Helen, although everyone called her 'Sugar,' was probably the reason why good old Harold was able to retire at the age of fifty-eight. By the time she and Harold met, Sugar had already been widowed twice and was worth a bundle because of it. They got hitched in 1986. In 1988, while on vacation in Australia, poor Sugar met with a fatal accident."

"What sort of accident?"

"She drowned while scuba diving."

We stared at each other for a minute. "Are there any more?"

"Maureen. 1992. She was fifty-eight and he was sixty-four when they got married. It was a second marriage for her and it lasted three years."

"What happened to Maureen? I mean, I assume *something* happened to Maureen."

"Oh yeah. She and her only child, a thirty-three-year-old

daughter, were killed in Chicago in a hit-and-run. The daughter was planning to move to Chicago, and the two of them were apartment hunting. They never found the person who hit 'em."

"Harold had an alibi?"

"An alibi would suggest that the man needed one," he said, a sparkle in his eye. "Yeah. Not only was he in New York but he was getting a root canal."

"Is that it with the harem list, or are there more?" I asked.

"That's it." He had good reason to be as pleased with himself as he seemed. However, what he had discovered so far was enough to have me anxious, because I didn't have time to focus on this problem, and time was of the essence, since Dorothy's wedding was only weeks away.

"Okay, let's look at what we have here." I gave Auggie a final rub behind her ears and rolled closer to my desk, where I grabbed a pen and made a list of the many wives of Harold Hardy. All totaled, there were five: Paula, Cissy, Maggie, Sugar, and Maureen.

After Miguel had filled me in on what he had on Harold, I shared what little I knew of him from his courtship with Dorothy. As we compared notes, a picture developed of a charismatic man who clearly knew how to woo women. However, four dead wives out of five were enough to raise a red flag. Aside from the repetition of loss, his history was unexceptional. Harold was just an ordinary guy and the facts were simple:

- He started in the construction business and segued into real estate development.
- He'd had five wives.
- Four wives had died:
  - one from food poisoning (Cissy, no. 2)
  - one from a heart attack (Maggie, no. 3)
  - one from drowning (Sugar, no. 4)
  - one from a hit-and-run (Maureen, no. 5).
- Three wives (nos. 2, 4, and 5) had left him very well off.

Though losing most of his spouses through death could have been a stoke of very bad luck or some nasty karma working itself out, none of it was particularly reassuring from my point of view, and I knew that it was something we had to investigate. Or rather, Miguel had to investigate. There was no way I could let Dorothy blithely walk into a potentially dangerous situation, but I also knew I was going to have my hands full trying to find Peggy's offspring. Miguel could devote all of his time to looking into the four dead wives of Harold the Hardy. Investigating a current death would be hard enough, but the four deaths had occurred in 1975, 1983, 1988, and 1995, which created a whole new set of challenges. It wasn't going to be easy, but I had every confidence that Miguel would be able to get enough of a handle on this that when I finally spoke with Dorothy and Harold, I wouldn't sound like a complete idiot.

"All right," I groaned as I learned back. "You know what you have to do. I'm sorry that neither Max nor I can help you on this, but you have carte blanche to use any of the operatives we have on staff. Just treat it as if I were the client. Fill in time sheets and reports, and do whatever you have to do to get the information. Be careful. And touch base with me on this at regular intervals, okay?"

"Yup." He launched out of his seat as if he had a spring on his bottom. After he put his notebook in his pocket, he shook out his hands. The action seemed to shimmy up his arms, through his shoulders, and down into his torso, then ended with him kicking his feet out like a sprinter getting ready for a run. "Don't worry. I'm gonna take care of this for Mrs. W. like she was my very own mother, you know what I mean?"

"I'm afraid I do. Look, just treat this as if it were any other case, okay? I don't want any heroics or jumping to conclusions because you're feeling protective."

He flattened his hand on his chest. "I don't jump to conclusions."

"We *all* do, Mickey. It's human nature. We make *assumptions*," I said, thinking of my conversation with Leslie before she'd left. "However, in our business the objective is to get to the truth, which is probably the most elusive thing in the world. It's only natural one would decide that if something looks dirty and smells dirty, it must *be* dirty. Unfortunately, that's not always the case. Remember: Be thorough. Be mindful. Be smart."

"Jeeze, you know how I hate it when you sound like a chaplain." He pulled a baseball cap out of his back pocket and slipped it on, effectively shielding the top half of his face. He ran a finger along the bill, which had been molded into a stiff arc that had an attitude all its own, which only accentuated his lean, graceful style. He wore snug jeans and a stiff white oxford-cloth shirt, which was unbuttoned low enough to reveal a white ribbed undershirt and a few errant chest hairs. His finishing touch was a pair of Revo mirrored sunglasses.

We agreed that he would keep in touch with me throughout the day and that if he wasn't able to connect directly with me, he would leave an update with Kerry. He was to have absolutely no contact with Leslie.

"What if she calls me?" he asked, letting his shoulders drop.

"Tell her you'll call back," I suggested.

"That ain't right, boss." He waited at the office door, his hand on the knob, no doubt expecting me to change my mind.

"What's not right?" I asked.

"Withholding the truth from Leslie. Your partner. My client."

"But you're not withholding anything, Miguel. You're just putting her on hold. And the reason you're doing that is because more often than not it's best to be sure of the information you're passing on. Otherwise, you could do a lot more damage than good. Do you understand?"

"Sure. You want to decide what she knows and when."

His eyes were hidden behind his glasses and shaded by his cap, but his words hit me like a slap in the face. Did he really think I was that controlling?

Finally, I asked, "Could you take off your glasses and cap, please?"

He did as I asked. When he unveiled his soft brown eyes, I was reminded that this was a man who loved me. Talk about seeking the truth and jumping to erroneous conclusions—hadn't I just made the assumption that he was castigating me for controlling Leslie, which made me think of the wedge that had been set between Leslie and me ever since I'd learned that she had tried to hire him without my knowing. I reminded myself that Miguel didn't know what had transpired between Leslie and me. It was all inside my own head, and my onslaught of thoughts kept me mute.

"Yo, Sydney, you okay?" He let go of the door and took a step toward me.

"Why do you think I want to decide what Leslie knows and when?" I asked, because I figured it would be better to hear his viewpoint than to create my own insecure possibilities throughout the day.

"Because you love her," he said, as if any idiot could see that. He studied me for a moment and added, "Hey, you gotta know what I like about you is that you wanna protect her. I also get it that if Leslie's mom knows that Leslie axt for a background search on this guy and he came up clean, it might create a problem between Leslie and her mother. I mean, it might anyway, but if you're gonna admit to being suspicious, it probably helps to have your suspicions validated. Right?"

"You are excelling at the fine art of bullshit," I said, not knowing if he was indeed bullshitting or being sincere, which really disturbed me, because it meant my instincts weren't working.

"I was taught by a couple of pros, boss." His smile only added to his charm, but I threw him out of my office nonetheless. I had work to do.

As he was opening the door to leave, Kerry was coming in. "There's someone out there who wants to hire you." She shut the door behind her and added, "I tried to steer her to Max, but she insisted on meeting with you."

"Why?" I asked with more than a trace of irritation.

"I think it's a woman's issue. I don't know. She wouldn't even discuss it with me. You want to see her?"

I didn't, but I also didn't have a choice, since business needs business to survive.

The woman who entered the office was stiff, her clothes tailored. She stepped over the threshold, where she paused and took a long hard look at the interior. Auggie, who was normally the self-appointed welcoming committee, stayed by my desk and eyed the newcomer.

"Hello, my name is Sydney," I said as I approached her, extending my hand.

She arched a brow and pushed her well-painted lips out, as if to illustrate that she was important and deliberate. It made her look like an old pig, but I shook her hand nonetheless. It was limp. Her skin was dry. I knew I had made a mistake. I offered her a seat on the sofa and closed the door behind her.

"My name is Grace Hauest." She was a soft-talker, the kind of person who spoke just loudly enough to be heard. It meant lipreading, which, given her lips, was a repelling thought.

"I beg your pardon," I said, cocking an ear in her direction.

Again she paused, then took a deep breath, jutted out her pointed chin, and repeated her name, although no more loudly than before. But this time, she added, "Have you heard of me?"

"No. Should I have?" I crossed one leg over a knee and made a mental note that I had to get clothes from home before returning to Peggy's.

"Well," she said, then paused, as if weighing her deep thoughts. "I am the vice president of the accounting firm of Polosi, Rose and Nellam." She graced me with a motherly smile.

"How can I help you?"

She took a deep breath, lowered her eyes, and ran a dry hand through her long strawlike hair. This was going to take forever, I realized.

"I have a . . . personal issue I would like you to look into, Ms. Sloane. . . ."

This was getting painful.

"Ms. Hauest, I don't mean to be rude, but I have a very limited amount of time right now, so if I could trouble you to get to the point, I'd appreciate it."

She slowly licked her gummy lips, closed her eyes, and nodded.

"I have had a problem for the last few years. It started out relatively innocuously, but over time it has become increasingly more pressing. . . ."

It was unfathomable that this woman could be the vice president of anything more demanding then the Slow and Soft Talkers of America. It took fifteen minutes, but I finally came to understand why she had come to see me.

"Let me get this straight. You have had a pain in your groin for the last two years and having exhausted all medical resources. You believe that during an alien abduction you were implanted with a device that remains undetected by all earthly technology. Is that correct?"

A very solemn nod was her response. "I know it sounds odd," she added.

Odd? It never ceased to amaze me that people could function socially and economically in the world and yet be absolutely bonkers. I couldn't help but wonder how the chairman of a company like Citicorp would feel after having signed on the soft talker's company, only to learn that they had entrusted their numbers to a woman who had aliens living in her body.

My first thought was to send her in to see Max, but neither of us had time to deal with this. I appeared to give her problem consideration, then told her that we were not the company for her. When she attempted to talk me into taking her case, I stopped her and gently but firmly explained that we were a detective agency, unversed in the paranormal. It took another ten minutes, but when she finally left, I decided I needed a couple of minutes of yoga in the morning sunlight. Focus can often be fleeting, and I had discovered over the last few years that yoga could give me the quick fix I needed.

In the middle of my meditation, Kerry stationed herself in the doorway. I knew her well enough to know that when she crossed her arms over her chest, not under it, she was making a subconscious statement that she was implacable. She planned to stay right where she was until I gave her my undivided attention. I took a deep breath, filled my lungs with cool air, exhaled slowly, and turned to face her.

"That woman was certifiable," I told her.

"Totally. But listen, I was just thinking," she said as she pulled a chair over to my desk and folded herself onto it. "Patrick has an adopted brother who went through a very long process of trying to find his own birth mother," she said, referring to her artist fiancé. "It can take forever," Kerry said. "Logan—that's his name, Logan—he always knew he was adopted, but it didn't seem to bother him until he hit his late twenties. Then he became obsessed with finding his birth mother."

"Why?" I asked.

She took a deep breath and recrossed her legs, putting her left ankle on her right thigh. "He learned he was sick and that his illness was hereditary. I think he wanted to know if there were any other surprises he should be prepared for."

"Were there?"

"Logan's a weird guy, Syd. He needs to have secrets, you know?" She held up a hand as if taking a vow. "I try to have as little to do with him as I can. I see him at family dinners and holidays, but not much besides that. I always encourage Patrick to have his own relationship with him. I mean, the guy gives me the creeps, which isn't because he's adopted, but just because he's creepy. You know what I mean? But who knows? Maybe his birth mother was like this Addams Family creature and the reason he gives me the willies is because he's genetically spooky."

I knew it bothered her enough that she had interrupted the transcribing of the tape to tell me about it.

"Do you know how he found his mother?" I asked.

"No. But I can ask. We're actually all supposed to get together tonight because it's Mrs. Mom's birthday," she said, referring to Patrick's mother. "I'll talk to him then."

"Thanks."

"Hey, anything for Peggy." With that said, she started back to the outer office to finish transcribing the tape, which we could then pass over to the police (once they knew about this event). But she stopped at the doorway. "This whole thing with Peggy is pretty scary, isn't it?"

She sounded as if she could use some reassuring, but I didn't have anything to give her.

"Yeah, it is."

"You think this nut is the guy who shot John?"

I shook my head and shrugged. "I don't know what to think."

I looked down to rub Auggie and heard the door close behind Kerry.

Peggy and I had left it that she would call me as soon as she had seen John, but I also knew that she had a high-pressure client who was demanding her immediate attention. The problem for me was that I needed some questions answered before I started my hunt for the wayward progeny. I dialed Peggy's cell phone and left a voice message. Then I called her at work and learned that she wasn't expected until noon, at the earliest. I called the hospital, where one of the nurses in the ICU told me that Peggy was in with John, whose condition was unchanged from the day before. I asked if she would have Peggy call me when she came out.

I turned to the computer and started a fresh file. I keyed in all the information I had on Peggy, John, and her son.

Then under a column titled "QUESTIONS." I wrote "When?" and "Who?"

I stared at the page a good long time before I connected to the Internet and started to research anything and everything that might educate me on organizations helping pregnant women in 1968.

Before I knew it, two hours had flown by and Auggie was nudging me for a walk. Peggy hadn't returned my call. Miguel wouldn't be calling yet, and Max had gone out, so I figured a walk in the park was just what I needed to clear my head.

NINE

Peggy successfully avoided me until we met up again at her apartment that evening. Though I hadn't done much more than research adoption centers circa 1968 all day long and swim forty-five minutes' worth of laps at the health club, I was pooped by the time my sous-chef, Lucy, and I started dinner, a simple fare of chicken Milanese, garlic potatoes, and salad. After camp, Lucy, Auggie, and I had picked up a little snack and then gone back to my office, because I'd felt that if I kept Lucy away from home, she'd be less inclined to worry about her dad. I'd let her be the boss, which meant that she could work at my desk, where she'd played a computer game. I'd had to pry her away from the computer when it was time to walk Auggie in the park and head home.

"You couldn't call?" I asked Peggy once I learned that John's condition was unchanged, which meant he was sleeping more than not and in no shape to deal with her news.

"Don't start," she warned.

"Peggy, I don't know if you realize this, but *if* this fella was responsible, we are losing valuable time in finding—"

"You didn't start?"

"Yes, we started, but talk about a needle in a haystack. We need more information. Again, I cannot stress how helpful it would be if the police were also looking for him. You know as well as I do—"

"Looking for who?" Lucy asked when she came into the room, waving her hands as proof that she had washed for dinner.

Looking for the lima bean thief," I said as I put dinner on the table. "Short green guy they say is eating up all the lima beans in town."

"Good! I hate lima beans." Lucy screwed up her face and shook her head to emphasize her point. Her mother and I silently agreed to put a hold on the conversation until Lucy was in bed. In the meantime, Peggy reassured Lucy, saying, "Daddy is doing just great. I bet you'll be able to see him by this weekend." Then mother and daughter had a lengthy discussion about little Jimmy Hurwith, a boy at camp, who apparently had Lucy tied in knots as to whether it was love or hate she felt.

As they talked, I considered what I had learned that day. Going on-line to research anything can take you through an amazing labyrinth, and though I had tried to stay on track, it had been hard not to get waylaid in the land of people searching for their birth mothers. So many of the postings were from people stating that they just wanted to know who they were, as if they needed to define themselves not by the person they were but by where they'd come from. There were hundreds of sites where people could post information about their birth, in hopes of connecting with someone who might remember their family. One person, for example, was looking for a couple by the name of Schmidt who had had three daughters in 1944, one of whom gave birth to an illegitimate child at the Chittenton Shelter in D.C. or the New York Foundling Hospital. Unexpectedly, I had discovered that there were many agencies in the mid-sixties that had helped unwed mothers, whether it was to assist in the adoption process or give them shelter for the final stage of their pregnancy. All religious denominations were represented, as well as government agencies, including the Department of Social Services and the Department of Child Welfare. And of course there were loads of private adoptions that were handled through attorneys and physicians. I knew, too, that when Peggy was pregnant, young women were made to feel dirty and ashamed, but what I didn't fully understand or appreciate was how very much the times had changed. Now people entered into open adoptions, where the birth mother/parents got a chance to know the adoptive parents, often entering into a lifelong union.

Though I now had a list of thirty different agencies and shelters that Rita might have used for her daughter, the day had really been spent acquainting myself with the lay of the land of adoption. Just reading the postings of people looking to connect with their beginnings had had an impact on me. The mystery of one's own history has to be profoundly compelling, I realized. "Who am *I*," was a common question, one that threaded through all of the sites and had made me that much more aware of my own roots.

I took Auggie out for a walk while Peggy tucked Lucy in for the night. When we returned, it was clear that Lucy would not even attempt sleep unless Auggie was cuddled next to her. As much as my pup was a mama's girl, when faced with the choice between a warm bed with soft sheets or a cold wooden floor, she was no fool. After circling the foot of the bed several times, she finally plopped down on Lucy's legs, let out a huge sigh, smacked her lips loudly, and shut her eyes. Ah, heaven.

"Why didn't you call me?" I asked again as soon as we were alone. I knew I sounded like a shrew, but I couldn't help myself.

"I told you I would call if I had something to tell you," she said as she shoved the dinner dishes into the dishwasher.

"No, you said you would call after you saw John. And I left you messages, Peg, so it's not as if you didn't know that I wanted to talk to you."

She made a noise that sounded like what a bull makes when preparing to charge. "I have been pulled in every single direction today, Sydney." She turned and faced me, planting her knuckles firmly on her hips. "It isn't bad enough that the man I adore is lying in the hospital—in the ICU, for God's sake—and I can't just drop everything to be with him. . . ."

"Why can't you?" I asked only somewhat innocently. I knew what it felt like to be so driven by my commitment to work that as a result you got accused of both myopia and self-aggrandizement. But I also knew what commitment to family and friendship meant.

Peggy ignored my challenge and plowed ahead. "It isn't enough that I can't be there for John every waking moment, or that I was in the middle of closing a business deal with a client who really thinks that his two-hundred-million-dollar investment is somehow worth more than my peace of mind, but now my best friend is on me like napalm."

"*Napalm?* Oh, that's very nice. Like I'm trying to hurt you. I'm sorry, Peg. I thought we were both concerned about finding your son's whereabouts. I thought it meant something to you. My mistake." I turned my back in frustration but then did an immediate about-face. "Listen, I don't care what you say or do to try to hurt my feelings and push me away. I am in this for the long haul, Peggy. And because it's me you're dealing with and not someone else, you are going to have to answer questions you would rather ignore. You are going to have to think about things that you would prefer to leave buried. But I promise you that together we will not only get through this but we will find him and, more importantly, discover what it is he wants from you. I will not let him hurt you. Do you understand?" By now, I was across the room and we were face-to-face.

"Yes." She stood there, not moving, her hands at her sides.

"Good. Now before we start, I need a cup of tea. How about you?"

Ten minutes later, back at the kitchen table, I asked Peggy how Rita had learned that she was pregnant.

Peggy shrugged. "I don't know. All I know is that she told me she knew I was pregnant."

"Did she know that you had been raped?"

Peggy said nothing for the longest time. Finally, she said, "Yes. When she told me she knew that I was pregnant, I told her I had been raped."

"And she didn't *do* anything about it?" I couldn't keep the surprise out of my voice.

Peggy rubbed the tabletop with her thumb.

"Peggy, I'm on your side."

She swallowed several times, as if avoiding nausea, before she said, "I guess we both felt that it was . . . I don't know, easier just to deal with the problem than to make it everyone's business."

"What happened after Rita learned that you were pregnant?"

"What do you mean?"

"Did you go to a shelter?"

"Oh, I see." She stared in her teacup, as if trying to reach into the recesses of her memory. Finally, she said, "Yes, I did, but not right away."

"Where was it?"

"The Bronx, which for me might as well have been Idaho. The only place I had ever been to in the Bronx before that was the zoo, and believe me, I don't know it any better now." She got up and pulled a box of Entenmann's chocolate-chip cookies from a shelf. "The idea was to place pregnant girls in areas where they wouldn't be recognized, but usually they weren't admitted to the shelters until they were about seven months along. As soon as I graduated from high school, I left the house. I was only three months pregnant at that point, but Mom didn't want to take any chances of Dad finding out." She put the box of cookies on the table, placing it between us.

"Why?" I popped a small cookie into my mouth.

Peggy shrugged and studied the contents of the box, as if one cookie might taste different from another. "Maybe she thought he would care."

"Was he the one who attacked you?" I held my breath, not knowing if I would get her wrath or her tears.

I got neither. She just shook her head as if she were in a fog, then said, "No. Dad was a horrible man, and I hate to say that I wouldn't have put raping someone past him, but he never touched me. Not like that." She nibbled on her cookie.

"Do you know who raped you?" I popped another cookie into my mouth, fully aware that as much as I wanted it to, it wouldn't keep me from asking the hard questions.

She was impossible to read as she took a sip of her tea. When the cup was secured on its saucer, she looked me straight in the eyes, as if to put an end to it, and finally said, "No."

I didn't believe her, so I asked the question again.

"I said no." She could have cut metal with her tone.

"I hate to say it, Peg, but I don't believe you." I halfheartedly held up my hands. "Before you start yelling at me, just listen. I've been a detective a long time and I have a sixth sense when it comes to people lying to me. If I'm wrong, then forgive me for pushing, but if I'm right, your withholding not only hampers the investigation but makes you look incredibly suspicious. John was shot, you get this call, and then you withhold information that could help us find him—how would you assess it?"

She gently ran an index and middle finger along the line of her lips, back and forth, back and forth, barely present at the kitchen table.

"I'm your best friend," I continued. "I can understand why you would be reticent to talk about it, but if you do know who raped you, now would be a good time to tell me."

"I was alone. He came up from behind me and threatened to kill me if I made a sound. I tried to fight at first, but he was stronger than I was. He had already hurt me and I was afraid that he would kill me, so I stopped fighting."

"Where were you?"

"We had a shed in the backyard that Dad had turned into a sort of study. I had been back there studying for a test. Actually, I had just finished studying and was headed back to the house when he attacked."

"Were there any witnesses? Did any of the neighbors hear what was happening?"

She looked baffled by the question. "I don't know. I don't think so. But I don't know for sure. Would that matter at this point?"

We looked at each other, both of us aware that it probably wouldn't matter a whit right now. But back then, it might have made a huge difference.

"Where was your family?"

She tapped the cookie on the tabletop and said, "It was Saint Patrick's Day. My folks had gone out for dinner." She studied the abandoned cookie. "By the time they returned, I had already showered. It wasn't the kind of family where I could rush into my parents' arms and tell them what had happened. I felt very much alone. And I was so angry. And scared. Mind you, I knew other girls who had gone all the way with boys by that point, but that wasn't who I was. I was smart, but I was pretty naïve. Hell, Rita hadn't prepared me for anything when I started to menstruate. I was twelve and I thought I was dying.

"But that night, after that happened, I knew things weren't right inside me. I was terrified about getting pregnant."

"When did you know you were pregnant?"

"That night, probably," she said. "When I didn't get my period the following month, I knew for sure. So I started looking for a way to get rid of it."

She stared at the tabletop as she continued. "All I could think about was that I was supposed to start at Columbia in September and that I had to have the abortion before too many weeks passed. A friend of mine, a girl named Dara, she had a sister who'd had an abortion, and she gave me the name of the doctor."

"A real doctor?"

Again, Peggy shrugged. "Who knew? Who cared?" This time, a smile pinched at her mouth, both self-conscious and endearing. I could see my friend as a teenager, a girl who was determined not to be stopped by this twist of events. "The way I saw it was that I didn't care if I lived or died at that point, but I was pretty certain I'd live. I don't know how Mom found out, but I do remember very clearly that the week before Easter she told me that she wanted to go hat shopping with me. You know how she was about her Easter bonnets. Anyway, we were sitting on a bench in Central Park and she said, 'Honey, I know you're pregnant and I don't want you to get rid of the baby.'"

Peggy exhaled at the recollection and said, "It wasn't like Rita to be so direct. I think she felt she had to because she didn't want me to play dumb."

"What did you do?"

"I started crying. I told her I wouldn't give birth to what was growing inside me, and she started talking about God. I mean, it was insane. I asked if she really thought that God wanted me to

73

have this thing inside me, and she said that the God *she* knew felt there was merit in all lives. Even in the life of the scumbag who did that to me." She briskly wiped the tears off her cheeks and continued. "Her sentiment enraged me, but I think part of me was relieved that I wasn't really alone. The trade-off was having to go through with the pregnancy, but I figured once it was done, I would never have to deal with anything like that again. Every day, I woke up hoping that I would miscarry this doomed thing inside me, but I had a healthy pregnancy. My mother kept telling me that was because this was happening to me for a reason. Not that I was bad, mind you, but I was meant to learn something from 'the event,' as she called it. The only good thing was that because my grades were so high, Columbia let me delay matriculation until the spring."

"Huh. I always thought you'd been working to save money for school."

"That's what I told you."

"And Rita never suggested that you go to the police?"

"She couldn't. It would have meant having her own son arrested." When Peggy breathed, her entire chest heaved up and out. She squeezed her eyes shut and rubbed her brow with her fingertips.

"So it was Karl," I said, not surprised.

"Yes," she whispered.

"When you left your parents' house in June, after graduation, where did you go?"

"I worked as a live-in maid for a family in Larchmont."

"Who arranged for it?"

Peggy shook her head. "I don't remember. My mother?"

"How long were you there?"

"Until my seventh month."

"Did you see your mom during this time? Did you go to the doctor for monthly checkups?"

"I saw my mom maybe three times." Peggy retrieved the cookie and continued nibbling around its edges. "But after the initial examination, when I found out for certain that I was pregnant, I didn't see a doctor until maybe the fifth or sixth month."

"Your mom took you?"

"No. I mean, there were only one or two appointments, because I went to the shelter in my seventh month. I don't know if I went alone or if the woman whose house I was cleaning took me. She was kooky, but she was very nice to me. I can't remember her name, but she and her husband had five or six children, all girls, and I think she had a revolving door for, cheap hired help—pregnant girls, you know? I was there from June through mid-October."

"Then what?"

"Then I went to this shelter in the Bronx. It was in an old building, very Gothic, and it just depressed the hell out of me."

"Did you make friends there?"

Peggy dropped her chin and stared at me. "What do you think?" She rubbed the crumbs off her fingers and said, "No, I didn't make friends. Not only did they discourage friendships but I really didn't have anything in common with these girls. Most of them were pregnant because they had been willing partners, and many of them really wanted to keep their babies, but they were too young or too poor or just single. I wasn't like the others there. I just wanted to get the whole thing over with." She took a sip of tea and added, "There was this one nun I became friendly with. Or a nun wanna-be."

"Nuns ran the shelter?"

"I don't know whether they ran it, but they were there."

"In full habit? Try to remember. Because if it was a Catholic shelter, then I can pare down my list by excluding other maternity shelters."

"I don't remember. The one I liked didn't wear a full habit. . . . I don't think any of them did. But since my mother made the arrangements, I would guess that it was a Catholic shelter."

"Do you remember her name? Was the hospital where you gave birth affiliated with the shelter? Was the shelter within walking distance of the hospital? Can you think of anything at all that might be helpful in tracking down the records of your giving birth?"

"I'm afraid," she said softly.

75

"I know. Did you talk to Detective Cooper again today?"

"No, but several of the top dogs called today to offer their support and see if there was anything that Lucy or I needed. Oh, and Gil called. He wanted to know if there was anything I needed."

"Jackson?" I asked, knowing that she had to mean none other than Gilbert Jackson, who had not only been a friend of the family for as far back as I could remember but had spent more than forty years in the Detective Bureau and was one of the more influential men on the force.

"Yes. He stopped by the hospital this afternoon. I had just gotten back after passing off this client to one of my associates. Now I can devote all my time to John. Gil's a very sweet man."

"He is, but I wouldn't tell him that. Just FYI: Gil can be an enormous help to us right now. As a matter of fact, my guess is that he's probably got his fingers in the investigation anyway. If nothing else, he has access to all the information. Actually, Gil is the one you should tell about your son."

"I'll tell him tomorrow."

"You promise?"

"I promise. Will you be with me when I talk to him?"

"If you want me to, yes."

"I do."

"Peggy." I studied her tired face and said, "I still have a few more questions before we can hit the hay."

"Okay," she said without moving.

"About the shelter . . . isn't there anything you can remember? The name? The street it was on? Was the hospital within walking distance?"

"Yes, I do know that. I remember walking there a few times, either for a doctor's appointment or just to get out of the place. But I also remember it was a brutally cold that year. It was hard to walk a block without feeling as if you were going to freeze to death. So I didn't go out much, but I do know that we were close enough to the hospital to walk. Does that really help?"

"Everything helps," I said, not at all certain that I was speaking any kind of truth. After a few more fruitless questions, I asked her to think about the nun she had taken a shine to. I told Peggy it would help if she could remember her name, because we were walking blindly into utter darkness and anything could be a guide.

"You want me to pick up Lucy from camp again tomorrow?" I asked as we began to melt to our kitchen seats, too tired to move. "We had a great time today. She's a terrific kid, Peg."

"I know."

"Everything is going to be okay. I promise."

"Some things you can't promise, Sydney."

She was right, of course. But I wasn't about to admit it.

"Yeah, well, I can promise you that if you don't get these friggin' cookies out of my reach, I'm going to be sick."

"Exercise a little self-control," she said smugly as she eased the box of cookies slowly past me and went to put them away. For a moment, there was a hint of the old Peggy there, and it felt good.

TEN

It's hard to admit some things. For example, it was hard for
Kerry to admit that there'd been a time when she was crazy about
the Carpenters. Max had a hard time admitting that he liked reading the occasional romance, and, if truth were told, it was hard for
me to admit that there were parts of Peggy's story that didn't sit
well with me.

It was reassuring that she had told me that it was her brother,
Karl, who had raped her. It was one of those things I would ultimately have found out, and it would have made her look bad if
she'd kept this from the police.

Unable to sleep, I took Auggie for a quick walk in the park and
then dropped her off at my office. By 6:00 A.M., I was at the gym,
jumping rope and pounding the weight bag as I tried to sort
through my objectives for the day ahead. But it was no use. As I hit
the bag, I couldn't stop thinking about the fact that Leslie and I
had not talked the night before. This disturbed me. Pattern changes
always had that effect on me. I'm like an old dog, a creature of habit,
someone who takes comfort in certain elements of routine. It
didn't matter that I knew Leslie was busy and that I was busy. We
were both busy people, but it wouldn't take more than a moment
to say "I love you." And as queer as it sounds, I had always been a
firm believer in the power of love. So it bothered me that we had
not talked.

No big deal, I thought.

Right jab.

After all, we're adults.

Quick left-right hooks.

I mean, the last thing I need or want is a codependent relationship, where independence and autonomy are lost. Right?

Right jab.

"Oh baby, what's eating you?" The very distinctive voice of my good friend and boxing coach, Zuri, came at me from behind.

I hit the bag one more time before responding. "Have you read the paper in the last few days? John Cannady was shot."

"I know. How is he?" I had known Zuri for more years than I could remember, and I was always taken aback when I saw her. Between her perfect mocha-colored skin and enormous eyes, she was strikingly beautiful.

I shrugged. "Ultimately, he'll recover."

"How's Peggy?" She tucked her fingers into the tiny pockets of her gym shorts, pushed her shoulders up, and scanned the nearly empty room.

"Shitty." I eyed the worn bag, but by now I had lost interest. "I suppose in the big scheme of things, considering what *could* have happened, they're incredibly lucky. That, however, doesn't make things any easier to deal with."

She nodded as she studied a slight man shadow boxing at the far end of the gym. "Too bad." She looked directly into my eyes. "Having incredible luck is just the sort of thing that should make anything much easier to deal with, don't you think? Especially with life-or-death issues." It wasn't a judgment, just an observation.

"I suppose so. Maybe good luck makes us greedy or entitled," I said as I started drifting back toward the locker room. "So give me some good news."

"I met a man." When she smiled, dimples dug little craters into her cheeks.

"Really? Tell me about him." I stopped and turned to her. Over the years, Zuri had had a slew of suitors, but no one who had been able to capture her attention in any significant way. Guys fell all over themselves for her, but Zuri was a self-reliant working mother of two sons and had never felt the need for just any man in her life. A glance at her was all I needed to tell me that this was different.

"His name's Chester. He's a retired restaurateur. He's strong, funny, smart, kind, sexy. . . ." Her smile was infectious. As Zuri described Chester and how happy he was making her, the cosmic equilibrium of life struck me. Here I had one friend who was falling in love for the first time in years and another who was terrified that her past was about to undo her present. And there I was, smack-dab in the middle—the center point of balance, as it were. Neither here nor there, I was uncomfortably aware of an imperceptible shift between the two different coasts of my emotional life. It was easier to focus outside of myself, whether it was on Zuri's joy or Peggy's grief.

When I left the gym, I wanted to call Leslie, to try to connect, but it was too early and I knew I would sound desperate or panicked, both of which confused me. So instead I went to the office, where Auggie and I settled in to do some research. Avoiding an exercise in futility (which would have been following the adoption path), I decided to learn as much about Peggy's brother, Karl Dexter, as I could. Meeting him was inevitable, and the sooner the better, but I didn't want to go in there completely empty-handed.

I started with some basic information: address, phone number, date of birth, and education. I didn't have much more than that when I exhausted what was to be found on him on-line. I knew he owned what had been the family house in Jackson Heights. He had never been married. He was a registered Republican. He was a bookkeeper for a printing house. He was a Vietnam veteran.

I was surprised when the first person to arrive at work was Miguel. He came in with his breakfast: a bag of Fritos, a Dr Pepper, and Twinkies.

"Yo, boss," he said as he poked his head into my office. "You wanna talk about Harold the Horny, or you busy?"

"Come on in." I warned him off sharing any of his breakfast with Auggie, who sat at his side and anxiously waited for a morsel of the garbage he was ingesting. Her ears twitched; her lips tensed into a smile and then loosened. She cast an occasional gaze in my direction, until finally I took a treat out of the desk drawer and suggested she let Miguel eat in peace.

"So, anything further on Harold's connubial catastrophes?"

"Huh?"

"How's the investigation going? You learning anything?"

"Oh man, like yeah. First, I decided it was going to be too much to focus on all four dead women, so I decided to start with the most recent, which is still a couple of years old, and work my way back in time. Smart, huh?"

I didn't say anything.

"Maureen Kelly Hansen Hardy was sixty-one when she and her daughter, Margaret, were hit and killed by a car in Chicago. This took place on the North Side, an area called West Rogers Park. The street where they were killed is real residential. I mean, all of them are one-family houses. Middle-class. Lots of Indians and Yids."

"What did you say?" I asked as he wiped a greasy hand on his jeans.

He looked confused. "Middle-class?"

"Yids?"

"Oh, yeah. You know, the ones who wear those big hats and have—what do you call 'em? Dreadlocks."

"They're called payess, and *Yids* is a derogatory term. That's like someone calling you a spick."

He pushed his lips into an exaggerated frown and shrugged. "I been called worse. Besides, sticks and stones, you know."

"Let's just try to refrain from overt prejudice, okay?"

"Okay." He took a sip of soda. "Can I finish?"

"Please." I gestured with an open hand as I lifted my feet onto my desk. "But before you do, just tell me who's your Chicago source."

"Kerry told me to call a detective there, a Debbie Phillips. You know her?"

"Oh yeah." Debbie was a Chicago private investigator I'd met years earlier when she was trying to track down an embezzler who had made it to New York. The guy ultimately got as far as Saint Thomas, but during the New York part of her investigation, she and I had become fast friends. The unusual thing about Debbie was that everyone liked her, from the top political brass to cops walking a beat, civil servants, religious leaders, and ex-cons. She was a happily married mother of two and was not only one of the best-connected PIs I had ever met but one of the best in general.

"I called her late yesterday morning and she got back to me in a few hours with the initial stuff. Like I told you before, Maureen and her daughter were the victims of a hit-and-run. Debbie remembered the case because it made it to the papers, and the reason it made it to the papers was because of the neighborhood where they got hit. So yesterday I axt her to get me just the bare-bones info and then tell me if she thought there was something fishy going on here. She went through newspaper archives and apparently talked to the detective assigned to the case." He crumpled his now-empty bag of Fritos and opened the Twinkies. "The conclusion is that Harold didn't have his wife bumped off."

"Why? What's the evidence?"

"The detective who was on the case was convinced that he'd found the person behind the hit-and-run, but because of the tight-knit community, he was never able to build a case against the driver." He paused and offered an apologetic smile.

"What?"

"The car belonged to one of them hotshot rabbis. He called the police after the women were killed to report that his car had been stolen."

"And I bet he had an airtight alibi."

"You bet right. The community protected him and turned it into this whole bogus bias issue. Debbie said she thought that if the family of the women who were killed had been willing to pursue it, they might have been able to get something. But it was becoming a political nightmare, and because no one except the detective cared, it got swept away."

"Harold didn't insist on an investigation?"

"Nope." Miguel shrugged. "The rabbi died a year ago. He was

mugged in Lincoln Park and beaten to death. And while I think his death might have been what you call 'cosmic justice'—because I do think the scumbag was responsible for the women's death—I don't think Harold the Horny hired him to knock them off."

"And you feel absolutely certain that the rabbi was behind the wheel at the time of the accident? There's absolutely no evidence that someone else might have stolen the car, hit the women, and run off?"

Miguel shook his head slowly but emphatically. "The Chicago police detective, who's retired now, told Debbie that he would stake his entire reputation on it."

I tapped my feet together and gave this some thought. Unless we knew the detective in question, the reputation card was a moot point. Miguel read my mind.

"Debbie said to tell you that he was one of the best and that you shouldn't waste your time trying to open a case that, while not *settled*, was nonetheless solved."

"So the rabbi got away with murder," I said.

"Looks that way." He polished off the second Twinkie and added, "If it's any consolation, it seems that his own death was pretty icky. He was mugged and left for dead, but apparently his mugger didn't actually kill him. He died slowly in the bushes just off a major pathway. They estimate he could have been there for close to twenty-four hours before he died."

"Huh." I glanced at the computer clock. It was after 9:00 A.M., a perfect time to wake Leslie. "Anything else on Harold?"

"I was able to track down his first wife, and I have a lunch appointment with her today. I've also started checking out the third wife's death. I know it was longer ago, but it was also local. I axt Kerry if she'd contact someone in Australia to help me dig up anything on wife number four, Sugar, but she said she was too busy." He rolled his eyes. "She suggested I start with the consulate, but I decided to start locally with Maggie's heart attack. I thought it would be easier."

"Probably." I planted my feet back on the floor and made note of a name for Miguel. "Here. When you're ready, this is Denis

Merreck. He's a local detective and has excellent contacts in Sydney, which is where he's from. You may not need him, but at least you have the number."

"Thanks." He stood and stretched, exposing his flat stomach as his T-shirt inched over his midriff. "Listen, can I take Auggie to the park? I need to think, and she can always use a walk."

I gave them my blessings just as the phone rang. It was Leslie.

"Hey, babe," she cooed into the phone. "How's my favorite detective?"

My initial reaction was to ask why she hadn't called the night before, given how she knew all that was happening here. But I didn't follow that. Instead, I went with my second reaction, which was to tell her as much as I knew about Harold so far.

"You have a gut reaction yet?" she asked when I was finished.

"Nope. I'm leaving this one to Miguel. The stuff with Peggy is enough for me to deal with." That's when I gave her a brief overview on Peggy's revelation of a son and his sudden appearance in her life.

I was deliberately sketchy, because details weren't necessary and I could tell she was distracted.

"Leslie, are you alone?" I asked, feeling a hole in the pit of my stomach.

"Sydney, it's six o'clock in the morning," she said.

"That doesn't answer my question," I replied coldly.

"Of course I'm alone," she said with equal frostiness. "What's that supposed to mean? You think I'm cheating?"

"I think I'm tired and I don't want to deal with my feelings right now. I think we haven't been connecting well just recently and it's easier to wonder what's up with you, because I know I haven't changed."

"You're suspicious. That's a change right there."

"You're right. I'm sorry. Look, as much as part of me wants to deal with this right now, another part of me knows that Peggy's brother might have some connection to John's shooting, and I don't have the luxury of being able to put that off."

"But you have the time to put us off?"

"Leslie, I called you twice yesterday, but you didn't return my calls. That was the second day in a row you neglected to call me back, which is a first in our relationship. It may mean nothing and it may mean something, but the one thing in my life I feel I can trust right now is you. . . ."

"Even when you think I'm cheating?" she asked.

"Yes. If you're seeing someone else, there's a reason. We'll either work through it or we won't. But the bottom line is, I trust *us* enough to know that we've always been able to talk about things—even the hard things—openly and honestly. I also know that you love Peggy and John and want their shit settled as much as I do. So something's got to be put on hold. You're in L.A. and I'm here, so the option seems obvious. Am I wrong?"

"You're wrong about a lot, but I agree that this is something we need to deal with together and not long-distance. Maybe we should give each other space right now."

"What does that mean?" I crumpled a piece of paper and kept squeezing it in my hand.

"I mean that maybe it will do us good not to talk to each other for a few days. I'll be back in New York in another two or three days. Maybe we need a little break so we can sort through things on our own."

I don't remember the rest of the conversation, just the feeling when it was over: as if I had been sliced in half with a very cold, long blade.

I don't know how long I sat there, unable to think or feel, but when the phone rang, I grabbed for it as if it were a lifeline, thinking that it was Leslie. I was wrong.

It was Peggy. She had told John. She was ready to move forward. I told her I would meet her at the hospital within twenty minutes.

I decided it wouldn't be a bad idea to take my gun, a Walther P5 Compact 9 mm. For the last several months, I had changed my routine and been leaving it in the safe at work, rather than schlepping it along with me, but I threw it in my bag before leaving the office.

I called Gil Jackson as I bolted to the nearest subway station. I didn't have to explain anything more than that Peggy and I needed to talk to him. Without any questions, Gil agreed to meet us at the hospital as soon as he could.

In my subway car was a boisterously happy group of children en route to a museum. I watched their interactions and thought about all that was happening in my life. Who would have guessed that the calm woman sitting next to a blind man wearing a bad toupee, surrounded by a gaggle of ten-year-olds, was cogitating on how strange life is and wondering how many times a day we have to juggle it all just to keep our equilibrium.

One subway car. Forty-odd people. A million ideas. I love this city, I thought.

ELEVEN

Peggy was pacing the corridor when I arrived at the hospital. John had been moved that morning from the ICU into a private room, and a uniformed police officer was stationed outside his door.

"Say hey, Fay Wray." Our usual greeting popped out of me before I could stop it. Her response would usually have been, "Holy cow, sow," but instead all she could manage was a weak smile.

"Have the police been able to question John yet?" I asked as I looped my arm through hers and led her to a private alcove where there were two chairs and a table. Since John was out of the ICU and was the only witness to the shooting, they would naturally want to get a statement from him as soon as possible.

She nodded. "Detective Cooper was here, but John couldn't remember much."

"Much or anything?" I asked, knowing all too well how easy it is to block out the bad and the ugly.

"Anything," she said.

"What *was* he able to remember?" I asked.

She shook her head. "That he had taken Lucy to camp." She looked up at me with bloodshot eyes.

"That's it?"

She nodded.

I wasn't surprised. Getting shot point-blank in the chest is something most people would want to forget.

"Did he remember you?" I asked as gently as I could.

She nodded.

"Did he remember buying a newspaper, or the elevator ride up to your floor?" I was grasping for straws in much the same way Detective Cooper probably had earlier with John.

Peggy shook her head, only this time she lowered her chin to her chest, giving me a fine view of the now-gray roots on the top of her head. She dug her fingers into her knees and rocked back and forth ever so slightly. I reached out and placed one hand over hers and said, "You talked to John."

She stopped rocking but kept her head lowered, as if she was studying both our hands on her knee. Finally, she murmured, "Yes."

"You okay?" I asked.

She slowly lifted her chin, and I saw that what little mascara had remained on her lashes was now streaked down her cheeks.

I wrapped my arms around her. Despite all the questions I had, I could think of no words of comfort. Her body was stiff at first, but when I held on and told her to breathe, it opened the dam and she cried until there were no tears left.

"I'm disgusting," she finally whimpered as she pulled away from me, her hand cupped protectively in front of her nose and mouth. I handed her a tissue and leaned back into the orange leatherette chair.

"Tell me what happened. It'll make you feel better. Trust me," I added, addressing the doubt written all over her face.

By the time she had arrived at the hospital, the staff had already moved John into a private room and Detective Cooper was just ending his visit. Cooper told Peggy that so far they had no solid leads. He also explained how he wasn't surprised that John couldn't remember the incident, but he asked Peggy to call him during the day if John remembered anything, no matter how insignificant it might seem.

John had seemed so strong when she saw him that she'd practically blurted out the news about her son, she told me. "I didn't want to frighten or worry him, so I tried to be as . . . as laid-back about it as I could without making him think that I was being blasé. You know what I mean?"

"How did he take it?"

"He's pretty drugged. But he knows, so—"

"He knows what? That you have a son? That you were raped by Karl? That this guy called and scared you? What?"

"He knows that I was raped and have a son as a result."

"Did he ask why you were telling him this now?"

She wet her lips and shook her head. "As far as I'm concerned, the important thing is that he knows it, because now I can tell the police."

"Peggy. Sydney." Gil Jackson's deep voice seemed to round the corner before he did.

"I called Gil," I told her as she shot me a look that would have felled anyone fainthearted.

"You couldn't wait?"

"No. Neither can you. Hey, Gil. Thanks for coming," I said as I watched him wordlessly wrap his arms around Peggy. She disappeared for a moment into his embrace.

"You okay?" he asked as he held her at arm's length and looked into her eyes.

I was standing behind her, facing him, and I saw the kindness in his expression. Dear old Gil. As cantankerous as he could be, he still had the power to instill one with the confidence that he could make things better. I was glad that I had called him. Glad to know that together we might be able to help Peggy.

The three of us went to John's room and I got a chance to see my friend for the first time since he had been hurt. He looked almost dwarfed by the hospital bed and his skin tone was pale. He had tubes attached to various parts of his body, but he still had a smile when he awakened and saw us standing around his bed.

Gil and I stayed only a few minutes because it was clear that John needed rest more than company, but a good dose of love from a handful of friends is always good medicine, I figured. Gil and I left Peggy with John and told her we would be in the cafeteria.

"So." Gil took a deep breath and cast a professional eye around the sunny hospital eatery. He stirred sugar into his coffee and finally looked at me. "I take it we have something serious to discuss." It was a statement, not a question.

"Thanks for coming so quickly."

He shrugged his wide shoulders and pushed the corners of his flaccid mouth down. "I've known you too long not to know when there's something important going on."

"Really?" I neatly cut a corn muffin in quarters and offered him a piece.

"That's right. Thanks." He daintily bit into his piece of muffin. "So, what's up?"

I shook my head. "Maybe we should wait for Peggy," I suggested.

"She could be up there with him for hours."

"No. She knows why you're here."

"Which is more than I can say for myself," he said gruffly, then gave me a wink.

We spent the next few minutes taking a stab at small talk, but it wasn't something either of us was comfortable with, so when he finally said, "Let's cut the crap and get down to business," I couldn't argue.

And so I started to tell Gil about Peggy's past, her son, and the phone call she'd received the night John was shot. Although Gil was like family, he was also one hell of a law-enforcement officer. His strength was twofold: First was his ability to delegate; second was his nearly unerring gift for sizing up a situation and knowing how to move forward. He listened without interrupting and nodded as I spoke. He kept his eyes trained on his coffee cup, which he never lifted off the white Formica tabletop.

Peggy joined us just as I was about to give Gil the details regarding the phone call.

Gil pulled out a chair for Peggy and asked what she wanted to eat.

"Nothing," she said as she sat.

"Sydney, go get Peggy something to eat. You have to eat," he said, squeezing her hand. "Think protein," he cautioned me as I was shooed away from the table.

I took my time going through the cafeteria line. Gil and Peggy needed to be alone for a bit, so I allowed myself a little detour down memory lane: my high school cafeteria. Unlike my friends, I had loved the spaghetti and meatballs, which were so heavy, they physically weighed a tray down. And I'd adored the hamburgers, which were probably made of either horse meat or oatmeal. I'd certainly never tasted anything like it since, except for a burger in Nova Scotia once that scared the bejesus out of me.

I returned with a tray, onto which I had crowded a cheese omelette, a tuna sandwich, spaghetti and meatballs, a small salad, and a bottle of sparkling water.

Gil and Peggy ceased talking when I returned. As unobtrusively as I could, I set all the plates on the table, slid the tray onto the chair behind me, and took my seat.

"What the hell's the matter with you?" Gil asked softly.

I set the water in front of Peggy and saw them both staring alternately at the plates and me in disbelief. "What?" I followed their gaze. "I didn't know what to get, so I got a bunch of stuff I know you like. Just keep talking, would you?" I reached for a fork and took a bite of a meatball. It couldn't compete with my memories.

"You have a transcript of the conversation?" Gil asked me.

Peggy had obviously told him about the call.

"Yes. Kerry typed it up. I can have her messenger a copy to your office."

"Why did you wait so long to tell me? Have you told anyone else on the force?" he asked the table at large.

"Sydney wanted to tell the police as soon as he called, but I asked her not to," Peggy said softly. "John didn't know about my . . . past. I didn't want him to find out through anyone but me, and I knew I couldn't tell him until he was out of danger. As soon as he left the ICU, I told him."

"This morning?" he asked.

"That's right, just a little while ago. And as soon as I told him, I called Sydney, who, in turn, called you."

Gil worked his jaw and asked me, "Have you started an investigation yet?"

"I wouldn't say that I've started an investigation per se."

" 'Per se.' What the hell does that mean?" He reached for a piece of the toast that had come with the omelette.

"It means 'as such,' " I replied.

"I don't mean what does *per se* mean, you ninny. I mean how far has your investigation gone?" He shook his head and looked at Peggy, obviously wondering how they could both be my friends.

"Oh, I see. Well, not far. I know that the hospital where she gave birth burned down several years ago and that most of the records were lost, though I don't know if the ones we want were lost. Quite honestly, I've been involved in all sorts of different missing-person cases, but I have never tried to track down a parent or a child who is looking for their roots."

"What do you have working?" Gil asked.

"Nothing worth mentioning. Max is trying to track down the number from which her son might have been calling, but you know how hard it is for private detectives like us to get that sort of information. He's also looking into what happened to the hospital files." I turned to Peggy and said, "One thing I forgot to ask is if you remember the exact date of birth."

"I told you either the fourteenth or fifteenth."

"You're absolutely certain it wasn't the weekend before or after?"

She paused and rubbed her forehead. "Yeah," she said lamely.

"Your folks alive?" Gil asked, flipping open a notepad.

"No."

"Family?"

"Not to speak of."

"What does that mean?" Gil asked.

"That means I have a brother, but we haven't been in touch for years, and I'd prefer to keep it that way."

Gil nodded. "You have his address or phone number?"

"I just said I didn't want him involved in my life."

"No, you didn't. What you said was that you would prefer it if *you* were not put in touch with him."

"That's the same thing," she practically hissed as she picked off a tiny corner of the tuna sandwich.

"No. It isn't." He took a deep breath. "My intention is to have one of my people talk to him, which they should have already done, considering the nature of the crime. However, this is clearly a sore point for you, and I respect that. If we don't have to include him in the investigation, we won't," he said unconvincingly.

"Of course you will, because you have to," I interjected. "I'm sorry," I said, apologizing to them for different reasons. "I don't mean to contradict you," I said to Gil. "And I don't mean to alarm you," I told Peggy. "But the truth is, Karl is a part of your family, whether or not he's currently a part of your life, and because of that, he should be questioned relative to the shooting. It's just that simple." I gave her a look that said, If you don't tell him about Karl, I will. But it was clear from the look she shot back that she preferred I take care of it. *Later.*

"Would you feel more comfortable if Sydney were to question him?" Gil asked Peggy, making it a point not to look at me. You could have bowled me over with a feather.

Peggy sat a little straighter and, with barely a moment's hesitation, said, "Yes. I think I would."

"Then that's what we'll do." The smile Gil offered Peggy was reassuring even to me. "I'll still need his phone number and address."

"I don't know the phone number, but the last I knew he was still living at the house in Jackson Heights." She gave him her childhood address, which she assumed was still Karl's address, then added, "He also used to be a CPA. For all I know, he's retired." She paused and looked Gil straight in the eye. "Despite my fear, you have to understand that my first concern is that John and Lucy will be safe. I don't care if he has a grudge against me, but if he's responsible for John . . ." Her voice trailed off, the only way to stop herself from crying.

Gil nodded as he flattened his hand over hers. "Peggy, the

objective here is to keep you all safe, even if that means working with Sydney."

She allowed herself a weak smile.

"Now do you think you're up for answering a few more questions?" he asked.

She nodded.

"You'll be back upstairs with John in less than half an hour, okay?" It was as if he were reading her mind.

With all the cards on the table, Gil started a professional line of questioning. He asked the questions in rapid succession. I didn't learn anything new, but it was an education getting to watch Gil work. When he was done, she had come clean with everything, including Karl's brutal act of incest.

We escorted her to the elevator, where she reminded me that she had called the camp and given permission for me to pick up Lucy. "Three o'clock sharp, okay?"

"Not to worry. I'm never late," I told her.

As Gil and I were leaving, he took my arm, drew close to me, and whispered, "What do you say you and I get some work done?"

I had mixed emotions about this. On the one hand, I was thrilled to have the opportunity to work with a seasoned old fart like Gil. On the other hand, I felt awful that this was somehow at my friend's expense. But there are times when it's best just to move onward without even giving it a thought.

I offered Gil the reins. "Where do you want to start?"

TWELVE

Just over an hour later, Max, Gil and I were wrapping up a meeting, wherein we had decided how we could work together without distressing official brass. The solution was simple: We would keep it to ourselves.

Unlike other officers on the force, Gil was very secure in himself as a police detective, and because of that, he said, he wouldn't feel threatened by a little outside assistance on the case, especially one that was so close to all of us. Before he left our office, he had already made a handful of calls and started the ball rolling on his end. One of his calls had been to Detective Sam Cooper, arranging for them to meet as soon as he was through with us. He wanted to tell Cooper face-to-face what Peggy had told him.

As he dialed Cooper, Gil said, "You gotta figure if I don't talk to him one-on-one, I won't be able to see how he responds to the new information, and that's important, since I could be stepping on toes, you know? Hell, he's the detective working the case, and Peggy told me and not him about this blast from the past, so, depending on who he is, he could respond badly to that."

"Ah, the male ego," I intoned omnisciently.

"The human ego," said Max, wagging a verbal finger at my gender bashing.

"Whatever." I smiled, but I couldn't leave well enough alone.

"Though even a quick glance at the world is all we need to remind us that the male ego is at the root of most of our woes."

"Sydney, I'd pit your ego against almost any man's," Gil said before connecting with Cooper and turning his back to us.

Kerry had given me copies of the transcript of Peggy's conversation with her son, but we had played the tape for Gil so he could get the full impact of it. Having heard it again, I realized that part of me would always be frightened by not only the substance but also Peggy's emotional recollection of the connection.

And I had to admit that part of me was relieved that we would be working with the police department on this case. I didn't want the full responsibility of this one.

"Okay, good. I'll see you in an hour." Gil sighed as he ended his call with Cooper. He handed Max the phone and held out his hand to me for the tape. "You will contact me as soon as you have met with and spoken to Peggy's ass-wipe of a brother, is that correct?"

"Cross my heart," I said, and I did.

"How soon will that be?" He glanced at his watch, which had a Pavlovian effect on both Max and me. Now we all knew that it was nearing one o'clock. I had two hours before I had to pick up Lucy.

"I could actually drive out there right now."

"*We'll* drive out there," Max amended.

I turned and gave him a look that said, What are you, nuts?

"I think it would be counterproductive if you came with me."

"Don't be silly. There's always safety in numbers," Max said with more than a hint of condescension.

"They haven't seen each other in years, Max. Do you really think safety is an issue?"

"Probably not, but . . ." He left the word dangling all by itself, crying out for "you never know."

"The last thing I want to do is approach this in a way that could be interpreted as threatening."

"I'm not threatening." Max flattened his hand on his chest and managed to look hurt.

"A big stranger and a very attractive woman show up at this guy's front door and start questioning him about things he probably hasn't thought about in years. Of course that's threatening," I said.

"Who said you're attractive?" Max asked. "Did I say she was attractive?" He turned to Gil, who was already making movements toward the door.

"You two play nice," Gil said as he folded the transcript and put it in his pocket. "I don't know how you two can get anything done if you work like Laurel and Hardy. Remember: Bottom line is, I want this guy questioned and I ultimately want him brought in for questioning, but I promised Peggy we'd do it this way. For now. Get as much as you can and get back to me ASAP.

"I'm out of here. I'm going to meet with Cooper and fill him in on how I think we ought to proceed from here. Which means that we're going to have a small army tracking down her son. We'll also get a bead on where the call came from. If this putz is the one who shot John, we'll catch him."

"Even if he isn't," Max reminded him. "I have a bad feeling about this guy. I think we'll all feel safer when he's brought in for questioning."

When Gil nodded, it was as if his head sank into his neck. I realized for the first time that as he aged, he looked a little like an inflated Robert Mitchum with sagging skin.

"Anyone ever tell you that you look like Robert Mitchum?" I asked as I walked him through Kerry's office to the front door.

"Yeah. That and Cary Grant. I get it all the time." I could hear his laughter long after he had left and closed the door.

"That was mean," Kerry said, admonishing me.

"What was mean?" I asked.

"The man looks like a bloodhound."

Before I could respond, Max came out of his office carrying my purse, which he handed to me as he said, "Come on. I know exactly where we're going and I can get you there with more than enough time to interview this guy, but we've got to move. Now!"

I let Max sweep me away, but first I gave Kerry the additional information Peggy had given me the night before about the shelter. It wasn't much, but every little bit could help us focus the search.

I gave Auggie a big kiss on the snout and yelled back at Kerry to have Miguel call me.

We had options: We could go to Karl's home in Jackson Heights or try his place of work in Long Island City, which was closer.

To go to his home in the middle of the afternoon would mean that we were courting the temptation of breaking and entering to get a handle on the guy before meeting him, often a useful ploy, but, like Gil had said, he wanted to interview Peggy's brother ASAP.

"Do you know what you want to ask Karl, should we be lucky enough to find him?" Max asked as he cut off a pink Mercedes feeding onto the Fifty-ninth Street Bridge, an amazing structure that has linked Manhattan with Long Island since 1909.

"I figure I'll play it by ear, but here's a question: Do you think I should approach Karl as an investigator or as a friend of Peggy's?"

"Well, seeing as though there's bad blood between the siblings—after all, one of the last times he saw her, he was raping her—I would probably opt for presenting myself as the stunning professional that you are."

The pink Mercedes honked as it sped past us and the driver shot us the bird with her long, painted talons.

Max whistled the first dozen notes from "Into the Woods." "The thing is, is our objective in questioning him John, or Peggy's progeny?"

"Both. Don't you think?"

Max chewed his lower lip before responding. "I think we need to focus on one, get a feel for him, give Gil a heads-up, and then let his people question him."

Max turned onto a side street just off the bridge, pulled into a tight space in front of a one-story building, slipped a police marker from the visor, and placed it on his dashboard. "Imagine that, a parking space right in front of his office," Max said as he took the key out of the ignition. "It's an omen."

"Okay, come on." I took a deep breath. "Let's give it a shot." I glanced at my watch, knowing that whether Karl was at work or not, we were on a timer because of Lucy.

Midas Printing, where Karl was a bookkeeper, was housed in a warehouse that shared the block with a correctional facility and a community college.

The printing house had its own entrance from the street, protected with frosted wire-mesh windows and a security system that halted visitors at three different locked passageways.

The receptionist was a tired redhead who seemed partial to sky blue eye shadow and false lashes. I imagined her name was Roz and that she smoked Winstons that she carried around with a disposable lighter in a little leatherette case.

"May I help you?" she asked, directing her question to Max.

"Yes, please." He flirted unabashedly. "We're looking for Karl Dexter."

She deigned to give me a quick glance, then turned her attention back to Max. "And you are?"

"Max. Max Cabe."

Three minutes later, the receptionist, Doreen, directed me through the labyrinth of printing machines, cutters, and enormous stacks of paper supplies to a row of small dark back rooms. In one of these was Karl Dexter.

Without discussing it, Max and I knew it would be best to divide and conquer, so while I went off to question Dexter, he stayed behind with Doreen, a woman who would obviously answer any question Max asked.

"Mr. Dexter?" I asked a large man lounging behind a cluttered desk. "Karl Dexter?" He was wearing a wrinkled shirt under a worn blue blazer, along with a tie that he had probably purchased in the seventies.

He squinted at me and let his eyes come to rest on my chest. "Who wants to know?"

I pulled out my wallet and flashed an ID at him from the doorway. "I'm a detective," I said. It was the truth, and I figured if he wanted more ID, I could show it to him and explain that I was private and not with the force, but until then, I would let him draw his own conclusions. "I was wondering if I could have a word with you." I didn't volunteer my name, because for all I knew, his mother,

Rita—whom I'd known—might have talked about me when she was still alive.

"What about?" he asked.

"I suggest we do this in private." I smiled, entered the room, and closed the door behind me.

"Do what?"

"Answer a few questions." I dropped the charm and glared at him.

"I'm a busy man," Karl said, exhibiting surprising conviction for a man who had the *Post* crossword puzzle in one hand and a Mars bar in the other.

"This won't take long," I assured him.

He let out a soft belch and asked again, "What did you say this is about?" There was a constant tension around his eyes.

"I didn't." I glanced around the cramped and cluttered office before my eyes came to rest soundly on Karl. His hair was thinning, and upon closer inspection, I noticed that despite his girth, there was a family resemblance between Peggy and her older brother. I couldn't tell, though, if this was due to bone structure or to the shape of their lips. The thought of him abusing Peggy couldn't help but hit me, a foul thought, and one I knew I had to dispel if I were going to get anywhere with him.

"So who are you? Waddaya want?"

"Mr. Dexter, where were you at seven-forty-five this past Monday morning?"

An uneasy smile played at the corners of his mouth before he snapped to attention. "What do you mean, where was I? I was at home, getting ready for work. I don't get up until seven-thirty every morning."

"Can you prove that?"

"What do you mean?" He tossed the paper onto the desk, leaned way back in his squeaky chair, and slipped the fingertips of his right hand just under his waistband. "Just who the hell are you, and what do you mean asking me something personal like that? You wanna know who I sleep with? Not a chance. I'm a gentleman." This was followed by a sour smile.

I gave him my best Rebecca of Sunnybrook Farm look and said, "Okay. If you prefer to answer questions down at the precinct, that's fine with me." I turned and placed my hand on the doorknob.

"Yeah, okay, wait a minute. I thought you and I were having a conversation here." He slipped his hand out of his pants and leaned forward, resting his elbows on the desk. "I mean, you come in here like I know you, like you own the place—*which you don't*—and then you start threatening me? Well, lemme tell you something. I don't threaten easy. You got that?" As he continued, he addressed the air just over my head, "So if you have questions for me, you gotta tell me why you're asking these questions. I don't know much, but I do know my rights. I fought for this country so people like you could walk into my life and threaten me? I don't think so." He finally looked me in the eye. "What do you want?"

Again I asked, "Where were you at seven-forty-five this past Monday morning?"

"I told you that I was at home. Alone. Which precinct you with?"

"I'm a private investigator working with the NYPD."

"Show me your ID." He held out his hand.

I slipped my ID out of my wallet and watched as he squinted at it. He grunted and nodded. When he handed it back to me, I had the distinct impression that he hadn't been able to see a word of it.

When he didn't say anything, I started asking questions. "Your name has come up in an investigation, Mr. Dexter, and we are simply following all leads. If you have nothing to hide, this should be quick and easy and I will be out of here in a matter of minutes. Is that all right?"

He nodded.

"Do you have any family?"

He shrugged. "My folks are dead. I had a sister once, but she's MIA, if you know what I mean." He raised his brows and took a bite of his candy bar. "So, why don't you get to the point?"

"The other day, a police officer was shot in Washington Heights."

"Yeah. So? What do you mean? You think *I* shot the guy? You got to be out of your frigging mind."

"I didn't say that, but it's interesting that you did. Do you own any guns, Mr. Dexter?" I asked.

"Hey!" He threw the candy bar onto his desk and spat, "I fought in Nam, unlike most fuckers, who were hiding between their mommies' legs."

I repeated the question. "Do you own a gun?"

"Of course I do. But it's legal. Look, I don't know where you're going with this, but I don't think I want to answer any more of your questions. I don't care who you are."

"The officer shot was your sister Peggy's husband," I said.

He barely glanced at me. "Oh yeah?" He nodded and said, "Well, that's too bad." He stared defiantly.

"Did you know you're an uncle?"

He paused, then finally drew the corners of his mouth down and shook his head. "Nope. And I don't care. Peggy's garbage, as far as I'm concerned. I mean, I don't wish her ill, but I just don't care about her and her rich life."

"Is she rich?" I asked.

He shrugged as he reached for the discarded piece of candy, which he popped into his mouth.

"I see. It's just that you said it as if you know about your sister and her life, when a minute ago you said that she was MIA."

"It was an assumption. I *assume* she's rich. I mean, I don't live in a cave, lady. I read the papers. I know she's got some hotshot job and he's a cop, and cops make good money."

"So you *did* know your sister's husband had been shot."

"Huh?"

"A moment ago, you seemed surprised that it had been Peggy's husband who was gunned down on Monday morning."

"There's a difference between knowing and caring."

Now it was my turn to offer a cryptic smile.

"Do *you* have children?" I asked.

He laughed out loud. "There're probably a couple of little slit-eyed bastards running around Nam with my DNA, but that's about it. I don't particularly like kids."

When he smiled at me, I was stunned by how much he looked like Peggy, if only for a moment.

"What? You wanna make babies with me?"

I ignored his offer. "When was the last time you saw your sister?"

"Long time. Before Nam."

"Were you drafted?"

"Hell no. I volunteered."

"Which branch were you in?"

"Army."

"What did you do?"

"I dug holes, got high, killed a bunch of gooks, and came home."

"When did you enlist?" I asked.

"May '68. Little Peggy left about a month later."

"Why did she leave?"

He arched a brow and cocked his head to the side, as if he hadn't heard.

"Did she get married or go to college? Did she leave for a job?"

Just watching the shift of thoughts play on his face was mesmerizing. Finally, he straightened his head and stroked his stubbled chin. "She was asked to leave the house, if you know what I mean. You see, poor little Peggy had a problem. It was one of those long-hidden family secrets, but I suppose it's safe to talk about it now." He paused. "She was a real slut, you know what I mean? I mean, she'd fuck anything with a dick, even the Chinese delivery guy, which I know because I used to watch her. One night, my dad found her going down on his best friend, so he threw her out. I tried to keep in touch with her, but she never wanted anything to do with us after that, like she was the one who had been hurt." He snorted.

Karl was lying, but knowing something and having proof of it are two very different things. Despite the fact that anyone who knew Peggy would know she wasn't the woman he had just described, the fact that she had already hidden so much of her past created doubt. Gil would want proof that this scumbag was lying, and I intended to get it for him.

105

"Have you had any contact in the last several years with your sister's son?"

"Nope. Why would I?"

I glanced at my watch and knew that if we didn't leave soon, we would run the risk of being late to pick up Lucy. I warned Karl not to do anything stupid—like trying to leave town.

"So, what do you mean? Like I should get myself a lawyer?" He pulled a cigarette from his desk drawer and rolled it between his fingers, tapped the filter on the desktop, brought it to his nose, and inhaled the aroma of something the law declared he could no longer enjoy in the privacy of his workplace.

"That's up to you, Karl. But like you said, you don't have anything to hide."

Karl was hiding something. I just didn't know what it was or if it had anything at all to do with the recent turmoil in Peggy and John's life. It was just as easy to think that he was trying to hide his insanity as it was to assume he was hiding something pertinent to the investigation.

Despite the fact that Karl Dexter was an obvious liar, one thing stood out in the questioning that disturbed me. I found Max talking to a man in a handsome turban and motioned that it was time for us to leave.

"Productive?" I asked as he waved good-bye to Doreen.

"Karl's not a particularly well-liked bookkeeper. How about you?"

"He's a pig."

"I want to hear everything."

THIRTEEN

From the car, I called Kerry and asked how many newspaper accounts she had read on John's shooting, since I had made it a point to read none. She had read them all.

"Did the articles make any mention of Lucy?"

"Only that John has a wife and a daughter. They mentioned where Peggy works, but they were surprisingly discrete about Lucy."

"What?" Max asked when I ended the call.

"Karl said he had read the newspaper articles, which means that he would know his sister had a daughter, not a son. But when I asked if he had any contact with Peggy's son—I never mentioned a daughter—he said no."

"I don't know if that's so strange. He might not have been listening."

"Maybe."

"Did he know he had impregnated her?"

"I didn't ask about that part of the past. I wanted to get a feel for him. I figure Gil's team will get a shot at that soon enough."

"What's your gut reaction?"

I shook my head. "He's a pig. He's angry. My guess is that he's antisocial, despite the fact that he can hold down a job in the workforce. But I can't figure out why after all these years he would have gone after John. I found out that he does own a gun, which gives him a method. As far as opportunity, he said he was home that morning, but who knows? It's the motive that has me baffled. It doesn't make sense."

"Sibling rivalry?"

"After all these years?"

"Things take time to fester."

"Maybe." I had no answer.

"Do you think it was Karl who called Peggy the other night?"

"As her son?"

"Yeah."

"I don't know. But it's a thought."

We drove across the Fifty-Ninth Street Bridge in momentary silence. The cityscape both downtown and up was an amazing vista from the bridge, in some ways as awe-inspiring as the Grand Canyon.

"You learn anything interesting?" I asked as we inched off the bridge.

"He's worked there for close to twenty years. He's not well liked, but apparently he's a good, cheap bookkeeper. I do believe Doreen slept with him once."

"Eeww, gross."

"She intimated that it was after a Christmas party several years ago, soon after her divorce."

"Excuses, excuses."

"We should meet with Gil after we pick up Lucy." He pulled onto Third Avenue to head uptown.

I called Gil and left a message with his assistant.

Max and I arrived at Lucy's camp five minutes earlier than I had the day before.

Peggy had called in the morning to let the staff know that I would be picking her up, so I left Max outside in a gaggle of screaming children and went to the office, where I had to show a picture ID in order to receive my little charge.

The day before, Lucy had been waiting for me in the office, but she wasn't there. I greeted the same woman from the day before and showed her my ID, then asked if Lucy's group had been let out yet.

She didn't know, but she asked a young woman who had seven gold hoops piercing the rim of her ear and was encircled by a gaggle of children.

"The Nightingales?" she asked as she was being pulled and tugged by three gleeful girls missing various baby teeth. "They got out about five minutes ago."

I wandered through the hallways, now thinning out as the kids raced outside to greet moms, dads, and baby-sitters. At the doorway, I saw Max waiting alone on the sidewalk.

Again, I went up and down the hallway, thinking that maybe she had gone back to an activity room or had to use the bathroom. Nothing.

I asked several kids if they knew Lucy or had seen her, but most of them were in hyperdrive as they streamed out of the building. They were too busy screaming to one another to hear an adult ask, "Do you know where Lucy is?"

After about five minutes of this, I started to experience a low-grade panic. I went outside and asked Max if he had seen her, which he obviously hadn't, or she would have been with him. "I know a cop has been stationed here to watch Lucy. Did you see one?"

"No."

"Shit."

I went back to the office. Still no Lucy. When I turned away from the clerk, I saw Max standing in the doorway, and the look on his face made my stomach pitch.

"Come with me."

I followed him out onto the sidewalk, where a woman stood holding the hand of a pretty little girl, the same girl I had seen link arms with Lucy the day before when I had dropped her off.

"Sydney, this is Gaby, and this is her mother. . . ."

"Ann Scott," she said as she looked up at me and held out her hand. When Ann Scott grasped my hand, she took off her sunglasses, revealing enormous brown eyes that were so focused, she could have had X-ray powers.

"Where's your dog?" Gaby asked as she squinted up at me and twirled a curl around her index finger.

"She's at my office, waiting for Lucy. Do you know where Lucy is?"

"Uh-huh." Gaby chewed on her lower lip and glanced to her right, which was east. "A boy came to pick her up."

"A boy? Did they go in that direction?" I asked, trying to keep urgency out of my voice so as not to scare her, but wanting at the same time to yank the words out of the kid and stop wasting what felt like precious seconds.

"Yeah."

"Did they get into a car, or were they walking?" I glanced at Max as I asked the question.

She strained over this one and finally said, "Walking, I think."

"Powerpuff T-shirt and backpack, hair in a scrunchie, black pedal pushers, pink socks, and fluorescent green sneakers," I said to Max before he took off in the direction Gaby had indicated.

"Did you meet him?" I asked Gaby as gently as I could, trying desperately to get hold of the fear that was starting to course through my body.

"Sorta."

Ann squatted beside her daughter and prompted her. "Honey, did you meet the man?"

Gaby's lower lip swelled out, but she didn't cry, just nodded.

"Did he talk to you?" Ann asked, wrapping a protective arm around her daughter's waist.

"Not really." She rubbed her right eye. "He had a puppy and he told Lucy that her mom'd told him to pick her up."

"Can you remember exactly what he said?"

"He said, 'Lucy, your mom asked me to pick you up.' He told her he was gonna take her to the hospital to see her dad. When she asked where you were—because you said you were gonna pick her up—he said that you were working but that you'd meet them at the hospital, too."

"Did she know him?" I asked, knowing that Lucy had been trained to steer clear of strangers.

"No. But then he said, 'Don't you want to see your dad?' " When Gaby looked up, I could see that she was ready to cry. I glanced at her mother to ask permission to press forward, and Mrs. Scott said, "Honey, do you remember what the man looked like?"

Gaby took a deep breath and described a man who was about the same size as her mother—which would make him about five five—with close-cropped hair, blue eyes, and a dark mustache. He was wearing blue jeans, a white T-shirt, and a black jacket.

"Do you remember if his hair was curly, like your mom's, or was it straight, like mine?" I asked, feeling my chest slowly turning to a frozen vacuum.

She squeezed her eyelids tightly together and said, "Straight. And it was light and dark."

"Salt-and-pepper?" I asked as I looked at her mother for translation.

"You mean like Sophie's?" Ann asked.

Gaby nodded.

"Highlighted," she explained.

"Oh, and he had on big black shoes like Tommy wears." This was said to her mother.

"Doc Maartens," Ann explained.

"What about the puppy?" I asked. Despite her fears, she smiled at the mention of the dog.

"It was really cute. It was about this big," she said, spacing her hands about a foot apart. "And it was all white and had big dark eyes."

I stood and scanned the street, looking for Max or Lucy or a little white dog, anything that might pull me back from what I knew was an unfolding nightmare. My eyes came back to Ann, who asked what she could do. She assured me that it wouldn't be a problem for her and Gaby to stay there for as long as they were needed.

"I'm just going to get Gaby a snack at the deli down the street. We'll be right back." She reached out and touched my arm before they turned to go.

I flew back into the building, went to the main office, and asked a matronly woman tucked safely behind the counter if she had seen Lucy Cannady.

Her face went blank, and I realized that she probably didn't even know who Lucy was. She turned to the clerk and asked her the same question.

"No," she said, turning back to me, and then pressed her thin lips together until there was nothing, not even a line, to betray the fact that a mouth was present. I wanted to yank her across the counter. Instead, I slammed it, the flat of my hand sounding like a shot.

"Listen to me, damn it. A child is missing, and I want to know where she is!" I stopped all activity in the large room. "I want to know where Lucy Cannady is and I want to know now."

The woman across from me looked frightened. I turned to the dozen or so people who were mulling around, checking schedules, in the green room with its high fluorescent lights and blond wood. "Please. Has anyone seen Lucy Cannady?"

"I did," a voice said from behind me. I turned and matched the voice with a kind-faced man in sneakers, khakis, and a T-shirt. "You said she's missing?" He approached me and spoke in almost a whisper.

"Yes. I came to pick her up and . . . You've seen her?"

"Lucy's one of our campers. I'm Ben Silverstein; I run the camp. And you are?"

"I'm her godmother. I came to pick her up, but when I got here, her friend Gaby said that she'd already left with a man who had a puppy. Did you see him?"

"No." He glanced at the clerks behind the counter. "It's not possible that she would have been allowed to leave with someone who didn't have parental approval."

"Well, then someone's screwed up here." As I said the words, my body was silently screaming.

"Have you called the police?"

"Not yet. I wanted to check in here first."

"And you're absolutely certain that her mother didn't make other arrangements?"

As positive as I was that the answer was no, I also knew that I had to confirm that Peggy hadn't, in a moment of dementia, given permission for another person to pick Lucy up without telling me. That meant that before I called the police, or Gil, I had to call

Peggy. The thing was, I didn't want her to be alone—or alone with John—when I spoke with her.

I punched in the numbers for Max's cell phone. He said he hadn't seen them but was still searching the area. Then, with Lucy's counselor and the head of the camp program at my side, I called the nurses' station at the hospital and asked the head nurse, Yolanda, to help me. I could have asked to speak with someone from the security detail protecting John's room, but I didn't want to leave John vulnerable, even for a moment. Yolanda seemed like someone who could be trusted, and at that point I didn't have much choice. She agreed to take Peggy to a private room, where they would call us. This way, if Peggy needed someone to help her, at least Yolanda would be a firm shoulder.

As Ben Silverstein and I waited for the call, it took everything inside me not to cry. What I needed to do was concentrate on my rage, which would allow me to focus, and not on my fear, which had me shooting off in all different directions right then.

I was afraid, because I knew what some people were capable of. People are probably the least evolved species on earth, I thought. After all, you don't see roaches or deer poisoning the planet, killing for pleasure or torturing others.

My cell phone rang, and I jumped, as if an electrical current had been shot through my body.

"Sydney?" I heard the concern in Peggy's voice. "Are you okay?"

FOURTEEN

My mother always used to say, "God doesn't give us more than we can handle." And while I figured there might be an element of truth to that sentiment for those who believed that God pulls all the strings, I couldn't help but wonder what she would have thought of her theory as I watched Peggy that night when she learned for a fact that her daughter had been kidnapped—and by whom.

I don't know what was worse, the waiting or the actual call, which came to Peggy's home phone just after seven o'clock. It was short and to the point: "I decided it was time to get to know my sister. Don't worry, Ma, she's fine, but she won't be home tonight."

He—who still didn't have a name—hadn't given Peggy a chance to utter a response, let alone ask to hear Lucy's voice just to make certain that she was all right. The call was over in less than ten seconds.

When he hung up, Peggy's scream pierced every inch of my soul. It was like no other sound I had ever heard before. And then her cry turned into sobs as she folded into herself and dropped the phone to the floor. Aside from Marcy, Max, Gil, and me, none of the other half a dozen people in the apartment knew Peggy. However, because none of the men and women present were strangers to the unspeakably ugly side of life (being that they were members of the Major Case Squad), they could invisibly continue going about the business of trying to set up a command post.

I retrieved the phone and handed it to Gil. Peggy's heavy sobs filled the large apartment, making each and every one of us feel helpless. If Max had been in her shoes, he might have punched a hole in the wall. Gil probably would have picked up a pack of cigarettes. I don't know what Marcy or I would have done, but screaming seemed like a pretty good release. In less than three days, her husband had been shot, a past she'd thought was buried had been unearthed, and her daughter had been kidnapped by a madman she had given birth to. Making matters worse, she couldn't even share the burden with John, because the doctors had warned her against anything that might impede his recovery at this point.

Out of the corner of my eye, I saw Cooper fill the doorway and motion for Gil.

Max and the others followed after him, leaving just Peggy and me in a small room that doubled as a den/office.

When the door was securely closed, Peggy cried—her words almost unintelligible—that it was her fault.

I tried to shush her gently and reassure her that it was no one's fault, but I also knew that if I'd been Peggy, I would have been going through the same thing.

After several inconsolable moments, I finally held her at arm's length and said, "It really doesn't matter what preceded all this. The thing is, we're here. And as hideous as it is, you have to be strong. You have to work from the premise that Lucy is fine and will be returned safely to us."

"The power of positive thinking," she said with contemptuousness as she wiped her cheek with the back of her hand.

"No. Outmaneuvering your opponent. This kid has an advantage right now because he has Lucy and we don't know where he is. But those people out there are a hell of a lot smarter than he is, and I have every confidence that they'll find her. The boy wants your attention, Peg, and he's got it. My gut tells me that he's not going to do anything to jeopardize that."

Whether or not I believed what I had just said, it seemed to have an impact on her. As I watched her leave the den and walk down the hallway to the bathroom, I wondered if I could be as strong as she would have to be for the next few—what, hours, days?

Because John was a police officer and because Max and I had called Gil as soon as we knew for a fact that Lucy was missing, things moved incredibly fast. Unfortunately, the call came in before the Major Case Squad had finished setting up command central in Peggy's apartment, so the call couldn't be traced. Once they were up and running, they would be able to trace a call in seconds, but it was still only a matter of hours since Lucy had gone missing, and not everything was in place. The officer running the show from the Major Case Squad was a woman named Florence McElroy, whom Gil had known for years and trusted implicitly.

Peggy and I joined Gil, Cooper, and McElroy. As different as their faces were, each one at that moment possessed a stony rage, which I knew couldn't be the result of good news. It was McElroy who explained to Peggy that despite the fact they hadn't been able to trace the call, they had been able to tape it, which could give them some vital information. In a gentle, even tone that commanded cooperation and trust, McElroy explained to Peggy how they would move forward in their search for Lucy. There would be no uniformed officers to call any further attention from the neighbors and, initially, they would hold off on any public mention of Lucy's kidnapping.

"*If* the man responsible is your son, Mrs. Cannady—and there is no proof yet that he is—there could be reason to believe Lucy is safer with him than with another kidnapper, if only because he's curious about his sister. For the time being anyway." McElroy, who was the only person in the room standing at this point, stopped Peggy before she could interrupt. "I'm not going to lie to you. There is no way of second-guessing what could happen in a situation like this. I think, however, that it's important to remain focused and as positive as we can. Detectives Jackson, Cooper, and I will be working in concert with one another. Now, this is how it's going to work." She motioned toward Detective Cooper. "Sam will continue the investigation into John's shooting, keeping in mind that your son *may* have played a role in this, but not limiting his investigation to that hypothesis. In the meantime, Detective Jackson's office has already started scouring through records to find out exactly who your son is, and, of course, where he is." As she outlined the game plan, it was clear that McElroy was not a professional who would ever get tripped up by her feelings, but she also conveyed the sense that if a building were on fire, she could lead you through the flames without ever getting singed. When she was finished, she asked Peggy if she had any questions.

"Yes. Do you have children?"

"I do, yes. A three-year-old son and an eight-year-old daughter." The corners of her mouth twitched. "Peggy, we'll find Lucy. I promise you. In the meantime, it's important that you keep up your strength and your stamina. If you can manage some toast or cereal—something, anything—it would be a good idea, as well as getting some rest. However, if you're more comfortable heading back to the hospital and spending time with John, I'll have one of my officers escort you there and back. For the duration of this investigation, you will be under twenty-four-hour protection. It might make you a little anxious, but that's the way it is."

"What about Lucy? I should be here for her," Peggy practically mewled.

McElroy nodded once but then said, "Given the tone of his call, I would say it's unlikely that we're going to hear from him again this evening. And while it's unfortunate that he called before we were ready, that doesn't mean we can't learn things from his call. Right now, we're running the tape through a series of tests for background noise and dialect, anything that might help us learn something about the caller and perhaps even get an idea of where he might be." She walked to the sofa and sat next to Peggy. "Let me explain how it works. From now on, whenever a call comes into this house—before you even pick up, as soon as the phone starts ringing—the number will register on one of our computers. Once the computer displays the number, then in a matter of seconds it will show us the person to whom the phone being called from is registered." She stopped, seeing the glazed-over look in Peggy's eyes, and said, "Look, you have an awful lot on your plate right now, Peggy. You're being pulled in several difficult directions, and each one of them is frustrating and frightening. You have a lot of good friends and capable people working behind the scenes to make things better, but the truth is, none of that can make you *feel* any better right now. And we all know that. You're in an awful and unusual situation, and the hard part is that you have to stay focused."

The sound of a throat being cleared interrupted McElroy's pep talk. A thin man in a pink shirt and blue tie held on to the door frame, leaned into the room, and muttered to McElroy, "Sorry to disturb, ma'am, but there's a call for you from HQ."

Not having told John about the kidnapping, Peggy was in a panic to get back to the hospital. She had no intention of telling him about Lucy, but she needed to connect with him, with her family. I offered to go with her to the hospital, but she asked me to stay at the apartment in case something happened with Lucy. "I can trust you, Sydney. Do you mind?"

Naturally, I didn't. As soon as she left, Max, Marcy, Gil, Cooper, McElroy, and I gathered around the kitchen table, where we went over each and every piece of information that we had to offer, whether it was what had been garnered by the detectives or what we could provide as friends.

So far, Cooper's group was having a hard time getting anywhere. "We did get the ballistics report. One bullet—a hollow-point thirty-eight."

"What about the shell casing?" Max asked.

"There wasn't one."

"The shooter used a revolver?" Marcy asked.

Cooper shrugged. "It's unlikely, since no one reported hearing a gunshot, which would imply that a suppressor was used. There is the possibility that he could have picked up the casing before he left the scene—after all, only one shot was fired." We looked at one another doubtfully before Cooper took a deep breath and continued. "We have identified and met with all of the people on the security videos. So far, nothing. But because of the camera glitch, we're missing a total of about five minutes per tape for the ones recorded at the main entrance."

Max and I described our meeting with Peggy's brother, Karl, whom Gil had already sent a team to pick up for questioning.

"Well, we know for a certainty that he didn't kidnap Lucy. First, I was with him in Queens at the time of the abduction. Second, he doesn't fit the description," I offered.

"So, what do we think—that these two events are not connected?" Cooper sneered.

"It seems unlikely," Gil said, "But we can't rule it out. I want every single possibility sniffed out here. Does anyone know if that son of a bitch was picked up yet?" he asked, referring to Karl.

"Not yet," Cooper said. "He wasn't at work or at home. We have detectives waiting for him at the Jackson Heights house."

"Is there any way to get a search warrant?" I asked Gil.

"Not yet. We haven't any cause. But it won't take long if we need to get one."

Gil told us that as soon as he left our office, he got together a team, which had worked throughout the afternoon, trying to track down the history and subsequent whereabouts of Peggy's son. But so far, they had come up blank. With the hospital records having been destroyed from that period, and none of the data having been computerized, it now meant an arduous search into state birth records. So far, they had learned from the Department of Vital Statistics that some 130,000 children had been born in New York in 1968. Only thirteen thousand had been born in December, though, which narrowed it down considerably.

"Talk about a needle in a haystack," Cooper murmured.

"We'll find him," Gil said, looking directly at Cooper.

"You figure if he found her, then we can find him," I said, echoing Max's mantra.

Gil tapped the table as if it were a drum. "On a more upbeat note, we were able to trace the telephone number from the call Peggy received on Monday night. It was placed from a cell phone that's listed to a Jean Silver in Brooklyn."

"And?" McElroy asked.

Gil shook his head. "Nothing. Apparently, Mrs. Silver doesn't use her cell phone much—only for emergencies or when she's running late from a bridge game and wants to leave a message for her cat."

"Her cat?" asked Max.

Gil nodded. "Puffer. Anyway, it wasn't until we arrived that she even discovered her phone was missing. Even a rookie could tell from one look at her that she's on the up-and-up, but I had my people do a rudimentary check on her anyway. She's not hiding anything. She's a relatively shy, genteel woman. She always keeps the phone in an outside pouch of her purse. It could have been lifted from anywhere."

"Does she remember the last time she saw the phone?" I asked.

Gil shrugged. "It could have been three days or three weeks. The only thing we know for sure is that she doesn't get out of Prospect Heights much, and in the last month she hasn't left that area at all because her father's been ill. Obviously, I have someone working to get the call log on that particular cell phone. I should have something by tomorrow morning."

"Did you have the phone deactivated?" I asked, knowing that once it was shut off, whoever had stolen the phone would either discard it or sell it to some unsuspecting idiot on the street.

Gil's eyes softened as a shy smile spread across his face. "No. We'll wait and see if he'll use it again. So far, he hasn't."

"He could have sold it," I suggested.

"Or given it away," Max said.

"Right, or left it on a bench somewhere," Gil said impatiently. "But if it's used again, we'll know, and that's what we want."

"How does it work when they trace a call from a cell phone?" Max asked.

McElroy explained: "It's much harder than a landline, because with a landline we can get an exact location. With a cell, it's the switching station and transmission tower that can give us a general idea of the location of the caller."

"Huh." Max nodded. "Have you considered the possibility that the person we're dealing with is in law enforcement?"

"What?" Cooper sneered again. "So now you think the shooter and the kidnapper are not only the same person but a police officer with a grudge against John?" He sounded angry at the suggestion.

"All I'm saying is that it would be dangerous to assume that he's not."

"Oh, I definitely think the shooter and kidnapper are connected," I said. "But my hunch is that Lucy's kidnapping has nothing to do with John or his work, and everything to do with Peggy's past."

"Hunches don't mean anything, Sloane," Cooper said, dismissing me.

"I hate to say it, but Sloane's instincts are usually pretty damned good," Gil said, glancing over his reading glasses at Cooper.

"The son *could* be a cop," said McElroy, glancing at Gil.

"That would be a nightmare," Gil said softly.

"He could also work for Verizon or AT&T," Cooper said, shifting his bulk in the chair.

"You know, you could run a search on how many officers in the force were born in December 1968," Marcy suggested.

McElroy and Gil both shifted their eyes toward Marcy and then back to each other.

"I don't think he's a cop," I said, shaking my head. "Baboons can learn police procedure from television any night of the week. No offense," I added when I saw my faux pas written on all the faces around me.

"It couldn't hurt to check it out," Gil said with an eye on McElroy.

"I agree," she said as she turned to Marcy and asked, "Do you know how to get that information?"

"Sure," Marcy said, and then turned to Gil. "With your permission and access to the computers and force files, I could probably have it for you by morning."

"Good. Do it. *Adamson*," he called out over his shoulder. In a flash, Gil's assistant, Jo Adamson, was two feet behind her boss's chair. "Give Marcy access to anything she needs or wants. Got it?"

"Yes, sir."

Gil ran his hand along the tabletop and said, "And Marcy, see if you can put together a secondary list of officers who are either recently retired or inactive. Use the same criteria to sort it by. Okay?"

"Will do." She lifted her chin in Max's direction and was gone.

"Okay," McElroy said, and then took a deep breath. "We got the last call on tape. We're isolating the sounds to see if there is anything that can give us some sort of direction." McElroy stopped and chewed her lower lip for half a second before directing her next question to Max and me. "You two know Mrs. Cannady fairly well, right?" She waited until we had either nodded or said yes. "In your opinion, is it possible that she could be withholding any information from us that might be useful?" She kept her gaze on me.

I answered with a question. "What makes you ask that?"

I caught her glance at Gil and knew that they had discussed this before our roundtable discussion. "As I understand it, she was the only person in the vicinity when her husband was shot, yet she saw and heard nothing. Then out of the clear blue sky, she tells you about a son she had given birth to over thirty years ago, a son who ostensibly descends upon her like a vulture and starts picking her life apart. If the transcript of her initial conversation with him is accurate—keeping in mind that it is all hearsay—he alluded to Captain Cannady's shooting, as if there might be some culpability, without actually claiming responsibility. And now this same man, who may or may not be her long-abandoned son, admits that he has kidnapped her daughter." McElroy squinted as she rubbed her thumb against the tabletop. "I know that instinctively it's hard not to want to protect a friend—indeed, someone who is more like a member of your own family—but as a professional, you have to see that she is the constant thread, always there, always interpreting, and yet she doesn't hear or see anything. It's just . . . curious."

"I would bet my life that Peggy is not knowingly withholding information," I said.

"I would have to second that," Max agreed.

McElroy nodded before adding, "I don't think we should lose sight, however, of the fact that Mrs. Cannady is as much aware of police procedure as any of us sitting at this table."

We both folded our hands on the table and stared at her. She, in turn, gave Cooper a glance, which made me wonder if it was he who had prompted her to ask about Peggy.

Gil pushed his hands against the table as he rose from his seat. "Sydney? Max? I think you could help us best if you were here for Peggy."

"You mean keep an eye on her?" Max asked coldly.

"I mean watch out for her." Gil paused and took a deep breath. "I'll tell you what I'm afraid of. This scum, whoever he is and whether he's responsible for John *and* Lucy or just one of them, whether he's a cop or not, he's clearly got a bug up his butt about Peggy. Things are bad enough right now, but I would like to think that we could avert a complete tragedy if we keep a vigilant eye out for our friend. And I do consider her my friend, too, Max." With that said, he told McElroy that he was going to get some air but would be back shortly.

I got up to follow, but my cell phone rang. It was Miguel and he was downstairs.

FIFTEEN

"Yo, Syd." **Miguel looked so** young when he smiled down at me in the doorway that I was reminded of when he first started working with us, several years earlier. Back then, he wore either baggy jeans, which made the mere act of walking a challenge, or, on a rare occasion, dressed in drag. Now he was wearing khakis, loafers, and a polo shirt. For a moment, I missed the bad-boy rapper look. Whether it was time or CSI that had cleaned him up, I was comforted in knowing that beneath the permanent-press facade lived a young man who understood how to work Lee press-on nails and why Eminem is a genius.

"I thought I'd find you here," he said with undistilled pride. But just as quickly, his smile faded and he asked, "Am I interrupting something?"

"Come on in," I said, stepping to the side to let him into the hallway. I led him upstairs and then through the apartment, past McElroy's team, and into the small den, where Max was looking out the window.

Miguel's brows pulled taut as he tried to understand what was going on.

I suggested he sit down, and then I proceeded to tell him everything—from the sudden appearance of Peggy's illegitimate son to Lucy's kidnapping. Max seemed to blend into the shadows so successfully that it was easy to forget he was there, until he offered a handful of details.

Miguel leaned forward onto his elbows and, as he shook his head, a patch of dark hair fell over his right eye. He looked up through the fringe of hair and asked, "How can I help?"

I sighed. Where to begin? "I think the only thing you can do is follow through with Hardy. Dorothy's wedding is in three weeks, and if there's something to tell her, I don't want to spring it on her at the last minute."

"Does she know that you axt me to check it out?"

"*Asked*. You mean Dorothy?"

He nodded.

"No. But Leslie knows what you've learned so far."

He sucked in his cheeks and shook his head. "You know, last night I was convinced this old man was guilty as sin."

"And now you're not so sure?" It took everything in my power to focus on Miguel and not speculate about where and how Lucy was.

"Nope. I mean, come on, man, four dead wives? All I could think about was, you know, like a Jekyll and Hyde."

"Jekyll and Hyde?" Max asked.

Is Lucy hungry or frightened?, I wondered.

"Well, you know, I figured he seduced all those women just to kill 'em. Good one minute, nasty the next. My cousin Caesar has this book about crimes of the whatever century, and you'd be amazed how many husbands and wives have almost gotten away with killing like, you know, dozens of wives or husbands. You know what I mean?"

"Well, I do, but it's not because you make it easy," I said. "So tell us what you learned today." Knowing Lucy had to be frightened made it hard to concentrate on the matter at hand.

"I met his first wife, Paula Bell." He tried to maintain his cool, but there was no denying his spike of enthusiasm, which I understood all too well. It was the "I got a lead and it actually panned out" kind of excitement.

"Where?"

"She lives on the Lower East Side." His voice sounded calm enough, but his leg was going a mile a minute and he could barely stay in his seat. "I mean, all I knew about her last night was that after Harold and her broke up, she took the kids and raised them in Maine. But then I found out today that she'd moved back here six years ago, when her mother got sick. She nursed her until she died. This Paula's a nice lady. Real nice lady."

"How did you find her?" Max asked.

"You know that guy Cliff who lived with my cousin Marga?"

"No," we said in unison.

"Well, Cliff and me are still friends, and he happens to work for the IRS, so I axt him to just see if he could maybe run a check on her whereabouts."

"Asked." I suddenly envisioned Lucy trapped in a coffinlike hiding place, something reminiscent of what kidnappers had done to a well-known industrialist years earlier.

"Yeah, and like I said, he's a good guy, so he said yeah, even though he and Marga broke up. She cheated on him. With a dwarf. He told me he couldn't go back with her after that, even though he still loves her."

I knew better than to engage in any conversation about Miguel's family. Instead, I asked, "Had Paula remarried?"

"No, which was why it was easier to find her. But like my grandma used to say, 'The Lord works in mysterious ways,' and as crazy as it sounds, I think the Lord wanted me to find her.

"So you think it was divine intervention that brought you to the first Mrs. Harold Hardy?"

"Yes, I do."

"And you're absolutely certain that this was the one and only bona fide Mrs. Paula Bell Hardy and not some other Paula Bell?"

"Absolutely." He turned his chair around and straddled it. "She only had good things to say about this guy."

"Is that so?"

"That's so."

"You sound disappointed."

"I am. I thought I was onto something."

"Did you ask her about the other four Hardy girls?" The book *Lovely Bones* popped into my head and I dug my nails into a sofa pillow. It's a sick world, I mused; people do unthinkable things.

"Yeah. She actually met two and four, but never three or five." I missed what he said but watched as he pulled a piece of paper from his pocket and unfolded his origamilike notes onto his knee. He scooted his chair closer and flattened out the paper so I could see his list of players.

> Paula: Married 1951. Divorced 1966.
> 3 kids (his only children).
>
> Cissy: Married 1970. Died 1975,
> Madrid. Food poisoning. Rich.
>
> Maggie: Married 1978. Died 1983.
> Heart attack. Drugs?
>
> Sugar: Married 1986. Died 1988,
> Australia. Drowned. Rich.
> 1 child from previous marriage.
>
> Maureen: Married 1992. Died 1995.
> Hit-and-run with daughter. Rich.

"Paula said the reason they got divorced was because he was fooling around and she didn't want to share him. I get the impression that Harold's one of those guys who just can't keep it zipped up. You know what I mean? She met his second wife, Cissy, and the two of them actually became friends—Paula and Cissy, I mean. The other one she knew, Sugar, she only met a couple of times, but she said she liked her, too, even though she was a whole different league as far as money was concerned. She said one thing about Harold is that he's always had good taste in women."

"She sounds pretty generous for a woman who never remarried," Max suggested, keeping his distance from across the room.

Miguel tucked his chin into his chest and looked at Max, his eyebrows raised, like one of Raphael's cherubs.

"What?" I asked.

He held his hands out, as if weighing cantaloupes. "I can't say for sure, because we didn't discuss it. See, there was another woman there. Paula introduced her as her *friend*, whatever that means."

"Maybe they are friends," Max said reasonably.

Miguel shrugged. "I suppose. But I happen to have excellent gaydar, and I would bet a thousand bucks that the two of them are living happily ever after." He smiled smugly and went on. "Anyway, I axt Paula if she thought Harold was capable of murder."

I stared at Miguel. "What do you mean? Just like that? Without preamble, you simply dived in and asked if she thought her ex-husband—the father of her children—was a murderer?"

"If he was *capable* of murder." Miguel had the good grace to look mildly uncomfortable.

My breath caught in my chest as I wondered if Lucy was alive. Don't think that way, I told myself. Be positive.

"Let me guess," Max said, crossing his arms over his chest. "She said no."

"Yeah."

I took a deep breath. "Why don't you give us the salient points of your conversation with her, okay?" I could feel tears burning as I struggled to listen to Miguel. Fury not fear, I reminded myself, silently repeating this mantra as I watched Miguel's lips as he spoke.

"She said that she probably knows Harold better than anyone else, because after all these years she's his best friend, and the one thing she could tell me without any question of a doubt was that he wouldn't hurt a fly." He paused.

I nodded, not having heard a word he had said.

"She also said Harold's no idiot and that he saw the pattern in his life. Three or four years between marriages, with most of them lasting about five years. He even talked to a psychic about it, but Paula didn't remember what the outcome was from that. She pointed it out only because she said that the deaths bothered him enough to send him to one and that that wasn't his usual MO." He rubbed his shoulders as he continued. "Sugar had a grown son by the time she and Harold hooked up, and Paula remembered that he blamed Harold for his mother's death. Paula went to Sugar's funeral to support Harold, and I guess the son—his name is Steve—made a huge scene. It sounded great."

"Great?" Max asked.

"Yeah," he said, as if Max didn't get the joke. "I mean, that shit doesn't happen in real life; that's the stuff you see on HBO. Anyway, the thing is, this guy went so far as to hire an investigator. It turned out that there wasn't any evidence to support his theory, so ultimately he dropped the investigation."

"Who was the investigator?" I asked.

"Guy named Jimmy Hogan. Died a year ago."

"Why did the son blame Harold?" Max asked.

Miguel shrugged. "Paula said she thought he had this epedeal thing going for his mom and he was real angry that she had died."

"Epedeal?" Max looked at me.

"Oedipal. Go on," I said gently.

"Whatever." He turned away from Max. "The thing is, we'll never know why he wanted an investigation, because he's dead." He paused, nodded, then continued. "That's right, Epedeal Oedipal died three years after his mother."

"Was he married? Did he have family?"

"Nope and nope. He left his entire estate to a couple of animal shelters and his best friend, a woman named Amanda Robbins."

"What? You sound as if the steam has seeped out of your engine, Mickey." I glanced at my watch, not wanting Miguel in the apartment when Peggy returned.

He spoke carefully and thoughtfully. "I dunno, Sydney. This is something I don't think I understand. I mean, I know I want to be a detective and I know you guys think I'm a pretty good operative, which means a lot to me, you know, but . . ." He sighed and rubbed his forehead until it started to turn red. "I've never had a case where I start to like the person I'm out to get. You know what I mean? After my talk with Paula, I met Steve's friend Amanda, who knew Harold. She's another one with big bucks, lives on Park Avenue, the whole bit."

"Did you ask her if she thought Harold killed her friend's mother?"

He squinted at me and mouthed "Ha-ha." "No. I told her I was a freelance writer for a magazine called the *Riveters Review* and was doing a story on Harold and his years in the construction business."

"And she bought that?"

"Yeah, she bought that." His tone was a cross between a whine and a snarl. "Man, don't you have any manners?"

"I'm sorry. I didn't mean it that way. I love that you came up with the *Riveters Review*. I'm just surprised that she bought it. It's great. So what happened?"

"Well, I eased into things, you know, like I reviewed what history I had about Hardy and his moving from construction into development when he was with Sugar, the whole thing. Now, this lady was like a member of the family. She and Steve had been best friends since they were kids, so I axt how much influence she thought Sugar had on Hardy with regard to properties he chose to develop. Anyway, she was talking real affectionately about him, and so when the time was right, I axt, 'Is it true, Ms. Robbins, that Steve hired an investigator after his mother died?'" Miguel smiled and wiggled his brows. "I'm not shitting you. I sounded just like Lois Lane."

"You did not."

"What do you mean? You weren't even there."

"You're right. But I do know that any writer who uses the word *axt* instead of *asked* had better be writing for the *Riveters Review* and not the *Daily Planet*."

"All right, all right. All I'm saying is that I was playing the part. I'm sitting there with this notebook and looking real casual while the woman turns every shade of red you can imagine. Then she says, 'It was a very trying time for Steve,' who, as it turns out, was in the middle of a nervous breakdown then. This Amanda was the one who told me that the local police and the dive captain agreed that it was an accident. She told me that Harold adored Sugar and said that maybe Steve was a little jealous." Miguel crossed his arms and nodded. "How do you look for skeletons when everyone and their grandmother love the guy? That's my real problem."

"Are you convinced he's innocent?" Max asked, joining me on the sofa.

He took a deep breath and shrugged. "I don't know. I keep going back to one question: Why didn't he tell Mrs. W. about his previous wives? See, maybe it's because it's Leslie's mom and I have a personal interest, but I keep thinking if *he* felt he had to hide his past, that should be cause for concern, don't you think?"

I bobbed my head from side to side in an attempt to look noncommittal, but my thoughts were elsewhere. "This is one of those situations that proves things are rarely cut-and-dry, black and white." Black and white, good and bad, innocent and evil. Lucy and whatever this cretin's name was.

"But then I keep thinking, What if he kills Dorothy?" He threw his whole body into the question.

"Do you think he will?" I asked, meaning Dorothy but knowing in the back of my head I couldn't wash away images of a broken and battered Lucy.

"How the hell should I know?" He shifted impatiently in his seat.

"What does your gut tell you?" I asked harshly.

He rubbed his mouth and cheeks with his right hand as he considered the question. "Okay." He shifted and leaned toward me. "My *gut* tells me that this guy is bad, but everyone seems to think the world of him. I know you always tell me to trust my instincts, but you also tell me that if something smells like corned beef and tastes like corned beef, chances are it is corned beef, right?"

"Right."

"Well, as far as everyone else is concerned, this dude is corned beef, but I smell tuna."

"So your instincts tell you that something is wrong."

"Yeah."

"What happened with the one who died of a heart attack?" I asked.

"Maggie. Oh yeah, that was a pretty easy one to trace, because there had been an autopsy done on her. Natural causes. Her family had a history of heart problems."

"So what do you want to do?"

He shrugged his shoulders and flopped back into the chair, kicking his long legs out in front of him. "What can I do? I suppose I have to axt Leslie what she wants to do. I mean, all of the evidence so far absolves him." He shook his head and avoided looking at me directly.

"But you don't have all the evidence, do you? Look, the way I see it is this: Either you care about a case or you don't. It doesn't matter to me whether you care about the client, the challenge, or the compensation; as far as I'm concerned, all three have equal weight, albeit for different reasons. You're right: You need to contact Leslie and see if she wants to proceed, but I also suggest that you trust your instincts."

"So, you wanna talk to her and lemme know what she says?" he asked.

I took a deep breath, unable to get Lucy out of my mind, not wanting Leslie in there. "No. She's your client. You handle the case from here on."

"So you're saying, what—that I should stay with it until I talk to her?" He eyed me carefully. "You sure that's okay?"

"Why not?" I asked, knowing that if I were Miguel, I, too, would have stayed on the case.

"And Leslie won't be pissed?" he asked.

Without even looking up, I could visualize his face morphing into a question mark. When I finally cast an eye on him, my suspicion was confirmed.

"Would that make a difference?" I asked more harshly than I'd intended, then tried to soften it with a smile.

"Well, yeah," he said with such sweet innocence that I was almost—but not quite—able to forgive him.

"She's your client; you handle her." I stood up and turned away from the two men I liked most in this world, reminding myself that all men weren't like Peggy's father, or brother, or son. There were decent men, too, those who railed against violence and injustice. I didn't want mine to see me cry, so I walked to the window.

"One thing, though," I said as I stared blindly at the street.

"What?"

"Does Paula Bell know about Dorothy Washburn?"

"She knows about her, but they haven't met."

I heard Miguel move the chair back into place and Max start toward the door. I shut my eyes and wondered how Peggy would survive this. That's when I felt Miguel's hands on my shoulders.

"Lucy'll be okay, boss. It'll all be fine." He hugged me from behind and then, without another word, he and Max left me in the den, alone with my thoughts, a terrifying place to be.

SIXTEEN

I don't know whether calling Leslie was a Pavlovian response to wanting just any comfort in the midst of distress, or if Leslie was truly the only one I knew who might have the ability to make me feel less shattered, but before I knew it I had my cell phone in hand and had dialed her number.

"Hey," she answered, sounding subdued.

"You busy?"

She paused. "No. Are you all right?" I couldn't tell if her tone was guarded or gentle, and perhaps because of that I burst into uncontrollable tears, gasping for air as I held the phone to my side.

When I could finally control my breathing, I brought the phone back to my ear and heard her sweet voice asking, "Honey, sweetheart, what's wrong? Talk to me."

And I did. In an outpouring of fear and frustration, I told her about Lucy and how a ghost from the past had taken her away from us. I talked and talked and talked, but what I didn't tell her was how frightened I was for us, because in that moment, when a child's safety was at stake, I couldn't let myself think I was so selfish and self-involved as to admit being afraid of losing the love of my life and not knowing why I felt that. Baring my vulnerability, I felt suddenly awkward. I hated not only that the feelings existed but that I was so keenly aware of them.

It's hard to be of much use to anyone else when you're busy hating yourself, I realized.

And I knew, though I had never said it out loud, that if Max and I had arrived only a few minutes earlier, all of this would have been avoided. Logic told me it wasn't my fault, but my head was only managing a whisper, while my heart was screaming, *IT'S ALL YOUR FAULT!*

Leslie wanted to come home. I didn't know what good it would do. It was a stupid thing to say, but the words were out before I could retract them. Again, a silence descended between us, born not from malintent but, rather, a naïve lack of communication.

I was overwhelmed. There was no way I could possibly sort through the feelings to find the words.

Apparently, neither could she. Both of us tried to break the silence at the same time, which was followed by an awkward politeness, both of us saying, "You go first." The stalemate finally ended with an admission.

"I'm frightened," I said, trying to distance myself from my feelings.

"I know, honey. Me, too."

"We'll be okay," I whispered.

"Of course she will" was her response. "Call me, Sydney. I know it's hard right now, but I need to know what's going on there. Okay?"

"Okay." I took a deep breath. "I love you."

"You, too."

I pressed the little red button to end the call, wiped my cheeks with the back of my hand, and turned the phone off. I stood at the window, looking out as the evening embraced the city. Usually, nightfall made me feel safe in this city, maybe because I was raised here in a different time and a piece of me would always possess a child's wonderment about the lives being led in the rosy glow behind the zillions of windows. But at that moment, the backdrop of the sky outlining concrete, metal, and glass only served to make me cold and anxious. Now every lighted window I saw held not the promise of what could be but, rather, the terrifying possibility of what some people were capable of.

Lucy was somewhere, perhaps as close as a block away, but who knew where and how.

By the time I abandoned my thoughts in the den, I was surprised to see that Peggy was back.

She was almost unrecognizable. Her eyes were beginning to recess into darkened cavities, her short hair was stringy, and she was ashen and outwardly fragile. Whenever she unclasped her hands from her lap, they shook like those of a junkie starting withdrawal.

I am rarely rendered stupid, and yet it was as if all my synapses were severed. Signals were going out inside one part of me to respond to Peggy, but they never connected with the other end of the configuration, which would have me actually stand and walk and speak. Instead, I watched as Max got up, wrapped his arms around her, and let her sob until she was still. He looked helplessly at me over her shoulder as I sat there feeling as if I had been hit in the gut with a boulder.

Peggy finally eased away from Max, patted his shoulder, and sank onto the living room sofa.

I held out a handful of tissues, which she accepted with a quivering hand.

"Peggy," I began, then stopped. What on earth could I say?

She shook her head and moved her fingers as if to brush away a bug or a thought.

"You know," she said, so softly I had to strain to hear her, "I want to kill him with my bare hands." She stared at the floor and chewed her lower lip. "I keep thinking about everything I've done wrong in my life that's led to this moment, knowing perfectly well that I can't change a fucking thing." She pressed the tissues to her mouth and squeezed her eyes shut. Max and I watched helplessly from the sidelines. "There is nothing I can do to make my baby safe. And I know I'm supposed to think positive thoughts, but all I keep thinking is how many milk cartons have pictures of missing children. How many innocent kids become victims of psychotics like him." She paused and I watched her face make the transition from anguish to steely rage. "They have to find this son of a bitch. I want my baby back."

"They're doing everything they can," Max said, glancing at the room where the team was set up; two agents remained on duty.

"Have you heard from Marcy?" I asked Max.

"About what?" Peggy asked, whereupon I explained how Marcy was doing a search for officers born the same year as her son.

"It's going to be a long night for her. There are close to forty thousand police officers in the five boroughs, and the database won't behave with a simple sort. She'll get it, though," Max said.

"Did Gil hear anything further from statistics?" We knew that the Department of Health and Vital Statistics had been able to assess the birthrate in NYC in 1968 quickly and had even narrowed it down to December births, but anything more specific—such as who was born at what hospital on what day—was confidential and, given that it was more detailed, would take longer to review. First, Gil was having them run a check for the weekend of the fourteenth and fifteenth, but he had also requested a secondary search into the weekends before and after, just in case Peggy's recollection was tainted by an event she would rather have forgotten.

"Nothing new yet," Max said softly. "With the manpower they have working on this, they should have something soon. You know Gil—he won't let his staff sleep until he has what he wants."

"What *does* he want?" Peggy asked softly.

Max leaned closer to Peggy and asked, "Who, honey? Gil?"

"No." She stared at a faraway place on her knees. "Not Gil."

Max nodded, turned toward Peggy, and rested his arm on the back of the sofa. "From everything you've told us, I'd be willing to bet that he just wants to scare you." Just a glance and I knew he was simply saying this to make her feel better, to try to calm her, even though he knew there was no way to make any of this better.

"Yeah, well, he's doing one hell of a job."

Max seemed to study Peggy carefully before he asked, "Look, I know you've been over this a dozen times with Sydney and the entire police force, but would you be willing to go over what happened back in 1968 one more time with me?" Max had an uncanny ability to make people feel safe and comforted, even in the diciest of situations. I don't know if it was the tone of his voice, his kind eyes, his solid build, or some mesmerizing quality, but his magic seemed to work with Peggy. She took a deep breath and nodded.

"It's not as if I'm about to sleep." She rubbed a dry hand over her mouth and cheeks and asked if I would make a pot of coffee.

As I started to stand, Max suggested that we all go to the kitchen. I knew his objective was to get something more substantial than caffeine into our friend.

Max's questioning of Peggy was more like a conversation. As they talked, he explored the kitchen, and before she knew what had hit her, Peggy, along with the two of us, was digging into a tomato, Brie, and asparagus omelette, toasted bialys, and decaf coffee.

By midnight, the only new information that Max and I had learned was that the name of the nun who had befriended Peggy back at the shelter was Sister Angeline. Peggy still had a mental block about the name of the shelter, but at least now we had a name, and that felt like gold. I made a note to have Kerry start a search for Catholic maternity shelters in the Bronx where a nun by the name of Angeline might have hung her habit in the late sixties. Every little piece made the search more specific.

Our conversation never veered from Lucy or John, not while I cleared the dishes, nor when I started a fresh pot of coffee for the officers in the other room. At one point, I mentioned that Max and I had met Karl earlier in the day.

At first, I wasn't sure if she had heard me, but then I noticed her eyes following me with the intensity of a wary cat.

"What's he like?" she asked almost indifferently, but I knew better.

Max and I exchanged a quick glance before he said, "He's a pig."

"He wasn't very pleasant," I admitted as I scrubbed the sink.

"He never was," she said.

"Tell me about him as a kid," Max asked.

"What's to tell? He was a schmuck, just like our dad."

"Was he violent?" I asked.

Her brows knit together as she stared in disbelief at me. "If you consider rape violent, then yeah, I suppose he was."

"What about with people other than you? Other kids on the

block or school chums?" asked Max, who was sitting at the table with her, stirring sugar into his cup.

"I suppose so, yeah. I don't think he had many friends." She sounded as tired as she looked, but I knew nothing we said could coerce her to sleep until it hit her unawares.

"I know you don't want to hear this, Peggy, but—"

"What?" She eyed me suspiciously.

"It's late, and tomorrow is going to be a tough day. I suggest you lie down, even if you can't sleep."

Max backed me up, even suggesting a hot bath before turning in.

Peggy was too tired even to feign an argument and was probably just as glad not to pursue more talk about Karl. While she was soaking in the bath, Max and I sank back down at the kitchen table and looked at each other.

"Do I look as bad as you do?" I asked.

"My guess is that you probably look worse." He yawned.

"Oh yeah?" I asked, resting my elbows on the table and my chin in my hands.

"Yeah. For example, what used to be eye makeup is now raccoon disguise. Very convincing, though. Fetching, you might say."

"Thank you. I try." I felt like a bus had hit me.

"I think I'll stay tonight," Max said, glancing at his watch. "You just never know what'll happen."

"Thanks. I think that's a good idea. Tell you something?"

He looked at me.

"I feel a whole lot better knowing that the police are tracing the whereabouts of her son."

"Amen to that. At least they have the resources to find him," Max said.

"You know I spent a lot of time on-line yesterday, looking into the whole process of adoption. It's pretty amazing how things have changed. I mean, nowadays in open adoptions, the adopting parents can literally go through the pregnancy from beginning to end with the birth mother."

"Open adoptions? Is that what it's called when you buy a baby from Romania or China?"

"No, that's an independent adoption." I leaned back in my chair and heard three vertebrae pop.

"Well, what about children from overseas?" Max asked. "Does the couple who purchase junior from Cambodia know anything about that child? And what happens when little Thai turns twenty and wants to know where he came from? Is that information more readily available because it's the twenty-first century?"

"You know," I said as I started to feel my energy returning, "I wonder if Peggy ever checked on-line to see if anyone was looking for her. I mean, I'm sure she didn't. But . . ." I sat straight up and saw that Max and I were obviously experiencing mind meld.

"Do you think that he could have posted queries for her on-line when he was looking for her?"

"My guess would be yes," I said, feeling the chill of excitement start in the center of my stomach. "Especially at the start of his search."

"Couldn't hurt to take a look," Max said, already halfway to the den.

I stopped in the dining room and asked the officer who was awake if she had a way to search this faster than we could. She didn't, but she offered to run a search on one of their computers anyway. I directed her to the pot of coffee I had just brewed for her and her partner, then hurried after Max.

In our first search, we keyed in Peggy's name, which provided fifteen pages. At least twenty of the articles were relative to Peggy and her work, but nothing connected her to adoption sites.

Because I had searched the Web the day before in an attempt to find maternity shelters in the Bronx in the 1960s, I wasn't nearly as surprised as Max that our first inquiry—"Looking for birth mother"—generated eighty-eight pages of listings, which directed us to over seventeen hundred sites. And that was using just one search engine. Two hours later, we seemed no closer to finding Peggy's son, which wasn't surprising, given that it had taken him four or five years to find her. Unfortunately, we didn't have that kind of time.

The last thing I remember was sitting on the sofa, just for a minute, just to rest my eyes.

SEVENTEEN

I awoke stiff and confused. After I peeled my face off a sofa pillow, a bleary glance at my watch told me that it was just before 7:30. I didn't know if that was A.M. or P.M. I didn't know where I was. I lay there trying to decipher the sounds just beyond the closed door. Voices. Someone had covered me with a soft plaid blanket, which I had managed to twist around my body like a cocoon.

I was in Peggy's den.

It was morning.

I couldn't will it away.

Dull traces of light inched past the slats of the venetian blinds. I listened hard and thought it might be raining. Great. I slowly eased my legs over the side of the couch and planted my feet firmly on the floor. Looking down, I saw that my shoes and socks had been placed neatly together, and were now poking out from under the sofa. Max must have removed my socks, I realized.

Twisting my body one way, then the other, I managed to issue a satisfying set of pops down my spine. Three deep breaths and I was ready to face the day. Or so I thought, but my body had something else in mind, like stiff punishment for another night on the sofa. It was one of those days where I had to be kind to my muscles, pamper them with a little toe touching and "down dog" exercises.

When I opened the door, I could hear voices coming from down the hallway, probably in the dining room. I headed in the opposite direction, having decided that I wouldn't be fit for public viewing until I had showered first. It was a good thing, too. In the bathroom, I saw firsthand what a mess I was. It's amazing how one's emotional life can be reflected so accurately on the surface, I thought. Staring back at me in the mirror was a relative stranger: a pale mess of a woman, whose dulled eyes reflected sadness and fatigue. I could only imagine what Peggy looked like.

Fifteen minutes later, I was ready to face the world, squeaky-clean and more or less alert.

I found Peggy sitting at the kitchen table with a cup of coffee, an untouched glass of juice, and the cordless phone in front of her. Gil Jackson was sitting across from her, and he looked up as soon as he saw me approach.

"Morning," I mumbled as I entered the room. Right away, I noticed that Peggy was studying a piece of paper flattened between her hand and the tabletop. An identical piece of paper was facing Gil. It was the artist's rendering of the man who had taken Lucy. Lucy's friend Gaby had supplied the police with a description of the man.

I slipped the page from under Peggy's hand and examined the photocopied sketch. I don't know what I had expected, probably a monster, but instead what I saw was a drawing of a very attractive man.

"This is him?" I asked no one in particular.

Gil grunted. "The police artist said that the kid was amazing in how detailed her description was."

"And they trust the accuracy?" I asked, knowing it was a stupid question, given the strong resemblance to Peggy.

Gil's look might have withered another woman. "Yes," he said with admirable restraint, reaching for his deli coffee.

"You okay?" I gently rested my hand on Peggy's shoulder as I stared at the picture. He had an oval face with seemingly gentle light eyes that were offset by dark brows and lashes. His nose was straight and unremarkable; he had a mustache, well-trimmed dark sideburns, and one of those Three Musketeer hair follies under his bottom lip.

"Yeah, great," she said quietly.

I couldn't keep from saying out loud how amazing the resemblance was. Under the picture, it was noted that the suspect had blue eyes, was approximately five six, weighed about 140 pounds, and had dark hair with blond highlights. It cataloged what he was last seen wearing. The only identifying mark noted was a tattoo—about an inch wide—that encircled his left wrist. It was believed to be of Celtic design, but that was uncertain. Apart from that, there were no other distinguishing marks or jewelry.

"Did anyone find out what kind of puppy it was he had lured her with?" I asked just as Max handed me a cup of coffee. "Thanks."

"They tried, but the little girl was on overload. It was little, it was white and had a black nose, and it was cute," Gil said as he was handed a slip of paper from his assistant.

"Did you get any rest?" I asked Peggy, who shook her head in response. I was impressed that she had managed to shower and dress for the day. Despite the fact that she was probably running on nerves alone, she looked a lot more composed than she had the night before.

"Okay," Gil said with renewed energy as he shook the page in his hand. "Where's McElroy?" he asked the room in general.

She was just coming in from the dining room. "What do you have?" she asked.

"Statistics have been able to pare down births at the hospital on the fourteenth and fifteenth. We have eight on Saturday and five on Sunday. No certificates, just data, but I have names, which means we have a place to start."

"How many were males?" McElroy asked.

"Let's see. . . . On Saturday the fourteenth, there were six, and on Sunday, four out of the five were male."

"This is good," I said, squeezing Peggy's shoulder. "That means we've narrowed it down to ten possibilities. That's excellent."

At that very moment, the phone rang, causing everyone to snap to and then freeze, except for McElroy, who was in the dining room before you could blink.

"It's the hospital," an officer said from the other room.

"John," Peggy practically cried as she fumbled with the cordless phone. She had asked us all not to mention Lucy's situation to John. "Hello?" She stood to leave and give herself some privacy. "Hey, what are you doing calling? You must be feeling better. . . ." She left the room.

Max shook his head as he watched her go. "I cannot imagine being in her skin right now."

Gil was already on a cell phone in the corner of the kitchen, checking in with his office to see if they had any updates for him. It wouldn't be easy, but there was a comfort in knowing that with these names in hand, we had a starting place.

"Did you sleep at all?" I asked Max.

"An hour, maybe two. You snore," he said as he handed me a powdered doughnut.

"Okay, the ball is rolling. Has anyone heard from Marcy?" Gil asked Max, who shook his head. "Wouldn't it be a slice of heaven if one of the names on *this* list matches one of the names on her list?" His eyes sparkled for a moment before his shook his head and said, "Nah. Never happen."

"Has Cooper learned anything?" I asked.

Gil shrugged. "Dunno. But he has a set of these pictures, so he'll be following up with this son of a bitch with regard to the shooting. Look, I'm going to talk to McElroy and then head downtown and see if I can speed things up. Call me if you learn anything—*anything*. Got it?"

"Got it," Max and I said in unison.

As he turned to go, I asked if they had learned anything from Karl the night before.

"Guy's as innocent as a babe," he said with unmasked contempt. "He admitted that he had relations with Peggy when they were kids but insisted that it wasn't rape. Said she had come on to him and that if she had a baby back then, it was someone else's. Based on your information that he owns a gun—which he denied— we were able to get a search warrant, but nothing was found on the premises."

"Is he still in custody?" Max asked.

Gil shook his head. "He was just brought in for questioning, but he knows not to leave town."

"You have a tail on him?" I asked.

"Oh yeah."

"Gil? Has the FBI been brought in?" I asked.

He looked at me, closed his eyes, and said softly, "They've been informed." Again he turned to leave and again I stopped him.

"One last thing. We have the name of one of the nuns who worked at the shelter where Peggy stayed." I gave him Sister Angeline's name and he managed a lame smile.

"Every little bit helps, kid."

This time, I let him go.

I poured myself another cup of coffee and found Peggy in the dining room, looking through the list of names Gil had left behind. She shook her head as she read through the list over and over again.

"Nothing. Nothing rings a bell."

I could see the muscles in her right cheek start to twitch, so I eased the paper out of her hand and asked for a look at the names. "How's John?" I asked as I glanced at the first names: Michael, Thomas, Howard, Michael, John, James, Mitchell, Robert, Kevin, Peter.

"He sounded great," she said, rubbing the back of her neck. "He was clear and sounded strong. They've reduced the dose of the painkillers he's getting, which is going to help him heal more quickly. He never did like drugs."

The ten infants were listed with first and last names; No Dexter was listed.

"Are you sure none of these names rings a bell?" I asked.

She shook her head.

"Did Gil tell you whether there was data relative to parents with this?" I asked.

"I think that's all they have right now."

McElroy was on a cell phone and the second officer was facing a computer screen, his back to us. Peggy touched my arm and led me into the kitchen. When we were alone, she said, "Listen, I know that the person behind this is my son. I have tried everything to avoid coming back to the one simple truth that because of that, this whole bloody mess is my fault. John being shot, my baby—" She stopped, dug her fingers into her eyes, and dragged her fingertips down the length of her face, where she pulled at her chin. She didn't leave a mark, just a fleeting red shadow of the path her fingers had taken.

"What I'm trying to say," she said, as if catching her breath. "What I want to say is that I know what a good friend you are, and as much as part of me wants you to, I know you can't stay with me twenty-four hours a day. That said, my fear is that if I go see John, no one will be here to answer the phone. But if I don't go see him, he'll know that something is horribly, horribly wrong."

"Maybe he should know, Peg," I suggested.

She shook her head. "No. Not yet. He's just not strong enough." She paused and looked at a faraway place on the backsplash of the sink, and I was reminded that her fears were a lot more complex than John's recovery.

"You're going to have to tell him at some point," I said gently.

"Not yet." She was firm. "I'm not looking for advice, Sydney. I want to know if you'll stay here when I'm at the hospital, just in case he calls."

"I promise. I also think it's a good idea if you have a friend around at all times, whether it's Max, or Marcy, or me, or . . ." I shot off a list of various friends whom I knew she could trust but who did not yet know what was happening with Lucy.

She held up her hands as if to end the conversation just as Max walked in.

The phone rang. We all jumped and Peggy raced into the dining room, where McElroy was holding the cordless phone and studying the computer screen at the same time. She handed the phone to Peggy and motioned for her to pick up.

"Hello." Peggy sounded cautious and breathless at the same time.

I checked my watch; it was not yet 8:30.

"Yes," Peggy said, and then shot a frightened glance at McElroy, who was listening in to the call on another headset. McElroy shook her head no and moved her right hand in front of her as if to signal Peggy to keep the conversation moving.

"No," Peggy said quickly. "You asked me not to and I didn't. Look, it doesn't have to be this way. Please . . ." She stopped and listened. "That's not true. It was a different time then, a different age. You haven't even given me a chance to tell you how much I want to meet you." Peggy shut her eyes and lowered her head for barely an instant before recovering. It was as if she were refusing to give in either physically or emotionally. "Please, tell me what I can do. You and I both know that this is between you and me, not Lucy. . . ." She looked like a soldier ready to attack as she listened to the voice on the other end of the line. "All I'm asking is that you and I meet. Why don't you just bring Lucy back here, and then—"

Again she listened.

"What does that mean? Why not? Please, where is she? At least let me talk to her."

I watched McElroy's face as she listened to the call and watched the computer screen to see if they had been able to trace it. Before my eyes could shift to Peggy, I knew they had identified the number.

"She's a child," Peggy said, showing her emotions now. She clamped her hand over her mouth as she listened to what was being said on the other end of the line.

"No, wait! What about Lucy? Where is she? Please, please, just let me talk to her. What do you want? I'll give you anything. Just bring my daughter back to me."

Peggy looked helplessly at McElroy, who nodded reassuringly. Then Peggy's head jerked almost imperceptibly to the left as she seemed to strain to hear the caller. Her eyes snapped open as she cried out, "No!"

It was clear that the conversation had come to an abrupt halt.

McElroy was on another line, delivering orders to another officer, her face somber and angry. The officer at the computer turned to Peggy and gave her a hopeful smile. "We have a number."

Peggy turned to me, grabbed my sleeve, and whispered, "He said, 'Plenty of people would pay top dollar for a kid like yours.' How could he say that? Is he serious?"

There was no way to know, no way to reassure Peggy.

The number turned out to be for a cell phone. Getting to the source would take longer than any of us would be comfortable with, even if it was minutes, which it wouldn't be, because despite modern technology, pinpointing a person would take time. My guess was that this cell phone, like the one used when her son had first made contact, would also have been stolen. It was easy to see the pattern emerging. In the back of my head I heard Gil and McElroy discussing whether the son could be a cop. Whatever he was, he was smart and he was sick. Listening to the conversation played back, McElroy pointed out the sound of a tugboat in the distance, a sound that had been identified in the background from the call the night before. Hearing the other end of the conversation sent a chill down my spine, because it was evident that the person we were dealing with was a breath away from losing total control.

The next phone to ring was mine.

EIGHTEEN

It was Kerry. I had called her the night before and asked her to take care of Auggie, but I hadn't told her anything about Lucy, just said I'd be in touch.

"I talked to Logan," she said. When I didn't respond, she reminded me that he was her brother-in-law-to-be, the one who had been adopted and was searching for his birth mother.

"He found her. Or rather, he found her gravestone. Seems that she died of this liver disease that can be passed down from generation to generation." Kerry paused. "It was weird, you know. I mean, Logan's not someone I have ever been able to connect with, but when I asked him about his birth mother and the whole adoption thing, it really seemed to make a difference for us. For the both of us. It's like it brought us closer together."

"How did he find her?"

"Believe it or not, he finally found a connection to her on-line. It took him about three years to get what he was looking for, and he told me that if he hadn't had a place to start—birth mother's name—he never would have found her. I tell you, though, talking to him really made me realize that there are things we just take for granted. I mean, I know how lucky we all are. We live in New York City, we have indoor plumbing, nobody's going to stone us to death for adultery or force us to have clitorectomys, but I have to say I never really thought about the fact that I know my family—or that at least I know *who* they are." She took a breath. "Talking to Logan got me thinking about how weird it must be, like *Clan of the Cave Bear*, you know?"

I was afraid to ask her to connect those dots, so I said nothing.

"I know my family thinks I'm weird, but when my dad looks at me and wonders why I dress the way I do, my mom always says that I got it from his side of the family, that I'm just like his aunt Harriet. I never thought about that before. But it's kind of comforting, you know?"

"Wow. There's another one like you running around? Do you know her?" I asked.

"No. She was my dad's aunt, and apparently quite a wild woman. She died in a hot air–balloon crash."

"Max and I were checking on-line last night," I said. "Of course we didn't get anywhere. Were you able to get anything on the Catholic maternity houses in the Bronx?"

"Yeah. Giving myself a ten-block radius around the hospital, I have learned that in that area there were four churches and two shelters—the Halpern House and the Caring Center."

"You are unbelievable," I said. Kerry's ability to rout out information while never leaving her desk had always amazed me.

"I know."

"Are the shelters still in operation?"

"Halpern has become a halfway house and the Caring Center is gone. It made way for a high rise in the early eighties."

"What happened to their staff?"

"I don't know yet, but I'm on it."

"Is Halpern still run by the church?"

"Yeah."

"Good. Look, I have a name for you. Sister Angeline. She worked at the shelter where Peggy stayed."

"Excellent. Anything else?"

It was then I told her about Lucy's abduction the day before. I gave her few details, reminded her unnecessarily that this was strictly confidential, and said I would be by the office as soon as I could get there. In the meantime, she said she'd try to get whatever she could on Sister Angeline, because that was the most promising lead we had. Knowing Kerry was on it gave me a somewhat increased level of confidence that we would find this asshole.

When Peggy left for the hospital with Max, I listened to the recorded conversation between Peggy and her son.

> —*Hello.*
> —*Hello, Mom. Were you waiting for my call?*
> —*Yes.*
> —*And did you call the police?*
> —*No. You asked me not to and I didn't.*
> —*Bullshit. Cop's wife's gotta call the cops. Yo, Officer, how you doing?*
> —*Look, it doesn't have to be this way. Please . . .*
> —*[A sigh.] But it does, really. I mean, you made it very clear a long time ago that you wanted nothing to do with me.*
> —*That's not true. It was a different time then, a different age. You haven't even given me a chance to tell you how much I want to meet you. Please, tell me what I can do. You and I know that this is between you and me, not Lucy. . . .*
> —*Lucy is fine.*
> —*All I'm asking is that you and I meet. Why don't you bring Lucy back here, and then—*
> —*No, no, no. It doesn't work that way.*
> —*What does that mean? Why not? Please, where is she? At least let me talk to her?*
> —*See, right away it's about Lucy.*
> —*She's a child.*
> —*I know that. I know she's a child. What do you think I am, blind? She's a child. She's a child and she's fine. She's having a great time. I happen to be a very good caretaker, but that's something you wouldn't know, isn't it? Look, I have to go.*

*—No, wait! What about Lucy? Where is she? Please, please
just let me talk to her. What do you want? I'll give you anything. Just bring my daughter back to me.*
[Long pause.]
*—You know, lady, plenty of people would pay top dollar for a
kid like yours. We'll call back at seven tonight. Oh, and Officer whatever the fuck your name is, if you interfere, you'll
never see the kid again.*

I asked McElroy if she thought, "We'll call back" meant that there was more than one person involved in the kidnapping.

"It could. Then again, it could mean that he's connecting with Lucy and considers them to be on the same side, as it were."

"Any feel for it?" I asked, sounding as pathetically lost as I felt. Of course there was no answer, and I knew it.

Feeling honor-bound to stay at Peggy's while she was gone, I set myself up in the den, out of McElroy's way. I had a copy of his photo, the list of the thirteen children born over a two-day period in a 1968, and Peggy's laptop computer, which I was able to get on-line with. But as soon as I sat down, I didn't have a clue where to start.

I studied his picture. He was a good-looking man. He actually looked kind, and, in a strange way, innocent. Right, what I didn't need at that moment was to see him as a sympathetic soul, be-cause there was no question that the man I was looking at was the same one who had taken Lucy from her family and had threatened to sell her. But as hard as I tried, I couldn't seem to hate the face I was looking at.

I picked up the page listing the ten boys. Michael Dwyer. Thomas Egan. Howard Nathan Epstein. Michael Hubbard. John Singleton-Watts. James Velasquez. Mitchell Nussbaum. Robert D'Angelo. Kevin O'Brien. Peter Wong. It was impossible to know whether the names were those of the birth parents or the adopted parents, because adoptions were done very differently back then. It was not unusual for records to be fudged, forged, and fabricated. All I knew for certain was that one of these kids had grown into a little monster, like Patty McCormack in *The Bad Seed*.

Again, I picked up the artist rendering.

The resemblance to Peggy was striking, especially in the eyes.

I turned on the computer and, going through the notes that I had been jotting on paper, made a cohesive list of everything we knew so far. There wasn't much, but we had more today than we'd had the day before. Then again, what with Lucy involved, it was a different race, and we were running out of time.

As I read through the overview of my meeting with Karl, several points disturbed me, but suddenly one jumped out and practically had me out of my seat.

I called Eddie Phillips, a grizzled photojournalist I'd been friends with since the beginning of time—or more precisely, since the beginning of the seventies, when I was a student at Columbia and Eddie had just returned from Vietnam. He might be a cranky old pain in the ass, but his mind was an amazing archive of information; everything from movie trivia to historical factoids banged around inside his cavernous cranium, just waiting to be called upon.

He answered in surprisingly chipper spirits, which was most unlike him.

"Sydney, little darlin', how are you this beautiful day?"

"It's overcast, Edwardo."

"I know."

"Am I interrupting anything?" I asked, not that it would stop me.

"Nah. I am simply lying here in bed with the most beautiful woman in the world."

"Inflatable?"

As low as I was, his laughter was a tonic.

"Believe it or not, no! What's up?"

"Quick question. Do I remember you once mentioning that in Vietnam they used suppressors on revolvers?"

"Oh sure. Smith & Wesson, a .357 Magnum. Nice gun. Only used by the Special Forces, though. It's not like it was regulation army issue, if you know what I mean."

That was the detail I was looking for.

"I owe you, Edwardo. Thanks."

"Anything for you, darlin'. Say, how's your friend John?"

"Improving. I gotta run."

"Wait! I want you to meet Anisha."

"Really?" This was a first. Eddie hadn't been serious about a woman since his live-in lover died in a boating accident a zillion years ago.

"Yeah. She's great."

"God, Eddie, you actually sound mushy. Good for you! Look, I'll call next week and we'll have dinner or something."

I called Max's cell phone, which was, not surprisingly, turned off, since he was at the hospital. Next, I called Gil to see if ballistics had learned anything on the gun used to shoot John, but he was in a meeting. Finally, I called Miguel. I may have been tired, but I knew that I was going to need backup, and he was my last lifeline. His cell had a recorded message, which explained that the number I was trying to reach was out of the service area.

Over the years, I'd learned never to ignore it when a hunch hit as hard as this one. It was time to head over to the hospital and grab Max.

NINETEEN

Walking to the subway, I heard a friendly voice behind me call "Hey!" to someone.

Or I thought he was calling out to someone else, until I felt a very firm hold on my right elbow, then my left. Thinking it was someone I knew—a perfectly reasonable thought—I started to turn my head to the right, but I was quickly stopped. The man warned me to face front as he deftly applied pressure to a point on the inside of my arm, just above my elbow. The subsequent effect buckled my knees, but two men, one on each side of me, made certain I didn't miss a step. When I had recovered my footing, the person on my left applied such intense pressure to a point just above my wrist that not only did the pain shoot straight up through my arm but I thought I would black out from my little nerves being pulverized. It was impossible to think that two fingers were causing such intense pain.

"Sydney, how are you? We have a message for you." The man on my right side could have made a fortune doing voice-overs.

"Sydney? What are you talking about? My name is Betty."

I could feel the one on the left falter ever so slightly, but the man on the right wasn't so easily fooled.

"Have it your way . . . Betty." He cooed the name as if we were lovers. He moved closer to my side as we all made a left onto a relatively empty side street lined with an odd assortment of buildings, from brownstones to industrial-looking three-story structures.

My peripheral vision allowed me to see that the man on my right was about six two, slender, with wavy dark hair and pock-marked skin. The left stepper was shorter and had stringy shoulder-length blond hair, big lips, and a tattoo of a knife between his thumb and index finger. He moved his right hand and cupped the base of my head with his pincerlike fingertips. It felt like if he wanted to, he could pop my head right off my spine, and I was terrified that he might. Suddenly, as if reading my mind and wanting to prove he could hurt me, he did something that made it feel as if he had skewered my head on his fingers. There was no way to pull free from his grasp, and the pain was literally blinding.

Wordlessly, he steered me up a three-step stoop and into a small, dark, musty vestibule. He was then ordered to wait outside.

"Betty, I have no intention of hurting you. Do you understand?" His voice was calm, almost lyrical, as he pressed me against a wall opposite one with an archaic intercom that was scribbled over with graffiti. He cupped his slender but potentially lethal hand around my neck and then, while applying an even pressure against my larynx with his palm, pinched my jaw between his thumb and middle fingers. The jawbone may be the strongest bone in the body, but it felt as if mine was about to snap in half.

"You know I could hurt you if I wanted to, right? Blink once for yes and twice for no."

I blinked once. They say that the eyes are the windows into the soul, which made me think that his green ones were window dressing, because they looked as kind as his voice was silken.

"You are looking for a young woman, and I have been asked to tell you it is time to stop. Okay?" He pressed the heel of his hand against my throat and waited for me to blink.

This was a dilemma: If I blinked once—which meant yes—did that mean I would stop looking, or that I acknowledged that he had been asked to tell me to stop? And who was the young woman? Lucy was a child, hardly a young woman. Language is sometimes a useless form of communication, and in a situation such as this, blinking can be even more useless. However, being wise to the

Pavlovian theory of pain, I knew that if I were to blink twice, it would hurt, so I blinked once, knowing that that was what he wanted.

"Do you know how easy it is to remove the eye from a socket using only one finger?" he asked quietly.

Q & A was definitely getting trickier. I blinked twice, but this was a question that required clarity. I mean, I didn't really know how easy it would be to poke out an eye, but I felt it was imperative that he know I didn't want to find out firsthand. However, as soon as I tried to utter a word, he showed me how easy it would be to crush my voice box, so I stopped.

"It's very painful," he added, glancing out the front door, and thus missing my one blink. When he looked back at me, he seemed to be memorizing my face. With his free hand, he traced the area around my right eye, starting on the underside of the brow, following the curve of the outside, then the underside again, and finally grazing over the eyelashes, as if his intention was to tickle. His jaw was slightly slackened as he peered into my right eye. A passerby might have thought he was tenderly searching for the cause of an irritation. I held my breath as he pulled my bottom lid down with one finger and rolled another finger along the bottom of my eyeball. The sensation of being helpless and violated stung almost as much as the saltiness of his skin against my cornea. He wiggled his finger into what felt like the bottom of the socket, making me fear that any further pressure would explode the eyeball. And then he stopped. He flattened his left hand over my entire eye, as if to soothe it, all the while never taking his other hand off my throat and jaw. I had completely stopped breathing.

There are times—even when the odds are overwhelmingly against you—when you should fight. And then there are other times when it's just plain stupid. This was one of the latter. I had no doubt that the man standing before me had the instincts of a psycho killer, but I also believed that he was an expert in the martial arts and clearly had training in the pressure points of the body. I don't know if it was his self-control or his in-depth knowledge of pressure points, which I had always associated with healing, but for some bizarre reason, as frightened as I was, I felt strangely safe with him, certainly safer than I would have felt alone with the blond on the stoop, even *after* my eye tuck. This conviction was in all likelihood born out of my understanding that there was absolutely nothing I could do to protect myself.

"I have been told that if you don't do as I ask, I will be commissioned to kill you. Now, you look like a nice lady. Perhaps you're even thinking about retirement in another couple of years, and I would hate to be the one to ruin that for you. Better you should die of old age or get hit by a bus, because, believe me, you don't want me coming after you. You know that, don't you?"

Nice lady? Retirement? *Retirement?*

"Don't you?" he repeated, clearly waiting for me to blink. Great, now I couldn't remember if one was yes or no. *Nice lady.* Women with white hair and droopy stockings who push walkers are nice ladies, I thought. I blinked once and held my breath.

"Good." He released his hold of my head and almost tenderly patted my cheek. "Now, between you and me, the individual who hired me would be very unhappy if he or she thought our meeting didn't make an impression on you. I am more evolved than most people, but that could simply be because I understand the power I possess. Do you understand the power I possess?" he asked as he straightened his cuffs.

I blinked once.

His crooked smile reminded me of Scott Glenn.

"You know, Sydney, it's because of your answer that I am not going to leave you in pain, even though I was instructed to do so. Instead, I am going to treat you with what you might call 'professional respect.' However, be warned that if I ever have to see you again, you won't have a chance to blink before it's over. Got it?"

I nodded.

"Good. Now, I'm going to make it look like I'm roughing you up. That way, when my associate and I return, he will be a flawless witness. After we have his attention, I will hit you in the stomach. You will double over, slide to the floor, and stay there for the count of at least sixty. Okay?"

"One question," I said, making sure my face was turned away from the door.

His look was enough permission to continue.

"Why are you being so nice to me?"

"It's a small world. A long time ago, you helped out a friend of mine. Simple as that."

"Just for clarity' sake, you should know that I'm not looking for a young woman."

The change in his expression scared the hell out of me.

"I'm looking for a child, a girl, but a little girl, not a young woman. I need to know if this is semantics or if perhaps your employer has been misinformed."

I knew I was taking a potentially painful risk, but I didn't feel as if I had a choice. He had clearly been sent to discourage me from pursuing a case, but it didn't fit.

He flattened his hands against the section wall on either side of me and leaned in. His breath was warm and his voice low. "I was told a young woman. If I have been misled, and you *are* trying to find a child rather than an adult, I assure you I will deal as harshly with my client as I promised I would you. Do you understand?"

I blinked.

"All right. This doesn't change things with us here and now. Are you ready?"

I was. We scuffled to get the blond's attention, which wasn't difficult, because he was standing sentry right outside the door. Perhaps the Voice really didn't understand his own strength, or maybe he did and his intention was to hurt me nonetheless, but either way, I knew his staged roughhousing would leave me with more than a fair share of bruises. Finally, he pulled his right arm back and brought his fist toward my stomach. I tightened my abdominal muscles. Contact was more than I had anticipated. When I went down, it wasn't staged. He towered over me, poked a threatening finger in my direction, and said, "Karma means you don't get away with anything. I've been good to you, Sloane. Don't mess."

I stayed in the vestibule for several minutes after they had gone, which was just barely enough time for me to get my breathing back to near normal.

"Nice lady," I mumbled as I struggled with the warped front door. I scrapped the idea of the subway and opted for a gypsy cab. But now, I wasn't sure where I was going, so I called Max again. This time, I got him. They had left the hospital and he was driving Peggy back home. I told Max to wait for me outside her building after he had dropped her off. I didn't explain what I had in mind; he didn't ask.

Though I was only a few blocks from Peggy's, I needed time to get my breath back. I figured a walk would be just the thing. Besides, I had to quell the deafening emotional melee of thoughts that was taking place inside my head as a result of my run-in. Who was the Voice working for? Who was the young woman? Who was the connection between the Voice and me that kept me safe? And who was he to suggest that I should retire, and why did it bother me so much?

Great, I thought. A tough guy who has the power to take me out with a simple squeeze calls me a *nice* lady, which everyone knows is just another way of saying *old* lady, and instead of concentrating on the important issues, all I can focus on is the age insult.

I slowly limped down the avenue, feeling the bruises popping out over my hidden flesh like measles without the itch. The thing that hurt most was that the Buddhist hit man was right: I was probably getting too old for this lifestyle.

Max looked surprisingly dashing with his tousled hair, two-day-old beard, wrinkled T-shirt, hole-in-the-knee jeans, and worker boots.

"Thanks," I said as I slid into the passenger seat.

"No problem." He waited as I clicked the seat belt into place. "So, my illustrious associate has had a brainstorm?" He turned and faced me, not knowing in which direction we were headed.

"I did. And even more impressive than that is that I actually called you for your help."

"My brawn?"

"Yes, and the fact that you had your car."

"Okay. Where to?"

"Jackson Heights."

"Aha," he said with a nod. "You want to fill me in?"

On the ride to Jackson Heights, I told Max my theory.

When I had finished, he asked, "And if he's not home?"

I paused. "Well, the last thing we need is to get caught breaking and entering."

"Shame on you and your foul thoughts," he said with a thick southern accent. "*I* have never been caught," he added, referring to the one and only time I ever got caught, unfortunately by the very man whose consulate I had broken into for a quick look-see.

"There are police watching the house," I reminded him.

"There are police watching Karl. If he's not there, chances are the police aren't, either."

Even a quick drive through Jackson Heights made it blatantly clear why the area had been declared a New York City Landmark Historic District. The first garden apartments in the United States were built in Jackson Heights by a developer who hired architects to design row houses and apartment complexes that were built to be situated around lushly planted interior courtyards. The buildings, which reflected Art Deco, Tudor, Spanish, and Italianate styles, all managed to create a unique neighborhood aesthetic. Naturally, there had been changes in the neighborhood since Peggy had lived there. Most notable, I suppose, was the heavy influx of Asians and Latin Americans who had settled in this area.

Max pulled up to the curb in front of a single-family house that was completely out of sync with the surrounding buildings and looked as if it had been plucked instead from Queens Village. The dirty two-story white structure had three concrete steps with rusted wrought-iron handrails that led to the front door. Four shaded windows faced the street.

We double-parked in front of Karl Dexter's house and scanned the street, which looked clear.

"Okay, come on." I took a deep breath. "Let's give it a shot."

I rang the bell and waited. Nothing. I rang again.

"Maybe he's not here," I said.

"He's here. He's in the living room, or what I will assume is the living room," Max mumbled under his breath. I looked at him and followed his gaze.

I rang again, this time leaving my finger on the bell an irritatingly long time. Still nothing.

Max went to the back of the house and I sat on the doorbell forever before opening the screen and starting to kick his front door. When the door finally did open, I was looking at Max.

"Don't tell me we missed him," I said, greatly disappointed.

"Nope," he said, stepping back to let me in. He nodded toward the living room, where Karl was rolling around on the floor, swearing and struggling to get up without the use of his hands, which, I was glad to see, were tied behind his back. In truth, I had no desire to have any physical contact with this blanched slob who smelled like he bathed every other week.

I was familiar with just about every profanity that he was spewing.

"What happened?" I asked Max, ignoring Karl's rage.

"Mr. Dexter only locked his front door. The back was open, so I took it as an invitation. As you can see, I convinced him it would be best to talk with us."

"Sure. Because you know, Karl, cops hate cop killers," I called out over his barrage. "Or, more accurately in your case, morons who *try* to kill cops."

"Fuck you both." Karl spat as a means of punctuation. "I got my rights. Get the fuck out of my house."

"I don't think you understand the gravity of your problem, but you should know that Max and I are the best that you could do at this point. If you don't cooperate with us, we'll just let the police deal with you again, and, believe me, they won't be nearly as understanding, especially with the FBI breathing down their necks."

This calmed the beluga down. He craned his neck to look up at me, and I could see a red patch under his left eye, no doubt compliments of Max.

"What do you want?" he huffed.

"Just a little chat, that's all."

"Fine. Fuck it."

I smiled and said, "I thought you'd say that."

TWENTY

I turned to Max. "*You* want to take a look around?"

"I think it will save time." The unspoken thought that what we were doing was both stupid and illegal was clearly communicated between us. We paused, shrugged, and then each walked in a different direction; I moved toward Karl, and Max started toward stairs that led to the second floor.

"I didn't try to kill anyone. Ask the cops. Those sons of bitches kept me at the fucking precinct half the fucking night. If you two crazy fucks—"

"Shut up, Karl." I sidestepped him as I entered the living room.

The inside of the Dexter home was as dark and dirty as one might have suspected, given the facade and the owner. The mustiness was redolent with old garbage and stale beer.

I imagined that—apart from the dirt—the house looked much as it had when Peggy moved out in 1968. The Chesterfield-style sofa and love seat were blue-green and threadbare. Mahogany side lamp tables were covered with dust and what looked to be years of detritus. The coffee table was buried under a sea of take-out food containers, magazines, hardware, beer cans, candy wrappers, a Mets baseball cap, and God only knows what else. Apart from a couple of family photos, the walls were covered with artworks you might find in a Motel 6. Faded velour drapes the color of absinthe were drawn and effectively kept out any semblance of daylight. The television was on and tuned into one of the shopping channels, where an ef-fusive blond couple was hawking a zirconium ring.

I powered off the TV and took a deep breath, which was a mistake, because one good whiff made me feel as if I had inhaled an army of spider mites and other microscopic things with invin-cible jaws.

When I sat on the arm of the plastic-wrapped sofa, I noticed how dimpled it was with cigarette burns. There were so many spots that it looked almost deliberate. I watched as Karl flopped onto his side and then struggled to push himself into an upright position. It's frightening what sloth, along with a diet of Budweiser and fast food, can do to the human frame after a couple of years, I thought. With no muscle tone whatsoever, the task to right himself was both fascinating and pathetic, like watching a group of sitcom has-beens competing in *The Weakest Link*.

In only shorts and a T-shirt Karl, his exposed flesh flabby and deathly white, was a good visual aid to illustrate why I don't like summer. I noticed that Max had tied his hands with the same necktie Karl had worn to work the day before.

"You mentioned yesterday that you're a vet and that you have a gun, Karl. I want to see it. As a matter of fact, I want to see every gun you own, every gun that's in this house. Can you do that with-out creating a stink?"

"I own a legal gun."

"Where is it?" I asked.

"None of your fucking business." Without the use of his hands, he was at a disadvantage, but he was working it.

"Where is it?"

Again, he muttered a garbled "Fuck you." He had made it to his knees, but he was facing the bay window, which looked out onto the street, and I was behind him, so he couldn't see that I had removed the Walther from my bag.

I repeated my question.

He said nothing, just continued to sit on his knees and breathe deeply. Because of his physical exertion, his hair, drenched with perspiration, was plastered to his thick skull, while errant strands hung limply over three rolls of flesh at the nape of his neck.

"Is your gun a souvenir from Vietnam?" I asked the back of his head.

It had been bothering me that the police hadn't found a shell casing where John was shot. Now, the logical reason for that would be that a revolver was used and not an automatic; however, none of the neighbors had reported hearing gunshot, which would lead one to believe that a suppressor had been used. Suppressors, or silencers, are fitted for automatics, not revolvers. Except, as Eddie had pointed out, for the Smith & Wesson revolver that was used by the Special Forces in Vietnam.

"What you're doing is illegal and you know it." He breathed heavily, but he was clearly getting control of himself.

"Is your gun a souvenir from Vietnam?" I asked again, ignoring his accurate observation.

When Karl didn't answer, I walked around him, pointed the Walter casually in his direction, and continued. "They're looking for the gun that was used to shoot Officer Cannady. I think it's yours. You were in Vietnam, and while I don't believe for one second that you would have had access to anything even vaguely related to the Special Forces, it is possible that you got your hands on a revolver that could have been fitted with a suppressor. Is that what you have, Karl?"

"I have rights. You can just suck my dick, you stupid cow bitch."

"No." I aimed the gun at his head, squeezed an eye shut, and whispered, "Bang."

"You don't scare me, Sloane. You're a pussy, and we all know what that's good for, don't we?"

I turned on the TV, jacked up the volume in case the police were sitting outside, aimed at the floor in front of him, squeezed the trigger, and scared him so badly that a little puddle appeared beneath him. "Apparently, I do scare you, Karl. And as far as rights are concerned, you have none, not when you shoot a cop and kidnap a little girl. That's when you stop having rights." I turned off the TV.

"You're outta your fucking mind!" he screamed, and his cheeks, which reminded me of his sister's, turned crimson.

"Maybe, but you're going to tell me everything you know about John and Lucy, or I'll just aim higher and higher each time you don't answer and call it self-defense, which they'll believe, since you shot a cop." I heard the calm delivery of my words and flashed on the Voice, who had terrified me only a short while earlier. Had I thought about it, I suppose I would have seen the food chain of aggression, but I had only one thing in mind at that moment, and none of me cared how frightened or hurt Karl Dexter got in the process.

Max's voice came from the hallway. "Sydney." I looked over and saw him hurrying down the steps. "What happened? Are you okay?"

"Yes. We're just peachy. How are you doing?"

As he walked into the room, I could see the pleasure in his eyes. He extended his right hand, in which he held a pencil. Dangling off that pencil was a gun, an automatic, but a gun nonetheless. "Lookie what I found in a bag that's all packed and ready to go."

"You fucking liar! You motherfuckers are setting me up!"

"That's not your gun?" I asked.

"Fuck you. . . ."

"Kind of makes you wonder how many more there are," Max mused.

"You know the feds are better at their searches anyway," I told Max.

"Is this yours?" Max asked.

The ensuing silence was telling. You could see Karl working the angles in his head. Finally, he admitted that the gun was his. "Yeah, but it hasn't been used in months. The last time I used it was at a shooting range with a buddy of mine. You can ask him. I'll give you his name." He was a disgusting mess of saliva, mucus, and urine from his scare at nearly having had his useless privates blown away.

"I am willing to bet everything I own that in this house we will find the gun that was used to shoot John Cannady. It's just a matter of time, Karl. And I just want to remind you that when we do

170

find it, it will be all the evidence the prosecution will need to ensure the death penalty for you. People don't like cop killers or kidnappers."

"I'm going to finish looking upstairs. Will you be okay here?" Max asked.

Acknowledging the Walther, I assured him I would be. When he was gone, I asked Karl where he had been planning to go with his packed suitcase.

"Up your ass."

I thought about this and said, "You know, Karl, until I met you, I don't think I really believed in the death penalty."

As I listened to Max's footfalls upstairs, I noticed an abrupt change in Karl's demeanor. His face flattened of any expression, except for his eyes, which he kept trained on me. I hardened mine in turn.

"You will suffer for what you've done to me, Sydney, for the position you've placed me in." Had I not been looking at him, I never would have known it was Karl Dexter speaking. The voice was about an octave lower and had a calculated edge. He took a deep breath as he looked down at the stain on his shorts. "You like humiliating people? So do I, but I'm better at it than you are because I have the stomach for it."

I was so mesmerized by his transition that I was completely taken by surprise when I realized that a dark object was flying directly toward my head. Karl had managed to free himself from Max's makeshift cuffs.

My reflex was to throw up my hands and duck to avoid being hit, but Karl had a surprising gift for pitching. The ashtray landed quickly, squarely, and painfully on the left side of my head, just above my ear. As I flinched and the ashtray made contact, I saw him jump to his feet. I mirrored his movements, but the pain and the cigarette ashes in my eyes slowed me down. The next thing I knew, he had the coffee table off the floor and was using it as battering ram, slamming me so hard that I flew over the back of the chair, my body going in one direction and the Walther going in another.

I was on his back like a rabid raccoon before he could even make it to the front door. The unexpected impact of me made him lose his footing, and together we slammed against the wall, my body hitting it first, which knocked some of the air out of me, but I was not about to be stopped. There was no way Karl Dexter was going to leave that house without a police escort.

"Get off," he grunted as he tried to keep his footing. I dug my nails into his cheek and right ear as I kicked us off the wall. We went careening first into a knickknack hutch and then ultimately hit the floor. That's when I went ballistic. A piece of flooring came up and jammed into my backside, feeling more like a shard of glass than a piece of wood. Inhaling the stench of the ashes and the foulness of Karl, I became a madwoman, kicking, scratching, slapping, and punching him with every ounce of energy I possessed.

Karl, however, was equally driven by the motive to get the hell out of there, and he was surprisingly adroit as a fighter. When threatened with arrest, the pale blob morphed into a dirty fighting machine. Often when things get emotional, they get sloppy, and he and I were no exception. Between his doing whatever he could to shake me off and my ironclad resolve to stay put, we managed to bring down just about every movable piece of furniture and gewgaw in the area.

By the time Max came tearing back down the stairs, the floor was covered with shards of porcelain, pottery, and glass. Karl and I were on the ground, a few feet from the front door, when I saw Max's foot fly past me and catch Karl squarely in the gut. I had never been so happy to see a boot before in my whole life. What followed wasn't pretty, but I was able to move fast enough to avoid being further soiled by Karl.

Max helped me up before grabbing Karl by the back of his shirt and throwing him into the living room.

That's when I saw the wooden floorboard that had come loose in the scuffle. It would have been easy enough to miss in a search, but now that it was exposed, it was impossible to see anything else. I bent down and, using the hem of my shirt, pulled out a tin box, which I then handed off to Max. It had a heft to it that made me think it wasn't secret buried treasure from the past, a box containing marbles, trading cards, and rusted skate keys, but that wasn't to say it wasn't. As Max opened it, I retrieved the Walther. Karl lay motionless on the floor.

Between the Voice and Karl, I was hurting, but because Karl was so determined to leave, I knew it meant that he knew something, which meant that I was willing to ignore any pain.

"Would you look at this," Max said softly. He held the lid of the box open, revealing a revolver and a suppressor. He brought the box to his nose, sniffed, and told me, "It's been fired recently."

Still no stirrings from Karl.

After several seconds, I wondered aloud if we ought to check for a pulse.

"Why?" Max asked as he placed the box on the stairs and took a few steps into the living room.

I shrugged. "It's hard to get answers from a dead man."

"He'll answer questions," Max said. "Because you know, Karl, if you don't answer them with us, if you don't show some good faith here, I guarantee you your life is going to be a misery when we hand you off to the feds."

"I haven't done anything," he choked out, his face still pressed to the floor.

"If that's the case, make it easy for yourself. Tell us everything you know."

"As God is my witness, I didn't do anything." He pushed himself up into a sitting position. "But I bet I know who did."

Max and I both knew that Karl had done something, but this was a starting point.

"Who?" Max asked.

"Frank."

"Who's Frank?" I asked.

"My sister's kid." He looked defiantly at the two of us and suppressed what looked like a smile.

"Go on." I was a block of dry ice.

"About a year ago maybe, maybe not that long ago, I got a phone call. It was this guy looking for Peggy. He calls and tells me that he's looking for Peggy Dexter and asks if I know her. I told him that if there wasn't more than one, I was her brother but that I hadn't seen her in a long, long time. So then he tells me that he's this son she put up for adoption, and then he asks if he can come over and meet me, since I'm the first relative he's found. I figured, What the fuck. It's not like I didn't have the time. Anyway, he comes over, and he's okay, you know? He's a nice kid, and if you think about it, he's my nephew, which means we ought to have a relationship. I told him upfront that I couldn't help him find Peggy, because not only did I not know where she was but I didn't care. And I told him that even though I was what you would call sympathetic to his quest, I just couldn't get all steamed up about finding the whore bitch Peggy."

I turned to Max and asked, "That list of names—do you remember seeing the name Frank on it?"

Max shook his head. "No. But it might have been changed by the adoptive family."

"Where does Frank live?" I asked Karl.

He shrugged. "One of the boroughs. I mean, he doesn't live in Connecticut or Jersey."

I pulled out the police sketch and handed it to him. "Is that Frank?"

Karl smiled. "Yeah. Yeah, that's him." He nodded slowly. "That is absofuckinglutely him."

"How can we find him?" I asked.

Karl shrugged. "Search me. I don't have a number or anything like that. He always just comes here, you know?"

"He calls and comes over?" Max asked.

Karl stopped and raised his chin to Max. "Before I give you any more information, I want to know what you're going to do to protect me."

"Before we can protect you, Karl, we need to know exactly what you need protection from. See, it doesn't help that you've withheld

174

information this long, and the feds will want to know why," I said as I perched on the arm of the sofa, feeling as if I'd been pounded from head to toe. Retirement. Huh. It was sounding feasible.

"I'm telling you, I haven't done anything. I let this kid into my life. That's it. He's the one you want."

"Does he know you're his father?" I asked.

"He's my nephew," he said quietly. When he spoke again, his voice was deeper and his expression was flattening, just as it had before. "I don't fuck family, no matter how bad they want it. No, I'm the one that gets fucked. My mother, my father, and that stupid piece of shit Peggy, they all fucked me over. And here I am, getting the blame whenever some little fucking thing goes wrong in their lives."

I wanted to kick him in the head, but instead I backed away and asked, "Did you use your gun to shoot John Cannady?"

"I'm not going to answer that." He straightened his back.

"Did Frank use it?" Max asked gently.

"How the fuck should I know?" He was getting irritated.

"Did he know you had this gun?" Max asked.

"Of course he did. I showed it to him."

"And he knew where you hid it?" I asked as I leaned forward and tried to shake the ash out of my hair.

Karl shrugged. "I don't know. Maybe. Fuck it, we spent time together, but I can't remember every frigging minute."

"Did he tell you anything about the people who adopted him or what his life was like growing up?" I asked, changing paths.

Karl sighed. "He didn't talk much about it. But I do know he didn't find out he was adopted until after the father was dead and the mother was about to kick the bucket. I don't think he liked his old man."

"And you know nothing about whether he did or did not use your gun?" Max asked.

"No." It was an unconvincing monosyllable.

"Where's the little girl?" Max asked, inching closer to Karl.

He paused. "I don't know what you're talking about."

Max grabbed Karl by the back of the neck and thrust his face inches away from Karl's. "If anything happens to Lucy, anything at all, I will personally kill you, do you understand?"

I knew that having the gun and the information that the kid's name was Frank was all we would get from Karl at this point and that it was useless to waste any more time with him. I called Gil and told him that we had found a gun at Karl's that would likely match the ballistics report, as well as a lead to Peggy's son, who went by the name of Frank.

Within minutes, there was a cadre of police cars outside and a gaggle of uniformed officers inside. Max handed over the revolver and suppressor as evidence. Then we gave the first officer all the information Karl had shared with us and promised to get to the station and make a statement later in the day.

As we were leaving, Karl yelled that he would get even with us. Somehow it didn't scare me.

As we walked to the car, I mused, "Karl hates Peggy. You know he filled his nephew's head with the 'whore bitch' routine and probably told him that his father was a delivery boy and Frank was nothing more than the result of a hefty tip. That sort of information could make an unstable person snap, don't you think?"

"Where to?" Max asked.

I asked him to drive me to Peggy's, where I could shower and be with her.

"Karl was headed out of town. If we hadn't shown up when we did, we might have lost him," he said as we pulled away from the curb.

"Where was he going?"

"Nebraska."

The only thing I knew about Nebraska was that it's in the middle of the country.

I exhaled a long, sad sound.

"Don't sound so dejected." Max shook my shoulder. "We're one step closer to her."

"Yeah, but how many more steps are there?" I stared out the window and tried to ignore the pain I was feeling in my chest. It had nothing to do with the Voice or Karl. It was the kind of pain you feel knowing that there are crazy people in the world who have no souls. "Frank. It has to be the name he was given when he was adopted."

"We'll find him," Max said. And because there was nothing else to say that could offer hope, he repeated himself.

TWENTY-ONE

While Max and I were at Karl's, two things had happened in our absence. Marcy had passed off her information to Gil, and Gil, with McElroy's prompting, had convinced Peggy to tell John about Lucy's abduction.

Marcy had been able to determine that several thousand officers were now Frank's age, and of those, about an eighth, approximately 250, were born in December. Not surprisingly, none of the names matched the ten on Gil's list.

The first thing I did when we returned to Peggy's was to wash the morning off me as best as I could.

I came in from the shower just in time to hear the tail end of Max telling Peggy, McElroy, and Gil about our meeting with Karl. "You guys have him in custody now, but my guess is that the ballistics report will prove that his gun was the one that was used to shoot John," he said as he watched me sit directly across from him at the dining room table. Having pounded my muscles with hot water, I was starting to feel the aftereffects of my run-in with both the Voice and Karl. Oddly enough, it was the bump on my head from the ashtray that smarted the most.

"You two make a statement yet?" Gil asked.

We both shook our heads and Max said, "We promised to stop by later and do just that. And what about you folks?"

I glanced around the table and noticed that no one could just sit still. McElroy clenched and unclenched the arm of her chair, Gil popped his knuckles, Max kept tugging at the tip of his nose, and Peggy chewed on her lower lip. I was deliberately trying to refrain from showing any outward sign of tension, but the truth was that just under my sternum, it felt like the inside of a dozen jalapeño peppers.

"My people have already been in contact with three out of the ten people on that list," Gil said.

"And?" one of us asked, but I was so absorbed with my heartburn, I didn't know who.

Gil pushed his lips down and shook his head. "All upstanding citizens with airtight alibis." He stared at the dregs inside his blue-and-white cardboard coffee cup and looked as tired as I felt.

"Did you tell them that Karl said his name was Frank?" I asked Max.

He nodded. "Yes, dear."

"Did your people get anything on the phone call?" Gil asked McElroy.

She took a deep breath and said, "We know that both calls were placed near the water and we're fairly certain that the last call was placed either at or near the South Street Seaport."

"It doesn't help that he uses a different cell phone each time," Gil said.

"Why is that?" Peggy asked as she flattened one of Frank's portraits between her fingertips and the tabletop, pressing so hard that her nails turned red.

"Because it's more difficult to trace an exact location on a cell phone," McElroy explained. "It's not altogether impossible, just difficult."

"What about GPS?" Peggy asked. "I thought that software was so advanced, they could pinpoint a needle in a haystack from outer space."

"Right, and they still don't have a cure for the common cold," said Gil.

"What about the last phone he used to call?" I asked.

"Another stolen phone," McElroy said. "Maybe Cooper will be able to get something out of Karl."

"So now what?" Peggy asked.

"It becomes a waiting game," McElroy said gently. "We know that he'll be back in touch with you."

"How do we *know* that?" Peggy asked.

"Because he hasn't yet asked for what he wants. It also seems that as much as he wants to hurt you, he also wants to win your favor. After all, you *are* his mother. You have to understand that this is an unusual situation. Most kidnappings are clear-cut: The abductors want money." McElroy chose her words carefully. "It's not that defined here. He called early this morning, rather than let you wait on pins and needles; to me, that is a positive sign. He also gave you a specific time as to when he would call back this evening."

"He did?" Max said.

"Yes." McElroy played back the tape. Despite the tension in his voice, he sounded clear and surprisingly young: ". . . I know she's a child. What do you think I am, blind? She's a child. She's a child and she's fine. She's having a great time. I happen to be a very good caretaker, but that's something you wouldn't know, isn't it? Look, I have to go."

Then Peggy's voice: "No, wait! What about Lucy? Where is she? Please, please just let me talk to her. What do you want? I'll give you anything. Just bring my daughter back to me."

There was a long pause at this point. And then in a very menacing, low voice, he said, "You know, lady, plenty of people would pay top dollar for a kid like yours. We'll call back at seven tonight. Oh, and Officer whatever the fuck your name is, if you interfere, you'll never see the kid again."

McElroy jumped in just as the tape had finished. "If you'll notice, he said, '*We'll* call back at seven tonight.' As Sydney and I discussed earlier, that *could* connote that he is working with someone else, but the sense that I got from it is that his reference is to Lucy, which could mean that he is cultivating a relationship with her. That's good, because he'll be less likely to hurt her, if that was his intention in the first place, which isn't the impression I get. He also made a prideful point to note that he is a good caretaker. That says to me that he wants you to know that he is not a bad man."

Just crazy, I thought as I tried to banish the thought that if Peggy's son cultivated a close relationship with Lucy, he might start feeling proprietary and think that since she was his sister, he had a right to raise her.

"Should I mention Karl when he calls next time?" Peggy asked.

McElroy took a deep breath and said, "I've been thinking about that. I think it's best to steer clear of it, because you run the risk of pushing him over the edge. If he knows Karl is in custody—"

"How would he know that?" asked Max, interrupting her.

"*If* they're working together, there has to be an open line of communication between them. I'm sure you understand that there is heightened paranoia in situations like this anyway. More often than not, partners like this don't necessarily trust each other. So if Karl was supposed to call or meet Frank at a given time and he missed it, Frank would have reason to assume that either Karl was in trouble or had fucked him over. In my opinion, if Peggy stirs up the pot, it would only make things worse," McElroy said, then rewound the tape.

"Right, and in the meantime the fucker will call on another stolen cell phone that we won't be able to trace." Max got up from the table, placed his hands on the small of his back, and stretched.

I got up and announced that I was going to start a pot of coffee, then asked if there were any takers. I enlisted Max's help. Once we were in the kitchen, I said, "Listen, we're all frustrated, but I don't think it's good if Peggy sees it."

"Peggy is Lucy's mother, Sydney. You don't think that she doesn't feel the same way I do, only more?" His tone exposed his frayed nerves.

"Of course I do. We all do. I just don't think it's real productive to focus on it right now." I started scooping coffee into a filter.

"Yeah, well, I'm a realist."

"Are you?" I stopped and faced him.

"Yes." His eyes were bloodshot.

"Then if you're a realist, you'll agree with me when I tell you it's time you went home and got some sleep. You need to remove yourself from this for a little while."

I could see all of his arguments playing out just behind his eyes, but he kept it to himself and finally nodded.

"I could just sack out in the den," he suggested.

"You could. But I have a feeling you'll rest better if you're away from here. I promise I'll let you know if anything happens."

An hour later, Peggy and I were alone, aside from McElroy and one officer who was left manning the phones. Gil had gone to question Karl, and Max was probably snoring soundly at home. Stillness settled in after everyone had gone. It was the kind of quiet that only happens in the afternoon—long stretches of nothing but the sound of intermittent elevators, water pipes, a distant door slamming, or the hum of a vacuum cleaner. Peggy's building was quieter than mine. Usually, I found this time of day comforting, but now it was unnerving.

"You know what frightens me most?" Peggy asked as she stared out the window. Her voice sounded dull against the hush.

I shook my head.

"He hasn't asked for ransom." She turned and faced me. "What do you think that means?"

Who the hell knew what it could mean? It could mean that Lucy was dead or that he planned to keep her, but I couldn't very well say that, so instead I said, "I think it could mean that he doesn't know what he wants to do. Lucy's his sister. Who knows? He might have a soft spot for her."

Peggy looked as if I had punched her.

"What?"

When she didn't respond, I asked again.

Wrapped up into a tight cocoon, Peggy's body language told me to stay away, but I couldn't. A million thoughts and questions collided as I tried to hug her.

When she looked up at me, she was dry-eyed. "This is all my fault. I never should have had him. I did what my mom wanted, and I did that because I knew if I didn't, I would have had absolutely no contact with my family, including Rita. And as much as

I hated Karl and Dad, I wasn't sure I would be happy without some kind of a relationship with her. You have to understand that she did what she honestly thought was best. She couldn't have known that something catastrophic would happen. But I did, or at least I knew enough to be afraid of my family lineage. Think about it: Genetically, this kid has a double whammy working against him. If he is anything like Karl or my father—and we know he is— there's no telling what he'll do to my baby."

"Listen to me. Using your logic, Frank has as much of Rita's genetic coding as he does your father's. Now, we know he's twisted— that's a given. But there's also every possibility that he's battling with his conscience, as McElroy suggested when she said that he had called you early to ease your worry and that he would call on time tonight. I mean, yeah, your father and brother are part of this kid, but so are you and so is Rita, and from what I can assess, you are a hell of a lot stronger than Karl."

She pushed one corner of her mouth up. "Let's hope you're right."

"Would Karl know that Frank is his son? He denied it, but what do you think?"

Peggy shrugged. "He should. He knew that Rita made me have the baby. As a matter of fact, Mom was so angry with him that she forced him to give me all the money he'd saved and then *suggested* that he enlist in the army."

"And he did it just because she told him to? Come on, we're talking Vietnam."

"Rita was a forceful woman. The only thing I know for sure is that she told him she would personally escort him to hell if he didn't do as she said. And believe me, she would have, too. I suppose she threatened to tell Dad, who would have killed him. She also believed that if he joined the army, he would learn discipline, and if he lived through Vietnam, that meant that God was watching over him and had forgiven him. I mean, it's convoluted bullshit."

"He must have been livid that he had to give you all of his money."

"I suppose. But he was always angry. Rita added to the pot, and with that I was able to start on my own. Nine thousand dollars—that was a lot of money back then."

"Did you ever talk to him about what happened?"

Peggy shook her head. "I never talked to him again after he raped me."

"Did Karl ever try to hurt you again?"

"We didn't overlap at the house very long, but Rita kept a vigilant eye on me until she shipped him off."

"I wonder if he told Frank he was his father."

"That's anybody's guess."

"But you think Karl knows?"

"Let me put it this way; he knows I had his baby. Now, he may have convinced himself that this boy isn't his, but somewhere inside he knows."

I knew it wouldn't do any good to tell her the trash that Karl was spewing about her sexual activity back then. Peggy was probably right: Chances were likely that he had told himself the lie for so long now that he actually believed it.

It was a good time to change the subject, so I asked how John had taken the news.

She took a deep breath. "You know, I was terrified to tell him, but just as afraid not to. When Gil insisted that I tell John and even offered to go with me to the hospital, I did. It was horrible for me, but John doesn't blame me for any of this. Can you imagine?"

"Yes."

She ignored me and continued. "He's an amazing man, you know. Here he is, stuck in the hospital, hardly able to help himself, let alone Lucy, but as angry as he is, he doesn't seem to be mad at me. He was trying to comfort me.

"And Gil was great. By the time we left, it seemed that we were all in control of the situation in a way, even though I know we're not. John and Gil agreed that it would be best for Lucy if no one knew. They also told me that it was imperative that I keep the kidnapper on the phone to try to find out where he is or what he wants, but I haven't been effective at doing that."

"That's not your fault," I told her.

"Oh, okay," she said, making it clear that my words had bounced off her like rubber. "Also, there's been one other complication. John's sister called and wants to come and see him." She shook her head. "John suggested that I stay home when she's at the hospital."

"That'll be tricky."

"Why?"

"She's from Buffalo. Won't she want to spend the day with her brother?"

"Helen's a good woman, but she's the kind of person who graces you with her presence for a minute and then moves on. My guess is that she'll spend an hour the first day, fifteen minutes the second. Knowing that her brother's going to be fine will make her comfortable enough to go shopping, or whatever it is she does with her friends."

"Won't she want to stay here with you?"

"Fortunately, no. Her best friend lives in Manhattan and she always stays with her. The only hard part is that she's going to want to see Lucy."

"She doesn't know about Lucy?" I asked, assuming that they would tell the family, but Peggy shook her head.

"John and Gil agreed that it was best not to tell anyone, especially Helen, because she's a compulsive talker and we know she wouldn't be able to keep it quiet. John suggested that we tell Helen that Lucy is on vacation with you and Leslie."

"Okay," I said, trying not to let the mention of Leslie wreak havoc with my already-frayed emotions.

"I promise you that they'll find her," I said. But my words felt like useless platitudes at that point, so I got up and wrapped my arms around my friend.

I felt like stone. She felt like a bag of bones.

TWENTY-TWO

I got Peggy to lie down and then went to call Kerry.

"Anything on Sister Angeline?"

"Yes."

"Really?" I couldn't keep the surprise out of my voice.

"I now know that she worked at the Halpern House and that she left in 1970."

"Where did she go?"

"I'm not sure. I'm working on it. What I do know is that she was in her second year as a novice when she left."

"Like Julie Andrews in *The Sound of Music*?"

"Maybe, though I always thought Julie was a postulate, not a novice, but that wouldn't have made any sense, either. Did you know that the real Maria von Trapp had been raised as an atheist?"

"No."

"It's true. However, I get the distinct impression that you don't know anything about becoming a nun. Do you?"

"No."

"As I used to understand it, there are three stages to becoming a nun. Postulancy—which is when the girls decide if that's the life for them—lasts a year. Then there's a canonical year, which can probably be likened to a year in solitary confinement. And then finally they spend another year or two as novices, only this time they're out in the world, teaching or whatever. That's where Sister Angeline was when she was at Halpern."

"You said she left. Did she leave the order, or did she just leave the Bronx?"

"The order."

"Okay. Anything else I should know?" I asked.

"Lots. For example, do you know that Thomas Jefferson and John Adams died on the same day?"

"I did."

"Yes, but did you remember it before I brought it up?"

"Not only did I remember it but I can tell you that they died on the Fourth of July, same year, hours apart. Tell me—how's my puppy?"

"She's asked several times if she can live with Pat and me from now on."

"Really? What did you tell her?"

"I told her we would have to do away with you first. She seemed amenable to it."

"Never. Any word from Miguel?"

"Not yet."

"All right. Well, you know where to reach me. Call me the second you get anything on Sister Angeline, okay?"

"Will do."

After that, I sat for a good long while with the list of names Gil had gotten from statistics. Thirteen children born over a period of two days, ten of whom were males. None of the children was named Frank. Michael Dwyer. Thomas Egan. Howard Nathan Epstein. Michael Hubbard. John Singleton-Watts. James Velasquez. Mitchell Nussbaum. Robert D'Angelo. Kevin O'Brien. Peter Wong.

So far, Michael Dwyer, Robert D'Angelo, and Mitchell Nussbaum had been cleared of any connection to Peggy. I had a feeling Peter Wong was going to be scratched from the list as well, which left six names.

A leaden wave of exhaustion washed over me as I circled the names of the six contenders.

"Eenie, meanie, miney, mo." I sighed. "So, is Frank your name or not?" I asked the piece of paper. "What if Karl made it up—made *you* up—and he's just leading us on to take the heat off himself? No. No, that's not possible, because we have your picture. Okay, so why would you lie about your name to the man you *think* is your uncle? When you first connected with Karl a year ago, were you already planning this, James? Kevin? John? Any of you boys use a fake name with Uncle Karl, with the intention of setting him up as a fall guy? Hmm? *Or* did this all happen as a result of Karl's influence on you?"

But it wasn't Uncle Karl, I reminded myself; it was Daddy. I wondered if Karl knew that. I figured he had to, and yet people rewrite history every day. Considering my first meeting with Karl, it was possible that he really believed that Frank belonged to his father's best friend or to a delivery boy.

My energy returned in a burst and I took a seat at the computer in the den. Searching on-line could now be narrowed down considerably by using the names on the list and a host of other words, like *adoption* or *looking for*. I came up empty.

Unable to sleep, Peggy joined me, and the wait for Frank's call began. By six o'clock, Gil had returned. He, Peggy and, I found ourselves back at the dining room table, going over all that had happened during the day, which was a lot. Karl was in custody, and while it hadn't yet been proven, it was presumed that we had the gun used to shoot John. We also knew that the son's name was Frank and that he and Karl had some sort of relationship.

"Has Karl given you anything?" I asked Gil.

He shook his head. "This yo-yo's certifiable, which in some ways makes it harder, because one minute he tells you one thing and the next another."

"And he hasn't given you any information on Frank?"

"Nope."

"He hasn't even tried to lay the blame on Frank?"

"Oh, sure, he insists we have the wrong guy, that we should be looking for this punk who used him—because you know Karl's just an innocent victim who wants legal protection and to press charges against you and Max for breaking and entering."

"Sure."

"Oh, and the Smith & Westson? Wiped clean of all fingerprints. Big surprise. Anyway, they've put a rush on testing ballistics. Good work."

"What about the list of names?" Peggy asked. "Have you learned anything more on them?"

"What we have so far is this: Michael Dwyer, Robert D'Angelo, Mitchell Nussbaum, and Peter Wong have been scratched as possibilities. Dwyer's a minister. D'Angelo is a teacher in Jersey and has an airtight alibi. Nussbaum lives in L.A., and Wong is doing time for embezzling from his father-in-law's business." He shoved the paper back into his pocket. "That's almost half the list, and we've only been working with it since this morning. We're working on this around the clock, so my guess is that we'll have more by the time this dick calls tonight."

McElroy came into the room and took a seat next to Peggy.

"Well, we have some good news, if you want to call it that." She had scratched quotes in the air around the word *good*. "While Frank is no idiot and he has been using the cell phones in a most efficient way, we were nonetheless able to pinpoint his earlier call. It was from the South Street Seaport. We canvassed the area and were able to get a couple of positive IDs when my people showed Frank's sketch at the various vendors."

You could feel the energy in the room shift up a notch. When you're starving, crumbs become a feast.

"Was he seen *with* Lucy?" I asked.

She paused and nodded. "One woman was incredibly helpful. She owns a kite store down there, and she remembered Frank and a 'sweet little girl he came in with.' "

"Lucy," Peggy whispered.

"Yes. The shopkeeper said that they came into her store just before noon, and Lucy was carrying a little puppy—a West Highland terrier."

"She knew the breed?" I asked.

"This woman was an incredible witness. The most important thing she noticed was that Lucy seemed very comfortable with the man she was with. The witness assumed they were siblings, not only because Frank had told her that Lucy was his sister but also because there was such a strong resemblance between the two. She was also touched by how close they seemed."

"*Close?*" Peggy choked.

"Yes."

"Is this unusual?" I asked.

"Very."

"Do kidnappers often take their victims shopping?" I couldn't keep the surprise out of my voice.

"Only if there was a custody battle and one parent has taken a child from the other. But no, not usually. In most kidnappings, the idea is to keep the victim well out of sight until the kidnapper's demands are met."

"But in this case, there are no demands," Gil said.

"So far," McElroy agreed. "Though this evening he did make it seem that he would be willing to negotiate for money."

"I'll do anything. I just want my baby back." Peggy's hands were balled into tight fists on the tabletop.

"What if he wants a million dollars?" I asked, leaning back in my chair.

"I'll get it." Her lips barely moved.

"So what?" I said to McElroy. "She gets the call from Frank, he tells her he wants whatever, and she says, 'Okay, where do I drop it?'"

"Essentially, yes. He may have a series of demands. He may ask for bonds instead of cash. It's impossible to try to second-guess."

We all sat there, momentarily mute.

"So let me ask you something. . . . You've been doing this a long time. What do you think it means that he's taking Lucy out on a shopping excursion and, more importantly, that she seems to strangers to be relatively unaffected by being away from her family?" I asked.

McElroy held her palm out to me, revealing a flat, delicate surface with a zillion dark lines. "Just because she's not kicking and screaming doesn't mean she's not affected," she said, obviously cautioning me. "Now, the owner of the kite store was the best witness we had today, but she wasn't the only one. Several people saw them together. That's very good, because it means that so far Lucy is safe. She hasn't been hurt or frightened enough to reach out to strangers. My guess is that he explained in a way that seems logical to her that he is her brother and because things are so hard for her mommy right now, he's helping out. Then he softens it with the dog and toys."

"Were you able to track the rest of their day?" I asked. "Or get fingerprints at the kite store?"

"No, we didn't get prints. With the amount of traffic she gets in her store, it would have been impossible. However, she thought she overheard them talking about going to the zoo."

"Central Park or the Bronx?"

McElroy shook her head as her eyelids fluttered shut for an instant. "As it turns out, neither, to the best of our knowledge. We showed his sketch and a picture of Lucy at both places but came up empty."

"So now we wait," I said with a deep sigh.

"Yes, we wait." She glanced at her wristwatch.

Gil shifted uncomfortably in his chair and cast a questioning look at McElroy, who nodded almost imperceptibly.

Gil started speaking with a gentleness that scared me. "Peggy, there's something you should know." He pinched his upper lip between his thumb and index finger, as if that could keep the words inside. I glanced at Peggy and saw her defensively sit up even straighter.

"Mac and I have agreed not to withhold any information from you," he said, glancing at McElroy. "There's no easy way to tell you this, but apparently Karl has seen Lucy."

Peggy and I froze. "When?" she asked.

"Before her abduction."

"He told you that?"

"No. Unfortunately, pictures of her were found when we got to his place after you and Max had left."

"But your people had been there before we found the gun," I said.

"I know, but that time we found nothing. We were only looking

192

for the gun, and we didn't know about the hidey-hole beneath that floorboard. Your find sped the process up. Then we ransacked the place."

"Does our having been there screw up the validity of the evidence?"

Gil shrugged with an air of insouciance. "You're not a police officer, so the evidence is still admissible."

"What kind of pictures?" Peggy's voice, as soft as it was, was cold and hard.

Gil pressed his lips together and scraped one thumbnail against another.

"What?" she asked, not taking her eyes off him.

"Candid shots taken from afar with a zoom lens. We didn't find any camera equipment in his house, so we have to assume someone else took the shots. Just the sort of thing you find in surveillance." He looked pained.

"What?" Peggy demanded again.

"He had drawn on several of the pictures."

"Drawn what?" I asked, not so certain I wanted to know.

"Mature female body parts."

The frightening implication shrouded the room.

"This is not to say that Karl has had any contact with Lucy," McElroy cautioned.

"Absolutely not," Gil quickly agreed. "To the best of our knowledge, Karl hasn't had any contact with her since the abduction. Remember, when it happened, he was with Sydney, and shortly thereafter he was brought in for questioning. After that, he had a tail." He shook his head emphatically. "No, I don't think he's even been in the same room with her. If he took the photos, that was probably the closest he's ever been to her."

Peggy started shivering. I went to her bedroom and got her a sweater, glad to be out of the room if only for a minute so I could try to collect myself. I needed to show strength, not the absolute terror I was feeling.

The bedroom clock revealed that it was after seven o'clock. The phone had yet to ring.

Seven-fifteen.

Seven-thirty.

Gil received a call about another name on the list: Michael Hubbard was deceased.

Seven-forty-five.

Still nothing.

At 7:53, the phone rang. McElroy's cool seemed to counteract the heightened sense of panic emanating from Peggy.

"Hello." Peggy's voice revealed her stress. But that was all she got a chance to say. Within moments, the call was over, without her uttering another word other than to scream, "*NO!*"

Peggy collapsed, and as I ran to her, I saw the expression on McElroy's usually unrevealing face. Whatever he had said, it wasn't good.

Gil and I led Peggy out of the room and into the den, where he left me with her and went back to McElroy.

I had no idea what Frank had said, but I was unable to maintain my own composure, and I cried as I held Peggy.

I found a bottle of Valium in her medicine cabinet and insisted that she take one. After she did, I lay with her in her bedroom, neither of us speaking, until I finally heard the gentle breathing of sleep. Tempted as I was to stay there and sleep with my friend, I dragged myself from the bed and joined McElroy, Gil, and the others.

An officer played back the tape for me when the call was over.

—*Hello.*

—*You're just like all the others, Mommy, aren't you? Well, fuck you; you're never going to see her again. Never. You lying sack of shit. You had to go and call the police. Well, she's mine now, and I'll be as good to her as you were to me.*

It ended with Peggy's scream.

"They must have been at his home, wherever that is," I said numbly.

Gil looked at me.

"In the background, there was a cartoon playing on the television. It was the *Powerpuff Girls*. That's Lucy's favorite."

McElroy was called back into the other room just as my phone rang. It was Kerry.

"I found Sister Angeline," she announced without preamble.

"When?" As I waited for her to respond, I wandered down the hallway, passed Peggy's room, and found myself in Lucy's room.

"About half an hour ago. I took the liberty of calling her."

"Did she remember Peggy?"

"Yes. Her name is Mary Sullivan and she's a therapist now down on Ninth Street."

"Excellent." I stood in Lucy's room and remembered the day that Leslie and I had helped John paint the room a soothing shade of periwinkle blue before Lucy had even been born. The wainscoting was white, like the furniture and her toy chest, which was now overflowing with stuffed animals, games, and books. I jotted down the ex-nun's number on a scrap of paper.

"What's happening there?" Kerry asked, sounding tired.

I told her, unable to hold back tears of frustration. There are times when words are useless, and this was one of them. Kerry assured me that she was there for all of us and that she would take care of Auggie. When the call was over, I studied the walls. It was only recently that Lucy had started adding more to the walls than her own finger paintings and drawings of the family and Auggie. She had taken an understandable shine to the *Powerpuff Girls*, and lately the souvenirs had started to accrue. A framed picture block on her dresser included Leslie and Auggie and me in one picture, her folks in another. Her paternal grandparents and other family members and friends were in a third photo, and finally there was one of Lucy on Santa's lap when she was three. I remembered her introduction to Santa as I carried the picture cube with me to her bed, where I looked at the picture as I slipped off my shoes. Lucy had been thrilled for two whole days before meeting Santa at his temporary office at Macy's, but when we got to Macy's, waited half an hour on line to see Saint Nick, and then it was finally her turn, she was afraid to go anywhere near him. Leslie and Peggy sat on

Santa's lap first to encourage her, and it had worked, but the photo recorded that moment in her life as traumatic and tear-filled. Fortunately, I had been savvy enough to take my own camera that day, so I had documentation that a mere moments later we had a very happy little girl discovering for the first time the intoxicating elixir of candy canes.

The bedroom smelled like Lucy—baby shampoo, bubble gum, and summer.

I sat on the edge of the bed and slipped the cell phone into my hand to call Leslie, but I must have fallen asleep before I could even flip it open. The next thing I knew, Peggy was sitting on the side of the bed crying.

In my muddled confusion of sleep and exhaustion, I reached out for her. Looking over her shoulder, I could see in the illuminated face of a clock shaped like a goldfish that it was four o'clock in the morning. Peggy was heaving words, but I couldn't understand her. Finally, it became clear: In her own confusion of half sleep, when she saw a body in Lucy's bed, she assumed it was Lucy.

I calmed her down and we fell asleep together in Lucy's bed. We didn't wake until four hours later, when the house was full and the phone was ringing.

TWENTY-THREE

Before the first ring had subsided, Peggy and I both had our feet on the floor and were halfway to the bedroom door. McElroy appeared, holding the phone, gesturing for Peggy to calm down. "It's John."

"Oh God, what am I going to tell him?" Peggy backed away from McElroy.

"The truth," I said as I gently edged her forward.

She balked. The phone continued to ring. I reached for it. Peggy grabbed it from my hand and disappeared into her bedroom.

Everyone was gathered in the dining room.

As I walked from the living room to the dining room and then into the kitchen, I noticed there were several more people at Peggy's than had been there for the last few days. I passed four strangers, who did a fine job avoiding eye contact with me.

"Hey," Max said as soon as he saw me. "Coffee?"

"I got it, thanks." I staggered into the kitchen and poured coffee into the biggest mug I could find. Back in the dining room, I asked, "What's happened?"

"We were able to check on all the names," Gil said rubbing his cheek with the palm of his hand. It sounded like it hurt.

"What?" I asked cautiously.

He shook his head.

"Nothing?" I asked, though it seemed impossible.

"The big goose egg." Gil sounded like a shadow of himself.

"How can that be? We had the ten names of the boys born at the hospital where Peggy gave birth on that specific weekend. What's that about?"

"If we knew, Sloane, we wouldn't be sitting here, would we?" Cooper's words were harsh, but just looking at the man told me not to take offense. He had deep dark circles under his eyes, a full day's beard, and his entire countenance was wrinkled.

I pulled the paper with the list of names out of my pocket and went over it with Gil.

Michael Dwyer was the rector of an Episcopal Church in a suburb of Chicago.

Thomas Egan was a DA in New Jersey.

Howard Nathan Epstein worked at a mattress store in Connecticut.

Michael Hubbard had died in 1989, the victim of a carjacking.

John Singleton-Watts was overseas, working with the International Medical Corps.

James Velasquez lived in Redmond, Washington, where he worked as a programmer for Microsoft.

Mitchell Nussbaum was a science writer who lived in L.A.

Robert D'Angelo was a teacher and high school football coach in Asbury Park.

Kevin O'Brien was a firefighter.

Peter Wong was doing time for embezzling funds from his father-in-law's insurance business.

None of them were adopted.

"What about Karl?" I asked.

"The people at ballistics were brilliant and had something back to us in a matter of hours. Karl's gun was used to shoot John all right. There's no mistake about it. Dexter swears that he didn't have anything to do with it, but we've arrested him on suspicion." Cooper wiped his hands on his slacks as he spoke.

"Do you think he did it?" I asked Cooper.

He shrugged. "As far as I can read him, Dexter's a coward, which means that he's more likely to talk big than actually do anything."

"But he's a nutcase," Gil added.

"That's true," Cooper agreed. "And a nutcase would be more likely to do something stupid, like shooting a cop. *But*," he added, addressing this to Gil directly, "the man has no real motive for shooting his brother-in-law after all these years, and nothing places him even vaguely near here before, during, or after the shooting."

"Does he have an alibi?" I asked.

"Nothing he can prove: he was at home, sleeping."

"But it was his gun that was used." Gil was clearly digging in his heels. I knew from personal experience that one place a person didn't ever want to be was on the other end of Gil's inflexibility.

"What? You think Karl shot John?" I asked Gil.

"I didn't say that. All I'm saying is that it was his gun that was used and I'm glad we've got him. That's all. But that's not the issue right now, is it?"

The room felt as if it was about to shatter.

"How's Peggy?" Max asked to diffuse the energy.

"Poor woman," I mumbled.

"Please," Cooper huffed. "The poor woman couldn't tell John about her past, which—let's be real—is the reason we're all standing here tonight with our fingers up our butts."

The silence that followed was absolute. Finally, Gil stood up and said, "Come on, son. I want to see if they've gotten anywhere with the list Marcy provided." He gestured for Cooper, who, I could tell, wanted to stand his ground but was facing a superior officer. He mumbled something I couldn't catch and lumbered out of the room, leaving Max, McElroy, and me.

"You heard about last night?" I asked Max after they had left.

"Yeah."

"What do you think?" I asked McElroy, who was also beginning to show signs of wear and tear.

"I coordinated with the FBI last night. They've been on the sidelines all along, but after last night's call, we escalated it. They'll be here in a little while to talk with Peggy."

"Should we be here?" I asked.

"One of you should. She's incredibly fragile right now, and I think it's imperative that she has family support."

"What do those photographs mean?" I asked McElroy.

She paused.

"What photos?" Max asked.

"It doesn't bode well. Karl's a sick man, but the good thing is that we have him in custody."

"Are you sure it was he who drew on them?"

"What the hell are you talking about?" Max asked, clearly upset now.

"I sincerely hope so," she said, leaving the other option—that it was Frank's handiwork—hanging in the air, an ugly possibility.

"Flo?" A young plainclothes cop poked his head in the room and motioned for his supervisor. McElroy excused herself and joined him.

"What are you talking about?" Max asked when she was gone.

I told him about the photos taken of Lucy, mature female parts drawn in.

I stopped when Max stood up as Peggy entered the room.

He embraced her and offered to get her coffee. She sank onto the chair next to me, looking like she'd been run over by a train.

"How did John take it?"

She was unresponsive. Max set the coffee and a doughnut in front of her.

Before Max could sit, McElroy was back. "Peggy. We were able to isolate various sounds from the call last night. I want you to hear something."

We all followed her into the other room and listened as she played a track that was muted, although it was Lucy's voice.

"The horseshoes are my favorite."

Peggy's hand shot involuntarily in front of her as she started to cry. "Lucky Charms," she finally squeaked out. "Play it again." She wiped her cheeks and drew closer to the officer playing the tape. On the computer screen were sharp green lines against a black background, jumping up and down as the voice repeated, "The horseshoes are my favorite."

"She's talking about Lucky Charms." Peggy was on the verge of hysteria, laughing and crying.

"Peggy." McElroy's voice was firm as she placed her hand on Peggy's arm. "I think it's important to note that she doesn't sound frightened. Lucy's voice is conversational. Do you understand what I'm saying?"

Peggy covered her face as she sobbed and nodded.

Max wrapped a protective arm around her and led her back to the dining room, then suggested I take a shower.

It was an offer I couldn't refuse. There was nothing I could do for Peggy at this point, and hiding in the bathroom seemed like a perfectly reasonable response to the day, which had barely begun. A brief but frightening glance in the mirror reminded me of my sister, Nora, who always made it a point to get up early and put on makeup before Byron, her husband of a zillion years, could see her. She would have been horrified that I had let strangers see me looking like a guinea pig in electroshock therapy.

My next thought hit like a cattle prod. *How could Leslie still be in love with this?* I couldn't remember the last time we had spoken, and I was frightened to call. Not a good place to be with the love of your life.

Fortunately, no one could hear me crying in the shower. The world was an ugly place, and no amount of time in the shower would wash it away.

TWENTY-Four

By the time I got out of the shower, the FBI had arrived. They, along with Peggy and McElroy, were talking in the den with the door closed.

"Miguel called you," Max said, gesturing to my phone.

"Kerry found Sister Angeline last night," I said, reaching for the phone.

"Wow, that's great."

"Yeah, I know. I want to see her as soon as possible. Can you stay with Peggy?"

"Sure." He waited while I called Mary Sullivan, once known as Sister Angeline. She was expecting a client but said she'd have some free time in another hour. She gave me the option to call or stop by. Since I preferred to question people one-on-one, I made an appointment with her for 10:30.

"Did you get any rest last night?" Max asked when I ended the call.

"Yeah. Peggy and I both fell asleep in Lucy's bed. Did she tell you anything about her call with John?"

"What's to tell? He's a cop. He knows when bad goes to worse. I can't imagine how he feels lying in that hospital, not able to be there for either his wife or daughter. Listen, I was wondering: Do you think it would be better if I went to question Sullivan and you stayed here?"

"Max, I have to get out of here," I said, looking for my bag. "I just need a break, you know?"

"I do. Sydney?" He stopped me as I started for the door. He opened his mouth, but nothing came out. Finally, he said, "Call me after you talk to her."

Because I had time, I decided to stop at my apartment for a change of clothes before heading down to see Mary Sullivan.

I was stunned when I walked into the apartment and found Leslie's suitcase in the hallway.

"Leslie?" I called out her name several times as I hurried through the kitchen, into the living room, and then toward the back of the apartment, where I could smell her perfume.

I saw from the bedroom doorway that she was sound asleep, her body curled comfortably around a pillow. Seeing her felt like Christmas and bad news all wrapped up in the same double-edged moment. And as much as I wanted to race across the room and pounce on her, I couldn't help but take a moment to enjoy her face, which was a reflection of utter calm. Her lips were slightly parted. I don't know why, but that alone was a reminder to me that there were some things in life that were absolutely perfect.

Half a second later, however, I slapped myself back to the ugly reality that my goddaughter was missing and I had an ex-nun to interview.

I sat on the side of the bed, watched her eyes flutter to a wakened state, and softly said, "Hi there. What are you doing here?"

"Is Lucy home?" She bolted into an upright position.

"No, not yet. I just stopped by to change. I'm surprised you're here."

"I tried to call you last night, but I couldn't get through on your phone. I left a message here, but then I thought you were probably at Peggy's, and I didn't want to bother you there." She squinted at me and wrapped the bedclothes around her bare body. "Hi," she said as she leaned toward me.

"Hi." Kissing Leslie was like coming home after a long absence. "So what are you doing here? Is everything all right?"

She rubbed her eyes. "I don't know." She eased out of bed and padded to the bathroom. "After our last call, I didn't know what to do. I mean, I was so angry . . . about Lucy, *and* about Harold not being honest with Mom, and . . . us. It just felt like my world was out of control." She came out of the bathroom wearing a robe and slippers. "Anyway, I told Christa what was happening here and she understood that I needed to be home, so I took the red-eye."

She opened her arms to me and I slid easily into her embrace. Not wanting to leave it, I nonetheless had to get ready for my interview with Mary Sullivan. I slipped into fresh clothes and followed Leslie into the kitchen.

"Have you told Dot anything?" I asked, admiring the sensual way the robe covered her body.

"Not yet. I will. I just want to talk to Miguel first. But the hell with that. What's happening with Lucy?" She pulled out a box of coffee filters.

I gave her the Cliffs Notes version and glanced at the time. "I have to go, baby. Auggie's with Kerry," I said, stealing a bite of her toast.

"I'm going to call Peggy and offer to be with her today. You think that's okay?" she asked almost shyly.

"I think that would be great." I studied her for a second as she poured equal amounts of orange and apple juice into a small glass. "I love you, Leslie," I said, aware that it didn't sound like my voice at all.

"I love you, too, honey," she replied, and then smiled before kissing me.

As I raced to the subway, I couldn't shake the feeling that Leslie's smile had seemed forced. I tried to reason with myself that I was under stress and imposing things on her that she didn't own, but it was there, tucked sloppily away in the back of my mind—the fear that something wrong was descending on our happy little home, that something I had no control of was slipping away from me.

I made it to Mary Sullivan's in half an hour. Laden with abbreviations like C.S.W., Ph.D., M.S.W., and Psy.D., the West Ninth Street lobby directory indicated that much of the ten-story building was dedicated to the fine art of emotional and psychological maintenance. It turned out that Mary Sullivan's office was part of her apartment.

I was mildly surprised when an attractive woman in a wheelchair answered the door.

"Not what you were expecting?" she asked with the air of a woman accustomed to waiting for people to shift their line of vision two and a half feet south.

"I had no expectations," I said, offering my hand. "I appreciate your taking the time to see me, especially on such short notice."

"Your associate was so persuasive, how could I say no?" She wheeled back to give me room to enter and then shut the door behind me. Since this was an old New York apartment, the foyer was a room unto itself. Three pine chairs, a table stacked with magazines, and a coatrack also indicated that this doubled as her waiting room. Once over the threshold, I faced a screened-off living room and a hallway that fed both to my left and my right. Standing in the doorway, assessing my options, I became quite an effective obstacle.

"To the right," came her voice from behind me.

"Oh, sorry." I stepped to the left and let her lead the way. The apartment, or what I could see of it, was a warm blend of ultramodern design in a traditional shell. The rounded archways, crown moldings, and wooden floors were from a time when craftsmen constructed buildings with materials meant to last.

I followed her down a long hallway, then into a room that was obviously the heart and soul of her business as a therapist. The twelve-by-ten-foot room was sparse yet attractive. Two windows framed with burgundy drapes took up the wall to the left as you walked in; they let in what little light the overcast day had to offer. Most prominent was the sofa, which resembled a plush orange arrow on four metal legs, and a red leather armless Barcelona chair complete with ottoman. A tapestry hung on the wall over the sofa and a Magritte painting within a painting hung on the opposite wall. It was not a poster but, rather, oil on canvas. I assumed it was a copy, and a good one at that, but the real deal, even if she could have afforded it, would have never been hung where the sunlight hit directly. Mary rolled to the right side of the room, which left me the sofa, the chair, or the ottoman upon which to sit.

I chose the sofa and felt a little as if I were sitting in the center of a section from a navel orange. Of course, I couldn't tell her this, because as a therapist she would ask why I felt that way, and instead of answering, I would feel compelled to ask why she had chosen such furniture for a room that should be all about the client and not the client's reaction to the therapist's choice of furniture. Then she would scribble something in a notepad—probably "Buy milk"—and I, unable to stop myself, would ask if perhaps the therapist's ego was getting in the way before the session had even started, forgetting completely that I was there as a detective and not a client.

At the rate I was thinking, I would be confessing childhood calamities before I even got to Peggy and Frank.

"So, how can I help you?" she asked as soon as we were both settled.

"As I explained on the phone, I am a detective and we are trying to trace the whereabouts of a child who was given up for adoption back in the sixties, when you were at the Halpern House."

"Yes. That much, your assistant told me." I tried to imagine who Sister Angeline was and how she came to be Mary Sullivan, therapist. She looked to be in her mid-fifties. Her shoulder-length hair was a cascade of dark curls. She wore loose-fitting turquoise slacks and colorfully layered tops, which might have been nearly transparent alone but together created quite an effect. She maneuvered her wheelchair well enough for me to know that it had been part of her for a long time. And now she was looking at me with anticipation written all over her face. "How can I help?"

"In 1968, a young girl who was staying at the Halpern House gave birth to a baby boy. During the time that she was there, she befriended a nun whose name was Sister Angeline."

"Yes."

"Do you remember a young woman named Peggy Dexter?"

I watched the color wash out of Mary's face as she explained the situation back then. "One of the objectives of the Halpern House was to protect the girls, and therefore no one ever used a surname. Only the administrative staff had that information, and perhaps the social workers, but I didn't. Why are you looking for her?"

"We're not. We believe that the boy she gave birth to in 1968 is responsible for several serious crimes, and we have to find him before someone else gets hurt."

"What kind of crimes?"

"Attempted murder and kidnapping."

She brought her hand to her mouth and whispered, "Oh my God. It's not possible that you're looking for the right person."

"Why?"

"Because Peggy Dexter gave birth to a girl."

For a moment, everything was utterly still. I could neither move nor speak, not to mention breathe.

"How do you know that? You're absolutely certain?"

" 'Absolutely certain'? No, but how many Peggy Dexters could have visited Halpern House in 1968?"

"You just said you never knew the last names of the girls," I reminded her.

"I didn't. A few years ago, I got a call from a young woman, Melinda Johnson, who was looking for her mother. She'd been searching for her for quite a while, going on information her adopted mother had given her right before she died. Anyway, she knew when and where she had been born and that her mother had stayed at the Halpern House prior to giving birth. This was a terribly tenacious young woman, one who was determined to find her mother."

"Who was Peggy Dexter."

Mary nodded and she said, "Yes, Dexter. At least that was the name Melinda gave me."

It felt as if all of the air were seeping out of me.

I pulled Frank's picture out of my bag, unfolded it, and handed it to Mary. "Do you know this man?"

She rubbed her brow as she studied the picture. She shook her head and said, "No. Well . . . " She paused and sounded as if she was ready to reconsider, but then she said, "No. No. Definitely not." Her tone, however, didn't fill me with confidence.

It didn't make sense. Finally, I said, "Mary, would you tell me everything you can remember relative to Halpern House, Peggy, and Melinda? Don't leave out anything, no matter how insignificant it might seem to you."

It turned out that Mary had only started at Halpern in October 1968. She remembered that Peggy wasn't well liked among the other "residents," as they were called, because she was smart as a whip and just as sharp with her tongue. It hadn't gone over well among the other residents that she was one of the few women who wanted nothing to do with the baby once it was born. "She didn't even want to know if it was a boy or a girl. So no one told her."

"But you knew? The staff knew?" I asked.

She furrowed her brow and said, "I suppose so. I must have." She looked up at me and shrugged. "However, I admit it isn't something that I can honestly say I remember. You have to understand— there were so many girls, so many babies."

Mary had left Halpern House in 1970, when a car driven by one of the resident's boyfriends hit and crippled her. Apparently, she had always hated it there; hated being a novice, hated the hierarchy at Halpern House, and hated the fund-raisers, where they paraded around the little pregnant girls as if they were waifs and not Georgetown debs shelling out a thousand dollars for a two-month stay. Despite the wheelchair as a daily reminder, she had tried to block out that time of her life.

But the call from a child looking for her mother had changed all that. Mary admittedly wouldn't have remembered Peggy's name if Melinda hadn't called a couple of years earlier and jogged her memory. She'd explained to Mary that back in 1968 she had been adopted by a couple in New Jersey. The girl's adoptive father had been abusive, and when he died, she and her mother moved to Brooklyn, where they'd lived together for several years before the mother died of cancer.

"It was on her mother's deathbed that the poor child learned she had been adopted."

"Are you still in touch with her?" I asked.

"Every now and then."

"Do you have her home address and number?"

"I should. Do you want me to call her?" She reached for the Filofax next to her chair.

"No," I said. "Something like this usually works best when we visit unexpectedly."

"What do you mean, 'works best'?" Mary paused, her hands wrapped protectively around the bulging date book. "You're not planning to hurt her, are you?"

"Mary, I don't even think she's the person we're looking for. We're looking for the man in that sketch. He's shot a police officer and kidnapped Peggy's five-year-old daughter. . . ."

"A police officer? Oh my God, that's not the police officer who was shot the other day, is it? I thought his name was Connelly, not Dexter."

"Cannady, but they're one and the same, so I'm sure you can appreciate how sensitive this is," I cautioned. "Look, for all we know, Frank is Melinda's boyfriend, or a cousin, or another boy she was raised with. But we have to find him, and it looks like the best way to do that is through Melinda. It's key that we don't scare her away. A child's life is on the line here."

As soon as Mary had finished the history of Peggy and Melinda as she knew it, I called Max. I gave him the address in the Boerum Hill section of Brooklyn and told him to meet me there. He wanted me to wait for him to pick me up, but I couldn't. I was too agitated after my meeting with Mary and knew that I needed, if nothing else, to move.

It didn't make sense. Frank had taunted Peggy with emotionally charged phone calls, accusing her of being a shitty mother, of abandonment. Maybe Max was right: Perhaps it had been Karl making the calls all alone, but that couldn't be right, either, because the last call had come in when Karl was in custody. Frank had been livid during his last call, accusing Peggy of being like all the others, a "lying sack of shit," ostensibly because she had called the police. But how had he known she had called the police? Was it possible that Karl had been able to make the call? Or had recorded one? But why? And who would he have gotten to play it? Frank? But who the hell was Frank? I had to trust the ex-nun about Melinda being the daughter, because that name had been on the list of girls born that December weekend, and Mary would have had no way of knowing that. As I passed a gaggle of doctors and nurses smoking outside of St. Vincent's Hospital, my phone rang. It was Max, who was already in his car, headed downtown.

"Sydney, I was thinking you should call Gil and have him do a roundup. Give him this information, Mary's address, Melinda's address, everything."

"I thought about that, but my gut tells me we should do initial reconnaissance and then call him. *If* this Melinda is with Frank and *if* Lucy's with her, I think it will be a whole lot easier on Lucy to see us and not a gazillion cops."

"Maybe, but I don't want to take any chances."

I didn't know what to say. I stopped at a streetlight and tried to think clearly, a seemingly impossible task.

"Look, at least wait for me. If nothing else, there is power in numbers. I can be there in ten minutes. There's no traffic," Max said.

True to his word, ten minutes later I was sitting next to him as we sped toward Brooklyn.

"I have a notebook and a pen with which to defend myself," he said as we entered the bridge connecting boroughs. "How about you?"

I felt the Walther in my bag and assured him that should there be trouble, that I would cover him. "But you know what they say, Maxo: 'The pen is mightier than the sword.'"

"Right. I'll remember that when I'm looking down the barrel of a zip gun."

TWENTY-FIVE

Because of traffic in Brooklyn, it took us close to an hour to get to the Boerum Hill address Mary had given me for Melinda Johnson. Underappreciated Boerum, like any other neighborhood within spitting distance of Manhattan, had been destined to make a comeback, and as we drove through the neighborhood, it was clear that its future was well secured. Unlike several of the surrounding communities, Boerum was still funky enough to be affordable, though brownstones that back in the sixties and seventies had gone for twenty thousand dollars were now on the market for half a million.

Such was not the case with Melinda's building. Like most on that block, it was a four-story brownstone with a big stoop and a street-level apartment, but this one looked as if it was either under siege or a squatter's paradise. A window on the top floor was shattered and covered with black plastic, whereas most of the others—except for those in one apartment on the third floor—were just opaque with soot. The dirt of probably more than a century encrusted the stones like barnacles on an old mollusk and several stones were either chipped or missing altogether toward the top of the building. The skeleton of a honey locust tree stood listing in front of the building, barely holding on to the earth in its four square feet of dirt.

Max motioned that he would check out the garden apartment, and I took the stoop steps two at a time. The front door led to a smelly enclosed entrance that had a buzzer system for eight apartments. I figured there were two apartments per floor, plus the garden apartment, which probably had it's own buzzer. The first buzzer I saw had a fully legible name beside it: Kopald. The name was neatly typed and covered with a protective piece of plastic. For a moment, I had a mental image of a mud-wrestling boy in a bubble.

The other names I was able to make out were Smith, Super, and Vijaya. Before trying the buzzers, I turned the knob of the front door. It was locked. I rang the super's apartment and waited. I rang again and the first door on the left in the darkened hallway just beyond the entrance opened. As the door swung open, the sound of a Spanish television station emerged, which was quickly followed by a woman of obese proportion standing in the doorway. She moved forward by swaying from left to right and pitching an alternating foot forward with each sway as she held on to the wall with her right hand.

I was ready to howl by the time she made it to the other side of the glass, wrapped her hand around the brass doorknob, yanked it open, and growled, "Waddaya want?" Despite her weight and the fact that she looked like she had dressed blindfolded, she had the most beautiful brown eyes. Her face was an erupted landscape of hair and blotches, crumbs and scars, but her eyes were untouched by time. I could see in her eyes the promise and beauty her mother and father probably saw when they held their baby girl for the first time.

"Hi." I smiled in a way so friendly, I could have been a Jehovah's Witness or a psycho killer. "Are you the super?"

She pushed her tongue against the inside of her upper lip, brought her hand to her mouth, scavenged around, and pulled out something from between her teeth, which she then wiped on her denim shirt, which was embroidered with the name Lew. Without looking directly at me, she repeated, "Waddaya want?"

"Melinda Johnson." I set aside the smile and moved forward just enough to stop the door with my foot if necessary.

"Who's asking?"

"Detective Sloane. Where is she?"

She plucked at the inside of her left nostril with the tip of her thumb and gave my question some serious thought. "Why do you wanna know?"

"Well, we can make this easy and painless, which means you tell me where I can find her and then you can get back to your television show, or you can make it difficult and we'll simply bring you down to the station for questioning, which, as I'm sure you know, could take the better part of a day. Choice is yours." I paused. When she didn't respond, I asked, "Where can I find Melinda Johnson?"

"Three B, but she ain't in."

"Where is she?" I asked, stepping over the threshold and squeezing past her.

"Who the fuck cares?"

"I do." My tone was as chilling as hers was indifferent.

The super was bright enough to understand that if she played along now, she might not have to be inconvenienced later. "I don't know where she is. She don't check in with me." When she swallowed, she pushed her lips up and back, exposing yellowed teeth.

Just at that moment, Max came sprinting up the front stoop, shaking his head. I nodded to the super and told Max to find out what he could. With that, I shot up the filthy steep steps and found apartment B on the third floor, which was the back apartment. I knocked, listened, but heard nothing. I knocked again, then pressed my ear to the door. Nothing. I pulled out a little cosmetic case I always carried and removed the tools I needed to open the door without a key. Normally in a building like this, I would have expected five locks, including a couple of Medecos, but there were only two locks, and both were frighteningly easy to pick.

I had the door opened in a matter of minutes.

The place was hot and smelled of patchouli oil and mildew.

I followed a short, dark corridor into the small one-bedroom apartment. At the end of the hall was a comfortable room that doubled as living room and dining room. The furniture was worn, but the place was well cared for, despite the need of plaster and paint. I scanned the room. A wooden Mancala game board lay abandoned on the floor, along with the colorful stones used to play the game. An empty Powerpuff lunch box had fallen to the floor just under the chair. Half a dozen framed pictures were propped up against three makeshift bookshelves. Both the television and stereo were placed on painted wooden crates.

I felt like Goldilocks as I entered the kitchen, where I found three distinct breakfasts in varying stages of completion. Two cereal bowls, one mug of coffee, a cup of tea, and a plate with one half-eaten fried egg sat in the sink, along with two half-empty glasses of orange juice. There was a forgotten bagel ready to be removed from the toaster. The coffee and tea were cool but not cold, so I knew they didn't have much of a head start, but I didn't know where they were headed, which was a definite disadvantage. However, I now knew there were three of them: Lucy, Melinda, and obviously Frank. At least it was something; indeed, it was a whole lot more than we had had half an hour earlier. Unfortunately, we were still in the position of having to find them.

I ran to the front door and called down to Max, saying that they had left within the last fifteen minutes and he should do a door-to-door check.

I then ran to the living room window to see if they had used the fire escape, but they hadn't; there were accordion grates pulled over the two windows that faced a surprisingly large oak tree in the backyard.

I dialed Gil and gave him a heads-up as I went through the rest of the apartment. I could practically hear his teeth fall out when I explained that Peggy's firstborn was apparently a girl. I explained that I wasn't finished at the apartment but that I wanted to get the police here ASAP. I also suggested that he have someone he trusted pick up Mary Sullivan for questioning. "She's an ex-nun who's stuck in a wheelchair, so I advise your people to be delicate with her."

As we talked, I found dog toys strewn throughout the apartment and remnants of Lucy—a drawing here, a T-shirt there—but it was the bedroom that stopped me cold. Once I realized what I was looking at, I bid Gil an abrupt good-bye and promised I would call McElroy right away.

I had deliberately called Gil first instead of McElroy because I wanted to buy myself a minute or two. I had hoped that Max and I would find Lucy before the police could surround them, scare the daylights out of Lucy, and probably damage her for life.

On the nightstand in the bedroom, there was a stack of photographs, which I leafed through as if they were a deck of cards. Only one picture stood out among the others. It was a picture of Frank, his hand caught, palm out, between himself and the camera lens. He was curled up on a bed, caught in a partial fetal position, as if he was trying to cover his body, which was bare. Half of his handsome, soft face was hidden from the camera, forever trapped in a fierce scowl, while behind him, in a mirror off to the side, was the reflection of the woman behind the camera. She, too, was naked, but, unlike Frank there was clearly no sense of self-consciousness about her. Her compact body was softened by curves you might have expected on a larger woman.

I held on to the picture as I took in the contents of the room: a crucifix over the bed; a ceramic lamp cast in the shape of a hula dancer, its red shade fringed; an inflatable armchair. A crack marred the white wall, which was grayed with time and city soot; the fissure stretched from one end of the wall, splintered into two deep lines, and ended at the other end of the wall. Then there was the walnut dresser. It was impossible to tell exactly what the piece had looked like before someone had taken a knife to it, but the end result was American folk art gone awry. And it was riveting. What had obviously started as crude gouges dug in rage had developed into a stunning magnum opus, which I couldn't take my eyes off of. Meticulously engraved scenes of violence, icons of pain, and lines of poetry were so carefully strung together that it gave the impression of physical movement. An intricately carved image of a creature half woman, half dog being sodomized by a man flowed into a quote from Balzac: "Who could determine the point where pleasure becomes pain, where pain is still a pleasure?" The first word of the quote flowed directly from the man's body; the *r* and *e* of *determine* became part of his back, legs, and feet. The question mark at the end of the quote morphed into clouds, which became rain, then a waterfall, which poured from a child's left eye and down the right side of the dresser until it became a rock, which began another quote.

The contrast between the lightness of the wood beneath the surface and the bloodred color of what little remained of the smooth walnut finish seemed to be as much a part of the art as it was a metaphor for the life of the artist, who no doubt was Melinda, given what Mary had said about her abusive father.

I called McElroy and we debated about whether Mary Sullivan might have given Melinda a heads-up, an assumption based on nothing more substantive than my own personal distrust. But if Frank knew we were onto him, it was likely that it would change the whole dynamic, for usually when people panic, they will do anything in their effort to escape the fear. I suggested to McElroy that I call Mary and simply ask her for the truth. "After all, she was a nun; she should know the power behind a lie."

"Come on, Sydney, we're Catholics. You sin, you apologize, you get to say a couple of Hail Marys, you're absolved, and then you're free to sin all over again."

I promised to call as soon as I spoke with Mary, but when I got the therapist's answering machine, I called McElroy back and told her.

"Okay. We're going to send someone over to talk to her—and we are already working on a warrant for the Boerum apartment."

"We'll try to wait for your team."

"Fine. It shouldn't take long."

"If we're not here, the super's a lovely woman. She'll be more than happy to help them, I'm sure."

"Great. Good work, Sydney."

"It's not over yet," I said as I saw Max filling the door frame. I said good-bye and turned off the phone.

"And?" I asked him, arching my brow.

He sighed. "And the super doesn't like Melinda."

I held out the picture. "And?" I asked again as he took the photograph but didn't look at it.

"And the only two people who are in the building right now

are the super and a retired tool and die maker who lives on the top floor. His name is Carroll and he lives with his fourteen-year-old Chihuahua, whose name is Señor Stanley. Stan likes to dance for grapes. But only green seedless ones."

I stared at my partner, unable to shift my gaze from his deceptively intelligent face. "Look at the picture," I suggested.

He did. And as he did, he let out a breathy whistle. "Son of a gun," he said, glancing up at me and then taking a look around the room.

"They left in a rush," I said, leading the way through the apartment and into the kitchen, hoping that they might have left a clue as to where they'd gone. "Did the super give you anything solid?"

"Only that Lucy was here with Melinda and a friend of Melinda's whose name she doesn't know."

"Did you show her the picture of Frank?"

"Yes. Positive ID."

"When did she last see Lucy?"

"Yesterday."

"And?"

"She didn't notice anything unusual. She complained about the dog and said she assumed that Melinda and Lucy were related."

"They are." I picked up the box of Lucky Charms just as we both heard a commotion on the landing outside Melinda's apartment. We raced through the short hallway and yanked open the door, where we found two men in very high spirits jostling to get their bicycles into the other apartment on the floor. The taller of the two men looked expectantly toward us, but when he saw Max and me, his face immediately retracted the welcome.

The second man glanced back at us, smiled, and nodded hello.

There was no doubt that they'd put a cap on their revelry because we were there. Max and I approached them and asked if we could have a word.

The taller man told his friend to go inside and start coffee. "I'll talk to them." He waited until the other man was inside before asking, "How can I help you?" He was good-looking in a rough-and-tumble kind of way.

We explained that we were looking for Melinda.

"Who are you?"

In the interest of time and knowing it would be a matter of minutes before the police arrived, I showed him my license and explained that Melinda was wanted for questioning in a kidnapping.

"I knew that wasn't her sister," he said as he shook his head. "What do you want to know?"

By the time we were through questioning him, we knew that Melinda had had a friend over that morning, a woman named Cheri Casoli, who lived in the Howard Beach section of Queens. He didn't have an address, but he was able to tell us that Cheri had a car—a 2000 silver Saturn SL—and that Melinda worked nights. "She tends bar somewhere in the Village," he said, his tone implying there was no keen friendship between the two neighbors.

Minutes later, we had Marcy and Kerry working on finding us Cheri Casoli's exact address. Then Max and I went through Melinda's drawers to see what we could find. Not wanting to mess with prints, I nonetheless picked up the phone and hit the redial button. A woman answered, so I asked for Cheri.

"She's not here right now. Can I take a message?"

"She's not? Oh gosh, I was hoping to catch her there. This is Marlee Lamm. I'm a friend of Frank's. Do you know when she'll be back? Is she at work?"

The woman on the other end laughed and said, "Work? Nah, they just left for the beach, so I don't know when they'll be back. You wanna give me your number?"

"The beach? Oh, great. Do you know if she went with Frank? We were all supposed to get together today and, well, I'm running a little late."

"Oh yeah, they're all together, even the sister, but they just walked out the door for Riis. Do you want me to check and see if they're still outside?"

"That would be great, thanks." I realized that I was trying to sound like an enthusiastic bimbo from Brooklyn, which was exhausting. I covered the mouthpiece and told Max what I had.

After a good minute and a half, which seemed like a day and a half, the woman returned, slightly out of breath, and said, "They was already gone."

I thanked her for her help, gave her the number for my cell phone, and practically flew out the door, with Max right on my heels.

"Jacob Riis Beach. You know how to get there?" I asked as we raced down the stairs.

"Sure. It's about forty-minutes from here, though. You want to call McElroy and give the police there a heads-up? There's a police station right on the boardwalk."

He pulled away from the curb as I stared out the window.

"What are you doing? Call McElroy," he repeated as he accelerated.

"I'll call Marcy and Kerry first, just so they don't spin their wheels."

I could feel his frustration, but much to his credit, he didn't say anything until I had completed the last drawn-out call and we were more than halfway there.

"Sydney . . ."

"Listen to me. The good news is that they don't know we're onto them; otherwise, they'd be headed somewhere other than the beach."

"*If* they're headed to the beach. Maybe the woman was covering—"

"You're making great time," I said, cutting him off.

"Call McElroy."

"At this rate, we should be there in what—another ten minutes or so?"

"Call McElroy," he repeated calmly.

"I don't want to scare Lucy. If she's there, I want us to be the ones who find her."

"Sydney, Riis Beach is a state park. Have you been there before?"

"Once." I kept my eyes on the blur of storefronts we passed at a good twenty miles over the speed limit.

"Then you know it's big. It's easy to disappear in a place like that."

"We'll find her," I insisted.

"*If* she's there! We could use help," he countered.

"I don't want to scare her."

"Christ, Sydney, you don't think she's not scared already, having spent the last two days away from her mother?"

"All right! Fine, I'll call McElroy." I knew Max was right, realized that at this point it didn't matter who found Lucy, simply that she be found. But despite what I knew, I felt an irrational panic. If Frank saw the police, he might hurt Lucy, and we were so close. So goddamned close.

TWENTY-SIX

As I pulled out the phone to call McElroy, it rang. It was Miguel. I gave Max a look, as if to say, I have to take this.

"Yo, boss, I found Cissy's niece, Janice Huffington. Cissy's the one who died in Madrid."

"I know. Go on."

"Janice married very old money and lots of it, and *she's* convinced that Harold was behind her aunt's death. She even has boxes of paperwork from her own personal investigation."

"*She* investigated?" I asked with moderate disbelief.

"No way, man. She hired four different investigators to check into it. See, Cissy was like a mother to Janice, who was nineteen when her aunt died in 1975."

"It doesn't bode well that Sugar's son *and* Cissy's niece both wanted to investigate when their relatives died. When did Janice start investigating Cissy's death? When she got married and had the money to do it?" I asked, trying to calm his nearly unbridled enthusiasm.

"No, it was her father, Cissy's brother, who started the investigation in 1975, and you want to know why?"

"Why?"

"Because she died while eating fish, which was one of the many foods she wouldn't touch. Apparently, she was what you would call a finicky eater, and fish was one of the things she had a phobia about."

"How did Harold explain her having eaten fish?"

"From what Janice said, he never even tried. All they know is that she ate a local dish called *parrilla de mariscos* and died."

"What is it?" I asked.

"Some kinda fish stew."

"Did other people have the dish? I mean, we're talking food poisoning at a restaurant. Did other people get sick at least?"

"No. I mean people ate it, but they didn't get sick."

"What was the upshot of her investigation? I'm assuming nothing came of it, since Harold's about to take another stab at marital bliss."

"Nothing did, but that's just it, boss. She wants to hire me. Us." Hearing his excitement reminded me of how I'd felt about this business when I first started. The possibility of making sense out of confusion can be an addiction for some people, and Miguel was becoming one of those people.

"Hire you? Her aunt's been dead for twenty-five years."

"Over twenty-five, but my showing up on her doorstep, poking around in what she called 'an unresolved piece of her life,' . . . well, she said she thought it was a sign to settle things once and for all. But listen to her terms: She would pay the usual fee, just for me to look through the files that she has had sitting around for a friggin' lifetime, and she added that if I'm able to prove that Harold murdered Cissy, she'll add one hundred thousand dollars to the fee."

"Good God."

"Yeah, I know. Cool, huh?"

It was staggering to think that kind of money was like Kleenex to some people. Huffington could have offered ten times less and it would have been equally stunning.

I relayed the information to Max, since that kind of money didn't often cross the threshold of our office in one fell swoop. Okay, maybe never.

"What did you tell her?" I asked Miguel as I watched Max's jaw twitch. I knew he wanted me to call McElroy and have her send in her army of professionals, but we were so close and I was digging in my heels.

"Well, at first I thought, You're shitting me. You know? But I just listened to her and figured this chick's either got one heavy vendetta against Harold or she really believes that Harold killed Cissy and she wants justice. Clearly, the investigators she hired, both here and in Madrid, didn't give her the answer she was looking for. The Spanish detectives—there were three, hired at different times—they all cashed her checks, filed useless, inconclusive reports, and then disappeared. The detective agency from the United States was Waters & Greene. You ever heard of them?"

"Sure, Jolly was a good detective, good man."

"Jolly? Jolly Greene? What about him?" Max asked when he heard his old friend's name. I filled him in on Miguel's findings. "If Jolly didn't find anything, then there's nothing to find, he said."

"Did she actually show you the report?" I asked Miguel."

"No. She said she'd show me the paperwork only if I agreed to take her on as a client."

I told Max, who sighed. I knew we were thinking the same thing: At a glance, this was a win-win situation, because no matter what we did, we would make money. Any other agency in the business would have leapt at it. But there were problems.

"I think it smells bad. Waters & Greene were too good to file inconclusive," Max mused as he slammed on the brakes to avoid hitting a family of tourists who were taking in the Brooklyn sites, completely oblivious to the world immediately around them.

I thought about it, shook my head, and waited as Papa Tourist hurried his clan to the relative safety of the sidewalk. "Max and I are debating," I explained to Miguel. "He's right: Waters & Greene would have never filed inconclusive."

"Right. Unless it *was* inconclusive, in which case, why would Huffington offer that much bounty? Because that kind of money *is* a bounty. I agree it's a red flag."

"Right. But first, do we really care if she spends a couple of hundred bucks to show us the files, and second, are you going to be comfortable sending Dorothy off into the sunset not knowing what another agency, one you respect, had to say?"

"Why won't she show him the files without hiring him? That really bothers me," Max said.

I asked Miguel.

"She's a little odd, you know, like a total control freak."

"Maybe she liked you," I offered as an explanation.

Miguel exhaled a breathy *"Ha."*

"Come on. Here you have an attractive, wealthy, lonely middle-aged women in a big, rambling house with nothing but time on her hands. Suddenly, this lanky, good-looking detective—"

Max interrupted. "Comes prancing onto the scene, and she is struck with the inexplicable urge to pull her Barbie clothes from the attic and dress the young stranger."

At any other time, I might have laughed. Any other time, Max might have sounded lighthearted, but at that moment, with Lucy so near and yet so far away, nothing seemed funny.

"What?" Miguel asked.

"Call McElroy," Max said as he zipped around a woman pushing a shopping cart filled with cans.

"Have you talked to Leslie?" I asked, ignoring both Miguel's question and Max's instructions.

"No. But I figured this isn't really about her, because this is someone else wanting to hire us, right?"

I thought about it. The one-hundred-thousand-dollar carrot being dangled in front of Miguel was cause for concern, but looking into old files could prove to be useful.

"Have Kerry draw up a contract for the initial stage of the investigation. Then go and look into those files. Leslie's with Peggy right now, so I don't want you to disturb her."

"She's back from California?"

"Yeah."

Max glared at me.

"Look, I have to go. Be smart, Mickey."

"Always," he said.

TWENTY-SEVEN

As soon as I saw the beach, I called McElroy and told her where we were.

Riis is a mile-long stretch of beach and concrete boardwalk. It has basketball courts, as well as baseball, softball, rugby, football, and soccer fields; a large brick bathhouse; and nude bathing on the gay stretch. Because it is so close to the city, in the summer Riis becomes a study in the spirit of New York—a wall-to-wall mix of every ethnic group you can possibly imagine, all coexisting happily within the boundaries of their beach blankets.

Fortunately for us, summer vacation had essentially come to an end. If it had been two weeks earlier, the parking lot, which holds six thousand cars, would have been filled and the beach would have been carpeted with bodies, towels, and radios, but as it was, we saw no more than two hundred people in front of the bathhouse.

Max dropped me off at the end of the bathhouse, near the old green clock that's been a part of the landscape since the thirties. I hopped out in front of the playground and scanned the handful of children playing on the jungle gyms. There was no sign of Lucy in the playground and no Frank at any of the oversized white stone picnic tables and benches that lined the side of the playground.

Max and I agreed that I would go it on foot and he would check out the area with the car, that way covering more space. If either of us saw Lucy, we would keep in touch with our cell phones.

"Don't do anything stupid," Max warned as I opened the door.

"At least I have a weapon," I said as a parting shot.

"What do you call this?" He lifted his hands off the steering wheel of his Saab. "This puppy is a whole lot of weapon."

In a situation like this, the detective's goal would be to blend in with the environment, not to call attention to his or herself. Despite the fact that I looked like a nerd in search of a computer in my black cotton sweater, white T-shirt, and black jeans, I blended in well enough on the boardwalk. However, there were pockets of people scattered along the shoreline, and I needed to get a closer look. Once on the beach, weaving through the sunbathers, I looked about as inconspicuous as a flying whale.

I was looking for Lucy. Not Melinda. Not Frank. Just Lucy.

As comparatively empty as it was, I was still surprised to see so many people enjoying a leisurely weekday at the beach. What do these people do? I wondered. Was it a day off, or did they not have to work until the night shift. Were they stay-at-home moms or nannies? Or were they welfare recipients, students, runaways, tourists? Or were they like Frank, kidnappers trying to make life surrealistically real for the children they had abducted?

Lucy. Lucy. Lucy. I knew I couldn't miss her. At close to four feet, she was tall for her age, with knobby knees, enormous brown eyes, and straight brown hair. She had recently forgotten how to walk, preferring to skip wherever she went. She could tie her own shoelaces, knew how to whistle, and could spell her name, both first and last. She also swam like a fish, though the ocean would be a new experience for her, one I didn't want her testing without one of us being with her.

We had told McElroy to instruct the police to be on the lookout for two adults and a child, but I didn't see any uniformed cops patrolling. I also didn't see many trios.

Sand was filling my already-clunky black shoes, and with each step I took, I grew hotter and more irritable under the beating sun. But I was determined; this son of a bitch was going to pay for what he'd done. Usually, anger wasn't one of those emotions I readily gave in to, knowing that inevitably it could be messy and nine times out of ten it had nothing to do with what you thought was the issue, but this time I was hooked.

I had to focus. If I let my anger lead me, I would be lost, so I forced myself to stop, take a deep breath, and divvy up the beach into segments, looking at it in a new way as I walked south.

That's when I saw her. Twenty feet from the shore, a little boy, a little girl, and a small white dog were in the initial stages of excavating a moat and building a sand castle. I squinted at the girl. . . . it had to be Lucy, except as I got closer, I could see that her hair was short and blond, not brown and shoulder-length. Not absolutely certain that it was Lucy, I decided to hold off on calling Max but I hurried toward the children, trying not to look as if I was attempting to cover the fifty yards in a single bound.

Less than twenty feet away, I was confident that it was Lucy. Upon seeing her, I experienced a totally visceral reaction, relief fusing with stone-cold rage that started in the pit of my stomach and coursed through my body. I stopped and called Max, gave him my location, and hung up before he could warn me to wait for him. I scanned the area immediately around Lucy and caught Frank's eye just as he realized that I might not be simply another sunbather. He was with a group of five other people: two women and three young men.

"Lu!" Frank called out as he scrambled to charge at her from a sitting position.

Hearing the familiar way in which he spoke to Lucy caught me off guard. Part of me just wanted to take the Walther out of my bag and shoot the son of a bitch the way he had shot John, without care or warning, but I couldn't.

Lucy's back was to the both of us, but at that point I, too, yelled out her name. She twisted around, squinted against the bright sun, and tried to see who was calling her. When she realized that it was Aunt Sydney, she called out my name and started to get up.

Frank reached her while I was still ten feet away. He grabbed her arm and went to hide her behind him. The white puppy ran a fast circle around them.

I waited. I didn't want to frighten Lucy, and I needed to catch my breath. I kept a safe distance so as not to cause Frank to act stupidly or call his friends into the fray. I smiled at Lucy, which made me feel nearly psychotic. The muscles used to grin seemed so contrary to the emotions I was feeling, which, I realized, is probably what schizophrenics feel most of the time.

"Hey. Didja miss me?" It felt good to say that again.

I could feel Frank's fellow group of sunbathers shift, which made me step back, however clumsily, so I could keep everyone in my sight at the same time.

I followed Frank's gaze and saw a short woman with large breasts sashaying toward us—not an easy feat in the sand, or perhaps because of the sand it was easier. Either way, Cheri, and there was no question that it was Cheri, was a woman who had studied the fine art of hip swishing. My eyes went back to Frank, who looked just like his image in the police sketch.

"It's over," I told him, absolutely mesmerized by the man in front of me.

"Hey, Lu, you want an ice cream? Why don't you go with Cheri and get some?" he suggested. The last thing I wanted was for Lucy to leave my sight again.

"Yea!" Lucy hopped from foot to foot and started listing the possible flavors she would want, starting with banana.

"Good idea," I said. "Come on, Lucy, I'll get us *all* ice cream."

"I don't think so." Frank trained his pretty blue eyes on me and smiled. He reached up to pull a pair of plastic sunglasses off the top of his head and onto the bridge of his nose. This brought attention to the tattoo around his wrist, which wasn't Celtic but, rather, a tribute to the bacchanal—naked bodies intertwined in various sexual acts. I assumed this meant that Frank was impotent and that this overt advertising was like everything else about him, mere window dressing.

Coming face-to-face with the person who had controlled things for the last few days and caused so much chaos and pain in our lives was not at all what I had expected. Immediately, I flashed to the picture I had seen in his bedroom, the one where he'd tried, albeit unsuccessfully, to conceal who he really was. He was several inches shorter than I, and though he looked tough, I was confident that if it came to blows, I would prevail. He may have had youth and strength, but I had training, and I wasn't about to let him walk away with my goddaughter again. The idea of protecting Lucy was probably enough incentive to give me superhuman strength, but it's never a good idea to underestimate your opponent, especially one with a gaggle of friends on the sidelines. He rolled his shoulders under his white T-shirt and squeezed his free hand into a small fist. He looked tragically pale in his baggy jeans.

"Your mustache is peeling," I said, flicking a finger toward his upper lip. "Spirit gum doesn't do well in the heat and humidity. Believe me, I know; I used to be in the theater."

In fact, his mustache wasn't peeling, but I figured it was a way to throw him off balance, to challenge the man covering the woman.

Cheri might have walked around me, but she chose a path that took her right past me. I reached out and grabbed her. Up close, she looked like the love child of Lanie Kazan and Joan Blondell. She was the sort of woman who likes to pretend to be helpless, so stopping her didn't take much on my part. She was wearing a skimpy two-piece suit, with the bottom half tied on the sides and the top held together with a tie at the neck and another in the back. She seemed to like it when I grabbed her, which made me just ever so slightly nauseous, but aside from taking out my gun and shooting the two of them, she was my only playing card to call attention to us. If we were the focus of attention, Frank would be less likely to slip away unnoticed.

Cheri exhaled a breathy cry: "Frankie."

"Yo, bitch. What the fuck you think you're doing?" An indignant young man from their crowd eased himself onto his two feet, but he didn't make a move to do any more than that.

I backed up two feet, effectively placing Cheri between them and me.

"I said, 'What the fuck you think you're doing?'" The young man, who was about nineteen, slender, tanned, and wore cutoffs pulled just low enough to reveal what little hair he had just below his navel, still didn't move.

"Nothing, really," I said, knowing I needed a distraction. I pulled at the strings of Cheri's top with my right hand and her bottom strings with my left. I then pushed her to get her hands off her suit and make her scramble to catch herself from falling. I was able to yank off her top and toss it to behind me as she squeezed her thighs together in an unsuccessful bid to keep the bottoms half of her suit in place. The young man's jaw dropped, while the two other men in their group lowered their sunglasses and smiled. It certainly didn't look as if they were interested in defending their friend's honor, but I took a step closer to Frank and shifted farther to my right anyway, just in case one of them decided to protect Cheri. I held out my hands in an attempt for calm and said, "Give it up, Melinda."

"Melinda? Who the fuck's Melinda?" A second young man in a short wet suit asked, and I realized that they didn't know. Frankie and Cheri had been able to convince their friends that Frank was a man. What a testimony to Melinda as a drag king, or perhaps she had joined the ranks of those in the process of changing their gender. It was possible, especially considering how convincing she was as a he. As I stared at her in the harsh sun, knowing what I did, I nonetheless had a hard time separating Frank from Melinda.

I couldn't help but wonder just how much Mary Sullivan knew. I could only hope that, as a therapist, she was more observant than most people, yet she had steadfastly referred to Peggy's offspring as a woman, calling her Melinda. Had she known about this alter ego, Frank, and simply kept this confidential, or was it only Melinda she knew?

The more I stared, the more obvious it seemed that under the short hair and glued-on facial hair was a pretty young woman who would have been a perfect Viola in Shakespeare's *Twelfth Night*. Then again, she might have easily been a pretty young man, perfectly suited for the role of the twin brother, Sebastian.

It was enough to wreak havoc with my sensibilities; I couldn't imagine what it was like to live within that skin.

Blood rose to Frank's cheeks as his rage replaced his deathly pallor with a healthy glow. He must have squeezed Lucy's wrist tighter in his anger, because she cried out for him to let go of her. The puppy stood on its hind legs and flapped his front paws in the air.

"They don't know, do they?" I asked, casting a quick glance at Cheri and her backdrop of friends.

"Know what?" asked the other woman, who had large hair and long nails, as she inched her way warily past me toward Cheri's discarded top. Cheri looked stricken, knowing better than I how her choice of partners would go over with this Howard Beach crowd. That they didn't know Cheri was gay was bad enough, but not to have known that Frank was a woman was going to make them feel stupid, which stupid people would find unforgivable. Had Cheri been upfront with her old friends from the start, she more than likely would have been rejected, but she'd added insult to injury by having tricked her chums into treating her and Frank as a couple. In a situation like this, the deception became the cardinal sin, because no matter how convincing Melinda was a Frank, her very success made those who bought it look like idiots. And in a tight-knit homophobic community like Howard Beach, it was going to take a long time for Cheri's family to come out from under a scandal like this.

I wasn't so sure I wanted to be the one to do the unveiling, because it was impossible to know how the friends would respond.

"Frank, I don't want to hurt you," I said as gently as I could. "You've been hurt enough. Why don't you and Lucy and I just go up to the bathhouse and—"

"Who the fuck are you?" His voice cracked as he held Lucy and started to back away from me.

"I'm Lucy's godmother. My name is Sydney."

"You're Peggy's friend," he said with contempt as he ran his fingers through his hair in the very same way Peggy always did.

"This isn't about Peggy," I said, moving closer as he backed away.

"Yo, Frankie, you want this bitch out?" This came from the third man in the crowd, who was much bigger and far more menacing than the others.

Frank glanced at his friend and then back at me. I moved still closer to Frank and Lucy. This put the trio of men slightly behind me, but I was determined that Lucy was not going to move out of my sight this time.

"Back off, boys. I'm with police enforcement. It's over, Frank. The police have this place surrounded."

"Yo, Frankie," the Menace prodded.

"What police?" asked the woman, practically yelping. "I don't need no police, Cher. My family's got enough trouble with my brother."

"Shut up, Vianne; no one's talking to yous." This came from the Menace, who was obviously in the mood for a fight.

"Frank, Karl's pinned everything on you. You have to understand that there's no way out of this. The police and the feds are here, and if you resist, it'll only look worse for you. Karl played you for a patsy to get back at Peggy. . . ."

"Karl's a good man. He had a reason to be mad. I know everything."

"Really? Then you know he's your father?" I said, knowing there was no good way to impart such ugly information, and yet there was no way I could have withheld it at this point. The shattered look on Frank's face made clear that whoever *he* was, the little girl was still inside, frightened, confused, and damaged. I was so angry that my hands were shaking, but I knew if I lost it, I'd only scare Lucy.

"What the hell do you know? I have thought of everybody else my whole fucking life, lady, because that's the only way I could survive. Well, now it's my turn. And let me tell you something: Lu could have an excellent life with me. Excellent! I know how to love, not beat up and fuck over or pretend like presents and shit are love, but real love. The real deal." He continued to hold Lucy and back away from me, but he was moving them toward the water, not away from it.

"Lucy, honey, don't you miss Mommy and Daddy?" I asked her directly.

Before she could answer, Frank had pulled her off the ground and was holding her to his chest. Lucy flinched as Frank turned away from me. "Nicky! Now! Stop the bitch," he called out as he started to run along the firmer sand at the shoreline. The dog happily bounced after them.

I got about five feet before Nicky tackled me from behind. I hit the beach hard but was able to squirm out of his initial hold by kicking the hell out of him. No one, not even this behemoth of a guy, was going to keep me from Lucy. I twisted to get away from him while still trying to keep an eye on Frank. Cheri scurried past us, wiggling like a hissing seal backing away from a curious dog.

I saw Frank cut to his right and head toward the bathhouse just as his friend Nicky yanked my leg back with one hand and slammed my head with the other. I didn't know which hurt more, the whiplash or the fact that it felt like I had bitten off part of my tongue. This idiot, whose hands were like metal clamps working their way up my legs, had no idea what he was doing. With every ounce of power inside me, I kicked at his head repeatedly and snarled, "Let go, asshole. I'm a detective. Your friend shot a cop." At hearing that, he stopped for half a second. I noticed that his nose was bleeding and that I had given him a good kick to his right eye, but before I could move, he wrapped his fingers around my right knee and pulled. That's when I took a fistful of sand and threw it at his face. Determined as he was to hold on, he was blinded by the sand and instinct took over: He let go of me to wipe his eyes. In a flash, I snaked out from under him and scrambled to my feet.

As I backed away from Nicky, I saw that his friends were still watching from the sidelines and had no obvious intention of jumping in. I also saw Max, who was slightly bigger than Nicky, come flying through the air and land on the kid, hitting him hard from behind. I tossed my purse at Max and yelled, "The Walther's in the bag," as I then took off after Frank, Cheri, and Lucy, who had just made it to the five concrete steps leading to the boardwalk.

Sheer fury propelled me up the beach, but it felt as if I were moving in a slow-motion nightmare; the harder I ran, the more the sand resisted me. Fortunately, Frank had been slowed down considerably because he was carrying Lucy, but he made it to the bathhouse, while I still had a good thirty feet of beach ahead of me. I kept hoping I'd see a cop, but there was none in sight, or at least no uniformed officer.

The darkness in the community bathhouse was momentarily blinding, but I could still hear Lucy crying and the puppy barking. I followed the sound and saw the silhouette of Frank and Lucy through the doorways that led to the front of the building. He had shot straight past the concession stands selling hot dogs, pizza, ice cream, and pretzels and was making a beeline for the main parking lot. That meant he still had a quite a distance to cover, but now that we were on solid ground and I had them in my sights, there was no way he would get away.

Cheri's heels clacked crazily against the tiled floor several yards in front of me as she chased after her lover. She screamed, "Frankie, drop her! For Christ sake, just leave her here!" Her voice reverberated off the bathhouse walls and unless you were listening she just sounded like a shock wave of frantic sound. Few people seemed to hear Cheri; indeed, no one seemed to care that there was anything unusual happening.

I shot past Cheri, who had stopped and was whimpering as she stamped her foot and flapped her hands at her side.

Even though I was a good twenty feet behind him, I pushed myself into high gear, because I knew that if they made it to the parking lot, I was in trouble.

Frank slipped on a turn and lost hold of Lucy. He went skidding in one direction and Lucy flew into some boxwood dividing the lot from the street. Lucy's scream muted every other sound, from the Atlantic Ocean to the fifteen-second intervals between low-flying airplanes heading to and from Kennedy Airport.

I bolted across the traffic lanes and made it to Lucy just as Frank was getting to his feet. In the spill, he had either sprained or broken his foot, but oddly enough, not a facial hair was out of place. A nasty long scrape covered the outside of his left arm and his sunglasses had been thrown several feet from where he stood.

The dog didn't know whom to console first, Lucy or Frank, so it dashed toward one, then the other, and back again.

I had Lucy in my arms. She smelled like Coppertone and oranges and her face was streaked with tears and dirt, but she didn't seem the worse for the wear. She had nasty cuts on one knee and on the palms of her hands and she was covered with sand, but she was safely in my arms. I held on to her as if someone were about to try to snag her away from me. She cried and squirmed to be free. I set her down and squatted beside her, holding on to her waist and taking her in.

"Are you okay?" I asked, knowing perfectly well that she both was and wasn't.

Enormous tears inched down her cheeks as she studied her bloodied palms.

"Hey, we can fix that," I said as I glanced up at Frank and saw that he, too, was crying. His fix wouldn't be so easy. As surprised as I was that he was still there, I was even more surprised that my rage had dissipated somewhere between the beach and the parking lot.

He looked so pathetic standing there that I had to remind myself that this person had tried to kill John. That he—she—had tried to murder a man, my friend, in cold blood. I hated her for having put all of us through such a painful week, and yet as much as I wanted to hold on to my rage, I couldn't help but feel pity.

There was the sound of a commotion behind me. I could hear sirens in the distance and felt pretty certain that they were headed our way, but it was as if the three of us were hermetically sealed in a dome, with a three-foot perimeter around us.

"Frankie?" Lucy's sobs had abated to sniffles and she twisted around to find Frank. She wiped her cheek with the back of her hand and her bottom lip was pushed out so far, it looked as if it might fall off.

"I'm right here," he said, limping the few feet back toward us. "I'm so sorry, Lu. I didn't mean for you to get hurt." He tried unsuccessfully to hold back his tears as he knelt before her. "Next time we go to the beach, it'll be better."

The puppy jumped around them and yapped, as if it was the happiest creature on the face of the earth.

"It's okay, Frankie. Don't cry." Lucy took a step closer to him, and though I knew I didn't need to hold on to the back of her swimsuit, I still did.

Frank held out his arms and Lucy stepped into his gentle embrace. She wrapped her thin arms around his neck, patted his head, and released him. Then she turned to me and said, "Frankie's my brother *and* my sister. Cool, huh?" She smiled as the puppy yelped for her to pick it up, which she did. The hold looked painful, but the dog seemed quite content.

"Yeah," I said as I watched Frank peel off his facial hair. Melinda Johnson was the spitting image of her grandmother, Rita. "Was Karl the shooter?" I asked, oddly hoping that was the case.

She shook her head. "No." She looked out at the horizon, which just happened to be the whole of Manhattan. The city looked as if it had been cut out of gray paper and set against a periwinkle blue scrim. Queens, Brooklyn, an airport, and several bridges stood between the city and us. It was an amazing sight.

"I did," she practically whispered.

"Why?"

The sirens were getting closer.

Melinda stared at me, but I felt as if she had somehow left the room, as it were.

As the police arrived and onlookers started to crowd around us, I lifted Lucy back into my arms and said, "What do you say we call your mom?"

When she smiled, I noticed that she had lost a tooth since I'd last seen her.

"Did the tooth fairy visit you?" I asked as I speed-dialed Gil's number.

"Yuh. I got a dollar and peanut brittle."

"Peanut brittle, eh?"

"Yuh. Frankie says the tooth fairy makes it herself because it's good for business."

"I bet it is," I said as I carried Lucy off to the side so she wouldn't see the police cuff Frank.

"Gil? It's Sydney. Where are you? Good. I have someone here who'd like to talk to her." I handed Lucy the phone.

"Hello? Yuh. Yuh. Uh-huh. Yuh, I'm okay. I hurt my hands.

Yuh. Uh-huh. I miss you too, Mommy. Is Daddy there? Uh-huh. Okay. I love you, too. Okay."

She handed me the phone and I told Peggy we would drive Lucy to the hospital, where she could see John and be reunited with the rest of the family.

I called Max next. He had already handed Nicky over to the police and was on his way to us.

The police had been alerted by McElroy to give Max and me custody of Lucy. Whatever was going to happen to Melinda and Cheri was out of my hands. The police swallowed up Melinda before I could remember to look around for her, and I never did see Cheri again.

Several hours later, after Lucy was given a clean bill of health and had been reunited with her parents, McElroy's team had packed up and moved out of the Cannady apartment, so as not to confuse or frighten Lucy any further. When we got back to the apartment, Peggy took me aside and asked, "What was he like? She? What was she like?"

I searched for words to sum up the miasma of feelings that had overwhelmed me. I shook my head mutely before finally saying, "I don't know what to tell you. He was a very handsome young man, and yet as soon as he removed the facial hair, I realized that your daughter has an uncanny physical resemblance to Rita. I mean, you wouldn't think a person could really do that, skate between the genders, and yet she did. I mean Sullivan thought she was a woman."

"She is," Peggy reminded me.

"Right. She is a woman. And yet—" I shook my head. "I can't imagine being stuck in that nightmare. She and Cheri managed to convince their friends *and family members* that Melinda was a guy named Frank. That's not an easy thing to do. And I tell you, Peggy, when I first saw her dressed as Frank, I wanted to rip her apart, but I found myself walking away from it thinking she's confused and angry. And clearly there's a part of her that is nuts, but she really did seem to . . . I don't know—she really did seem to care about Lucy. Mind you, I don't know if that caring was love or her own need to be loved. But when I saw them together, I honestly didn't think she would have hurt Lucy. Then again, a professional might tell you something completely different, especially after what I saw at her apartment." I then explained the dresser and how it had made it abundantly clear to me that Melinda Johnson had become Frank because she had been so brutalized as a young girl that she needed another persona. "That she chose to become a man makes sense to me, because men have power and men—or a man, probably her father—had controlled her life in a very brutal, ugly way. My guess is she thought that if she became the very thing that was at the center of her rage, then it could never hurt her again."

"When did you get so smart?"

It was good to see Peggy smile again.

"A year ago. It was a Wednesday, as I recall. November, I think. Yeah, definitely November. About six o'clock . . . six-fifteen. It was a stunning moment."

"Shut up," she said as she wrapped her arms around me.

"So, what are you going to do about Lucy's hair?" I asked, motioning to the den, where Leslie was watching TV with Lucy and her new dog, Brutus, whom her parents had said she could keep. "Or does it bring back fond memories of the first time you colored yours?"

"I was four and it was shoe polish. It washed right out," said Peggy, reminiscing.

Oh yes, it was very good to have things back to normal, whatever that was.

TWENTY-EIGHT

That night, Leslie and I were reunited with Auggie. I wanted nothing more than a normal evening—dinner, conversation, a little television, a walk in the park—but I was so tired that I was sound asleep by six o'clock and didn't budge until long past dark.

When I awoke, I was disoriented, which frightened me. At first, I didn't know where I was, but as my eyes adjusted to the dark, I remembered I was home. I was also sweating and parched, so I threw off the duvet and made my way in a fog to the kitchen where Auggie followed me, not so much out of love as in the hopes of a midnight treat.

I couldn't remember the last time I had eaten. Before I knew it, I was sitting at the kitchen table with Brie, grapes, an apple, toasted sourdough bread, a bottle of water, and a juice glass filled with pinot gris.

"I thought there was a hole in the bed," Leslie said as she stood in the doorway. "You cold?" she asked.

Sweating when I left bed, I hadn't wanted to return, for fear of waking her.

"A little, now that you mention it."

She disappeared and returned with my robe.

"Thanks. Some wine?"

"I'll get it." She waved me back to my seat, took a glass from the cabinet, and joined me. "Amazing, isn't it?"

"So many things," I said, not knowing what precisely she was referring to.

"That family has a lot of healing to do." She reached for a grape.

"I would imagine yours will, too. Have you talked to Miguel?"

She nodded. "He came over after you fell asleep."

"I'm sorry about that."

"Why? You were exhausted."

"I still am," I said, leaning back, fighting the usual routine of putting my foot in her lap.

"You look better, though."

"Thank you. What did Mickey have to say?"

Leslie took a deep breath and stared into her glass as she pulled back her hair with her free hand. "He told me everything he's learned so far. Tomorrow, he's supposed to start rummaging through that woman's papers in New Jersey."

"And what would stop him?" I asked.

"Me." She brought the glass to her lips and took a long swallow.

"Why?" I reached for the wine and replenished my glass.

She shut her eyes and rubbed her forehead. "I had a talk with Dorothy tonight after you fell asleep. I wanted her to know that Lucy was safe, and I knew it was time to talk to her about Harold."

I studied the hard lines that had started to etch into Leslie's beautiful face over the last six months. They weren't unattractive; in fact, they gave her face a sense of character she would undoubtedly grow into, but it was a wrinkle, as it were, I'd never seen before in this particular light. I waited for her to continue at her own pace. No prompting this time. Things were changing between us, and while I didn't know how or why, I knew I had to trust my instincts.

"Mom knew that Harold had been married before. She also knew that he had outlived several of his wives." She poked her tongue against the inside of her cheek and sighed.

"What does that mean?" I asked.

"It means what I said. It means that she knew but she hadn't told any of us. Not Marcia or Paul or me." The sharpness in her tone was reflected in her face.

"Did she know that some of the deaths were questionable?" I asked with a calm that I hoped would offset her resentment.

Leslie nodded. "Seems so."

"And your mother was content to enter into this marriage, to start a whole new phase of her life by lying to her family?"

"Well, that's just it; she still doesn't see it as lying. She insists that there is a difference between lying and withholding, and she says that as long as *she* has all the facts, that's what's important."

"It just doesn't sound like your mom."

"She's in love." Leslie looked away from me and shook her head. "I mean, she's *really* in love. And so is he."

"So what are you saying?"

"I'm saying my mom is old enough to make her own decisions without having to answer to me, or Marcia, or any of her kids, for that matter."

"Even if it means jeopardizing her safety?"

Leslie lifted one shoulder and looked sullenly at her lap. "People make decisions, Sydney, and the only thing that I can hope for is to be responsible for my own choices. I had a very honest talk with Dot, and that's the best I think I can do. I told her that as happy as I am for her, it concerns me that she felt she couldn't be honest with her own family, and that by concealing something from us about Harold, she was starting her new marriage by putting her own children at a disadvantage. An emotional disadvantage, because there is going to come a time when Marcia and Paul will find out, and they're going to feel betrayed, just like I did."

"What did she say?"

"What could she say? I think she understood that I was right, and she told me that she was going to tell my brother and sister the truth in her own good time."

"How do you feel?"

"It is what it is," she said, swirling the wine in her glass. Unlike me, she had always been able to walk past emotional doors left ajar, which I had never understood, although I believed it had helped the balance in our life together.

"I don't understand that," I said, biting into a grape.

"It *is*. That's all, Sydney." This elucidation could easily have been followed with a breezy "Jeeze, you're stupid," but it wasn't. Instead, Leslie added, "Apparently, Dot was the one who had asked Harold to keep his marital history from us."

"Why?" I asked.

"Because she didn't want to deal with Marcia, who was already against the whole thing. I've decided to let go. She made her bed; now she has to lie in it."

"But Miguel told you about Janice Huffington. She's so convinced that there was something underhanded that she wants to hire Miguel to look into old investigative files to see if he can find anything viably incriminating." I studied her face. "Does that make you feel any differently about your choice to let it go?"

She shook her head. "No. People are on paths, Sydney. Mom's made a choice, and for all I know, Huffington's this crazy woman who's looking for excitement in her life and this is it. Is it too late to ask you to stop the investigation?"

"It's not my investigation to stop. It's your choice and Miguel's. Now that Huffington wants to hire him, it becomes a matter of whether he wants to take her on as a client. I know he'll honor your wishes, but you should know that he has a hunch that Harold's implication in his wives' deaths is less than innocent."

I knew if she called Miguel directly, he would back off, because he'd do anything for her and she was, in fact, the person who had hired him to investigate in the first place. However, I also knew what it felt like to sink your teeth into a case and want the answers, if only to satisfy your own curiosity. The choice would have to be Miguel's. Besides, I didn't know how I would feel if anything did happen to Dorothy that we might have been able to prevent.

"You don't approve," she said.

"I wouldn't say that. I just worry about Dorothy, that's all. Look, Harold might just be a man with the kind of karma that has him outliving his spouses. On the other hand, he could be a very charming, clever killer, someone who makes his wives deliciously happy for five years and then murders them. Now, you believe that

244

people are on a path and the choices they make will result in consequences already predestined for that path."

"I didn't say that, but go on." She tightened the sash on her robe.

"At seventy-two, your mother has found passion, which we both know is an amazing gift at any age. I'm guessing that part of you is thinking that if her life is joyfully filled with love for the next five years and then, at seventy-seven, she suddenly dies of a heart attack or food poisoning, at least she will have had those five years, ones that she might not otherwise have enjoyed, so it was worth the risk. And for all I know, it might be. You have to understand that there's no judgment here, but the decision is yours—and Miguel's. And it's a tough one. Are you okay with that?"

"Yes." She pulled her dark hair back and asked, "What would you do in my shoes?"

"I would look for the truth."

"Even knowing you might not find it?"

My life had always been predicated on looking for truths, so I knew how elusive they could be. As an actor, a cop, a PI, I'd like to think, as a sentient being, I had learned how easy it was to try to package truth and honesty as the same thing. More often than not, they're as disconnected as the Bush administration and integrity, I reminded myself.

"What is it you want?" I asked, rather than answering directly, because what I would or wouldn't do didn't really matter in the scheme of things: This was her ball game.

"I want everything to be easy."

"What does that mean?"

"It means I took on a burden I think I regret now." Her eyes darted in my direction, and for a fleeting instant I didn't know what burden she meant.

We sat in silence for several seconds and I felt the weight of exhaustion wash over me. I thought of all the things I could have said, all the directions in which I might have taken the moment, but each and every one I considered would have brought the conversation around to us and the anxiety I was feeling. Boundaries, of my own making or not, were sprouting up around us. Truth. Honesty. I needed to be honestly true to myself.

"Lez, are we okay?" I finally asked.

"This isn't about us," she said, shifting in her seat.

"Funny thing about life: So many things coexist within our psyches simultaneously, so while one thing has nothing to do with another, it doesn't negate the presence of the other."

This at least brought about a smile.

"I love you, you know" was her laden response.

I did not doubt this was true. Nor did I doubt it was an honest statement. But with our boundaries neatly in place, I was unable to reach beyond the emotional barbed wire and ask why I was so scared. Instead, I put away the wine, the cheese, and the dishes, hoping she would say something more, but she didn't.

We fell asleep spooning, with me holding on to her as if proximity had anything to do with distance.

TWENTY-NINE

I awoke to barking. It seemed miles away as I tried to swim up from under Caribbean waters in my sleep. I opened my eyes, to see Leslie sitting up, as tired and confused as I. I asked what was happening and she told me someone was at the door.

"If it's the newspaper delivery guy, he's in a peck of trouble," I said as I wrapped myself into my robe and headed off in the direction of the noise, Auggie close on my heels.

"Shut up," I yelled at the door when I was a dozen feet away. It worked.

I looked through the peephole and saw Harold's convexly distorted face. I opened the door. The big man looked uncomfortable.

"I'm sorry to wake you, but . . ." He went to step past me over the threshold.

I held on to the doorknob with one hand and blocked his way. "No, you're not. Do you have any idea what time it is?" I asked. I certainly didn't.

"Around six-thirty," he said as he tried to see into the apartment. Auggie was trying to get past me and greet our visitor with kisses.

"Six-thirty, and you have the gall to wake not only us but everyone else in this building? What's wrong with you?"

"I want to talk to Leslie," he said through clenched false teeth.

"Is Dorothy all right?" I asked, pushing Auggie back with my foot.

"Yes, of course."

"Well, in that case, what the hell are you doing here so early?"

"I told you. I need to talk to Leslie."

"Harold . . ."

"It's okay." Leslie's voice sounded like a whisper behind me. "Let him in."

I turned and saw her standing at the end of the hallway, looking both implacable and vulnerable. Auggie had moved to her side and was half-sitting protectively at her feet, a smile etched on her goofy face.

I didn't think this was a good idea, but the call was hers, so I stepped aside and opened the door wide enough to let him through. He smelled like aftershave and cigars and moved like a big man with the weight of the world on his rounded shoulders.

Without a word, Leslie led the way into the kitchen, where she busied herself with making coffee. Harold kept his distance and stayed in the dining area, his hands tucked into his pockets. I had grabbed the paper from the hallway and settled at the table, the demarcation line between them. I pretended to be interested in the front-page news.

"Your mother told me about your conversation last night," Harold began.

"So?" She filled the coffeepot with water.

"So I don't appreciate having someone who's not yet part of my family poking into my private life." His voice was deliberately measured.

Leslie stopped, looked at the man, and said, "Fine." She returned to the task at hand.

I glanced up and saw that her simple acknowledgment would have had the ability to make him sputter if he were a sputtering kind of guy, but he wasn't, so he squinted instead and took a deep breath.

"Leslie, you and I are going to be family. I'd like it if we got started on better footing."

"Really. Well, banging on our door at dawn hardly seems like the best approach." She turned her back to him and counted scoops of coffee.

"I'm sorry about that. I'm an early riser, and I tried to wait as long as I could before coming over here. If you had an issue with me, you should have talked to me, instead of asking your girlfriend to try to unearth old lies about me."

I looked up from the paper and caught Harold's glance before he looked away. There was no question that despite underlying anger, he was uncomfortable. Now, he might have been uneasy because he had just acted on impulse and felt justifiably stupid standing in our kitchen, or he could have been—in an equally stupid act of macho bravado—trying to protect himself. If that were the case, then what was he protecting himself from?

Without stopping her coffee-making routine, Leslie told Harold, "I think it's interesting that you feel so threatened that you had to come over here, Harold. I think it's interesting that Mom chose to hide things from her family. I also think that whatever transpired between my mother and me is our business, not yours. And now I think I want you to leave." She pulled two mugs from the cabinet.

He shifted his feet a few inches farther apart, as if to stake his territory. He wasn't about to budge. "You should know that the losses in my past have been unfortunate but not deliberate."

"Then you have nothing to hide." The aroma of coffee started to fill the air. I heard Leslie fill Auggie's bowl with dry food and then open the fridge to get the canned food. Without looking, I knew that Auggie was drooling and that Leslie would have a paper towel under her foot to wipe up the slippery ooze.

"This whole thing has upset your mother. Don't you care about that?"

"The death of my father upset my mother, Harold." She paused in the breakfast-making process, which made Auggie whine. "My brother's incarceration upset my mother. She's lived through and survived a lot of upsets. And believe me, I don't need you to tell me how to have a relationship with my mother."

The paper in my hands was a blur as I shifted in my seat to

prepare to rise. Leslie's tone was ripe for an explosion, and I didn't blame her. I was also hurting from the day before, so I felt grateful that, as far as I knew, neither Harold nor Leslie was the kind of person to physicalize anger. Okay, Leslie wouldn't. Who knew what he would do?

"I'm an old man, Leslie. And I'm in love with your mother. Now, I'm sorry she didn't want you or Marcia or Paul to know about my marital history, but that was her call, not mine. I don't have anything to hide."

"Then you shouldn't mind a simple investigation."

"It's not a good way to start a new family."

"You know, Harold, I was going to let the whole thing go today. But your coming over here reinforces the fact that we're not family. Certainly not yet. You and Dot may both think I'm a shit for doing this, but you know something, Harold? Dot's my mother, and I will do whatever I need to do to make sure that I can trust the man she's marrying. And if you don't like that, I don't care. My family has been through too much for me simply to ignore the fact that you've lost three wives under suspicious circumstances. I mean, think about it. If this were your mother, wouldn't you do the same thing?" She vigorously mixed the dry and wet dog food and placed it on the floor.

Harold jiggled the change in his pants pocket and nodded. "Well, I'm sorry you feel this way, Leslie, but there doesn't seem to be anything I can do, does there?"

I was fascinated. Leslie had presented a perfectly logical, reasonable defense for looking into Harold's past, and apart from the fact that it was threatening, one couldn't ignore that if he had nothing to hide, he wouldn't have been standing in our kitchen before the birds were even awake. Despite the fact that this was even more engaging than my usual morning fare of NPR, it also meant that after a week from hell, I would be rolling up my sleeves and joining Miguel's journey into the past wives of Harold Hardy.

I saw Harold to the door. When I returned to the kitchen, Leslie was sitting at the table crying. I came up behind her, bent over, and wrapped my arms around her.

250

"I just don't like him," she snuffled.

"Me, neither."

Auggie joined us and laid her head on Leslie's lap.

"I tell you what," I said, releasing her and reaching for the coffee she had brought to the table for me. "You make breakfast while I take a quick shower, and then I'll get started on this right away."

"Really."

"Yeah. I don't like that he came over here."

"You just didn't want to get up."

"True." I sipped the wonderful dark brew and moaned. "I mean, you would have thought he'd be smart enough to know this would be a red flag. But who knows?" I said, topping off my cup for the shower. "Harold could be just a stupid old man who looks like a Teamster but has the innocence of Pooh. It's possible. But I think we need to find out—if we can. There are no promises, honey. No guarantees."

She nodded. As I passed her, she took my hand, squeezed it, and brought it to her lips.

I tried to avoid looking at myself in the bathroom mirror, but it was impossible, since the wall over the sink was one big mirror. Had I been a superficial woman, my reflection might have disturbed me enough to keep me indoors for the next week, dieting, exercising, primping, and pampering. Had I been a superficial woman, a face-lift might have been an option, or even an injection of Botox between the tired old eyes, but the thought of inserting botulism into my system or going under a knife to stretch my face just made my skin crawl. I drew closer to my reflection, like a scientist in a grade-B movie examining the seemingly harmless pod that will a moment later horrifically suck the life right out of him. Huh. Maybe a lift wouldn't be such a bad idea. Something simple.

Oh self-esteem, you nasty little demon, I said silently to my reflection.

As I showered, I sang "In the Merry Old Land of Oz." It seemed somehow fitting.

THIRTY

"So we've ruled out Sugar and Maureen, right?" I asked Miguel, who was lounging in the big red easy chair in my home office, which had been my brother's bedroom when we were kids.

"And Maggie, the heart attack."

Leslie had called him when I was in the shower and he had arrived in time for breakfast, to bringing chocolate doughnuts, which he continued to eat long after the dishes were cleared and Leslie had taken Auggie to the park.

"That's right. I forgot about her."

"So we can focus on Cissy," he said, licking chocolate off his fingers.

"Right, the most difficult one. Did you have a chance to look through any of Huffington's papers?" I asked as I reached for the tattered list of names he was studying with his free hand.

"Christ, Sydney, I didn't even know we were gonna take her on till an hour ago."

"So the answer's no."

"That's right. No."

I looked at the list, where only Cissy's name had not been deleted.

"Well, this is good. I want you to call Huffington and arrange to pick up her papers ASAP. I can't remember—did you ever get an autopsy report from Madrid?"

"No. I could only get a death certificate."

"There was an autopsy, though, right?"

He shrugged and flew out of the chair. "Lemme call this lady." He pulled a fistful of crumpled bits of paper and bills from his pockets, sorted through them, and finally found what he was looking for, but my phone rang before he could reach for the receiver.

It was Peggy. Miguel motioned that he would use his cell phone and then left me to talk with her privately.

"Hey," I said. "I wanted to call you before, but I didn't want to wake you."

"No way you could wake me, 'cause I don't sleep anymore. Listen, I wanted to thank you again. I don't know what I would have done without you."

I could hear Brutus yapping in the background.

"Peggy, we're family. I'm just glad it all worked out. How's Lucy?"

"She's okay. She was treated well, but you know how traumatizing all this was. Right now, she has the dog to distract her, but I know my baby. She did sleep through the night, though, which surprised me."

"How about you? Are you okay?"

"I'm ecstatic. I'm exhausted. I'm numb. I'm angry. I'm everything. How about you? I would imagine you're wiped-out."

"No rest for the weary." I filled her in on the early-morning visit from Harold and my current involvement with trying to learn how a woman died over a quarter of a century ago. It sounded daunting even to me. We agreed to have dinner together and I ended the call as Miguel was coming back into the room.

"And?" I asked as I cradled the phone.

"There was an autopsy report, but she doesn't remember exactly what it said. I'm gonna go there and pick up a couple of boxes and bring them here, okay?"

"Good." I gave him my car keys and told him I would see what I could rummage up on my side. I would start with Jolly's agency, Waters & Greene, since it was local. "Oh, wait. Did you get the names of the Madrid investigators?"

"Yeah." Again he emptied his pockets.

"That's one hell of a filing system you've got there."

"Thanks." He gave me the list and took off for Jersey. I didn't lose any time placing the call to Waters & Greene.

I explained to the receptionist who I was, that I had been a friend of Jolly's, and what I was looking for. She transferred me to Jolly's son, Michael, who had taken over the reins when his father died.

"That was more than twenty-five years ago, Sydney. Those files would either have been destroyed or placed in storage."

It made sense.

"Is there any way to check storage? I hate to be a pain, but this has become personal." I explained about my partner's mother.

"Let me put someone on it and I'll get right back to you."

"Thanks, Michael. I appreciate it."

"No problem."

Boy, was he wrong: This was a huge problem. No matter what the outcome, this was sure to cause a divide between Leslie and her mother, who had always shared a uniquely close relationship. It would have been easy enough to blame Harold, but it really had nothing to do with him. This was about trust, probably one of the most complicated tasks for the soul.

THIRTY-ONE

I tried to wait for Leslie and Auggie to return, but the longer they were gone, the more trapped I felt. I tried calling her on her cell phone, which rang in our bedroom. I left a note, telling her I would be at the office. Combining forces would be the only way to approach this Harold matter, and I knew I needed Max's and Kerry's help. I also needed to be with friends. The last several days had taken something from me, and while I wasn't sure exactly what that was, and as thrilled as I was that Lucy had been returned safe and relatively sound, I knew instinctively that I needed to be surrounded by people I loved.

Both Kerry and Max were sitting in his office. She was on the sofa, dressed in Betsy Johnson hot-pink tulle. Max looked rested.

"Hey," I said, flopping down onto his guest chair.

"Hey," they said in unison. "This is so great about Lucy," Kerry added. "But how weird is that about the he-she."

"The world is weird. The important thing is that she treated Lucy well."

"So, which lockup did she go to, men's or women's?" Kerry asked.

"Women's, I suppose. I mean, I didn't look at her sex parts, for crying out loud."

"It's an interesting point," Max mused. "Let's say that she had started the transgender process and right now she has a little penis between her legs. Would that mean, then, that she's a man?"

"She would still have a uterus, though, wouldn't she?" Kerry asked. "So what is it that defines the sex of a person?"

"The penis," Max said definitively, smiling like the Cheshire cat.

"You're an idiot," I mumbled.

"I talked to Gil this morning," he said, changing the subject.

"And?"

"And Melinda pulled the trigger, but from what she said—and Gil believes it—Karl was the puppeteer. The original plan was for her to hand Lucy over to Karl when the drop was made, but our showing up put a crimp in that."

"That's good. Could you imagine what he would have done?"

"I wonder why they put off making their demands?" It was a rhetorical question, but Max surprised me with an answer.

"Apparently, they hadn't gotten that far. Melinda was trying to take some sort of control, not to mention acting out her rage. There were even scripts that Karl had her write out, but she was too emotional to stick to them verbatim."

"But why would Karl want to attack Peggy after all these years?" Kerry asked.

"He had a fall guy," I said just as Max said, "He needed the dough."

Both Kerry and I looked at him.

"It seems that Karl's only recreational activity over the years has been the casinos. He's as much a loser on the tables as he is in life, and he was getting further and further in debt. Gil found out that the bank had started foreclosure proceedings on the house."

"Didn't he own that outright?" I asked, since I knew it had been in the family for a zillion years.

"Once upon a time. But he had refinanced a few years ago *and* taken out a second mortgage. Despite his job, his credit-card debt is so high from gambling that he never could have qualified for a new refi."

"So by kidnapping Lucy, he could finance his future and hurt Peggy."

"*And* if it worked out as he thought it would, accomplish the whole thing without ever having to leave a traceable fingerprint."

"See, that's what kills me," Kerry suddenly blurted from the sofa.

"What?" I asked.

"The world is filled with sick people. People who have children and then spend the next however many years making them insane. People don't get love, and then they begat little people and make them crazy."

"What are you talking about?" Max asked.

She shot off the sofa and started pacing. "All of these people were born, and maybe their parents thought they would grow into good people, but maybe they really just didn't care. Or they adopted them just to have another little victim." She was working herself into a state. "I mean, did you ever stop to think that the dregs of society float through our lives, day in and day out? What kind of cosmic effect does that have on our fragile psyches? This is not what you would call an emotionally healthy environment. Think about it." She crossed her arms over her chest and nodded, as if she were a lawyer resting her defense. However, one glance at her feet, shod in a lime green mules complete with plastic toe-strap daisies, blew the image.

"You want to tell us what's really on your mind?" Max asked at the same time I asked, "What's up?"

"I'm pregnant," she said with a distinct chill.

"Oh my God. That's great!" I practically jumped out of my seat.

Kerry smiled lamely and flattened the tulle of her skirt down. "You think so? Really?"

"What are you, crazy? Of course we think so!" Max was on his feet and aiming for Kerry. "This is wonderful!" He held out his arms to Kerry, who let him give her a bear hug.

"When are you due?" I asked, getting into the hugging action.

"May, I think." She started to cry.

I couldn't understand why she seemed to be so reticent about it, so I asked.

"Because I'm scared!" she yelled as she physically retracted from our embraces.

I had always assumed that women who wore Betsey Johnson were fearless, but I kept this to myself.

Max, on the other hand, tried to reassure her. "There's nothing to be afraid of," he said with the reserve of a maharishi.

"Oh really? And when was the last time you squeezed eight active pounds out of your smallest portal?"

Max tucked his hands in his pockets and nodded. "Okay, yes, I suppose I'd be nervous if I were in your shoes."

I couldn't help but glance at the daisies accenting her fuchsia toenails.

Kerry stared at Max, making him look a little like Wylie Coyote momentarily suspended in midair after having just run off a cliff, but he was undaunted. "A lot of women who don't have half your courage, strength, or fashion sense have had babies and will continue to do so. Let me tell you: If they can do it, so can you."

She looked as comfortable as a fifteen-year-old on a blind date.

Learning right then and there that Kerry was pregnant was reassuring in a way, as if the ugliness we'd all been surrounded by over the last few days was now sharing center stage with something wondrous and right.

Of course, my cell phone rang. It was Michael at Waters & Greene, so I took the call in my office.

"That was quick," I said, thanking him.

"Yeah, I'm surprised they found it at all, but our filing system is excellent."

"Obviously. So . . ."

"So, the coroner's report, while inconclusive, stated that the evidence present suggested anaphylactic shock, the result of an allergic reaction."

"Really? I thought that the death certificate stated food poisoning as the cause."

"Well, the original documents were in Spanish, but Dad had them translated. I see here that the Madrid detectives concluded that she had died from food poisoning, but that's not what the autopsy report says. I don't know why they said that, because the autopsy indicated dilated blood vessels, raised edematous patches of skin, and swelling in the esophagus. It looks like she suffocated as a result of an allergic reaction to something she ate." He paused. "I'm reading Dad's report, and while the coroner's report is somewhat inconclusive, with what we know now, I'd have to say I agree that it was an allergy gone awry. I suppose the only way to be one hundred percent sure would be to run further tests." He paused. "You said your client was Janice Huffington, but this report was filed for a client named Mort Benson. Who's that?" he asked.

"Must be the dead woman's brother, Janice's father. He initially hired the detectives. Does it say in the paperwork?"

"Let's see. . . . Ah, yeah," he said. "Initial interview. It was her brother who hired us."

"So the only way to be absolutely certain that she wasn't poisoned would be to exhume the body, right?" I asked, thinking out loud.

"That would be the next logical step," he agreed. "Anything else you need?"

"Would it be possible for you to fax pertinent documents to my office?"

"Sure, what's the number?"

I gave it to him.

"I hope this has helped," he said.

"Absolutely. I owe you one, Michael. If you ever need anything, just give me a call, okay?"

"Will do. Good luck."

I still didn't like it. I picked up the phone and called a friend at the local coroner's office.

"Jamie, I hate to bother you, but I have a quick question. Is it possible that a coroner could mistake anaphylactic shock for poisoning?"

"What kind of poison?"

"That's why I'm calling you. I don't have a clue."

"Sure, it's possible, but the only way to find out would be through blood tests. Essentially, you look at the electrolytes in the blood. Why?"

I told her my situation.

261

"Can you exhume the body?"

"I don't know."

"Was there a significant loss of bodily function when he or she was brought into the ER?"

"I might be able to find out, but she died over twenty-five years ago."

"With today's technology, it wouldn't be impossible to make a determination. Look, I've gotta run. Let me know if you need my help, though, okay?"

My next call was to Miguel. If he was at Huffington's I wanted to find out where Cissy was buried.

"Hey, boss, what's up?" he said when he heard my voice.

"Are you with Huffington?"

"Yeah. Just packing up the last box. Why? Whatcha need?"

"Ask Janice where Cissy is buried."

I waited, listening to the muffled conversation in the background.

"She was cremated."

"Shit. Whose choice was that?"

Again I waited.

"Cissy's. It was in her will. Why?"

"I'll tell you later. Just come back to the office."

When I got off the phone, I was feeling disappointed. It's not that I was hoping to find Harold guilty so much as I was seeking resolution so I could know with certainty on which side of the fence to stand. Here I was, still looking for absolute truths in life—the good and bad, black and white—as if they really existed.

Cremation brought an end to the search. It meant that there was nothing to test, nothing that modern technology could work magic upon and thus answer long-buried questions. Unless there was significant information that Jolly Greene had overlooked years ago, cremation meant we would never know what had happened in Madrid in 1975.

Sometimes you don't mind if an ending is left dangling, like in a romantic comedy or *His Dark Materials* trilogy by Philip Pullman, but this wasn't one of those times. I called Leslie at home, but there was no answer.

I wandered into Max's office and told him what I had learned.

"So what does that mean?" he asked.

"It means we'll never know if Harold had a part in Cissy's death or not."

"Well, if you look at probabilities based on the deaths of his other wives, the odds that he killed her are unlikely."

I stretched.

"What?" he asked.

"I don't know that it's that easy. Also, I'm thinking about the impact that all of this is going to have on Dorothy and Leslie."

"It has nothing to do with you."

"My company investigated his history. My involvement is assumed, and based on my personal history with Dorothy Washburn and her family, it's sure to open old wounds." There was no need to elucidate; Max knew the past as well as I did.

"Have you told Leslie?"

"I can't find her."

"Listen to me: Leslie and Dorothy have to deal with their stuff. As far as you're concerned, you'll handle it openly, honestly, and with great tact."

"That sounds like a pat answer."

"Not for everyone."

"I'm going to go work out. If Leslie calls, tell her I'll be back in a little while."

It felt good to be out on the street. The mild air felt like a second skin, and as I walked to the subway, I realized how good I felt, despite the Harold factor. Lucy was home. John would recover. Life was returning to normal.

At the corner of Broadway and Eighty-sixth Street, I saw Leslie and Auggie across the way, walking with a woman. Leslie's head was down and the woman was leaning into her, clearly making a point, given the gesturing of her hands. I watched them, watched as the woman laid a protective arm over Leslie's shoulder and squeezed it.

It was as if I were frozen in place. I crossed the street. Leslie didn't see me. I realized that the woman she was with was an old friend of ours, Fern, a woman I had known for years. As I neared them, Auggie started tugging at the leash to get to me. It seemed that both Fern and Leslie looked startled to see me.

"Hey," I said with a coldness I couldn't conceal. "I've been trying to reach you," I said to Leslie, as if Fern didn't exist.

"Oh. I bumped into Fern and she joined me for Auggie's walk. We were catching up."

"Hey, Syd."

"You live in Chelsea," I reminded Fern. "What are you doing up here?"

"I had to drop off some film at this woman's apartment. New project. Cool documentary, actually. *What?* You look pissed."

I turned back to Leslie as Auggie jumped up on me. Suddenly, I didn't like Fern or her messy "I'm too cool to brush my hair" style. Having felt distanced from Leslie over the past week and seeing her from a distance connect with my old friend sandwiched me between jealousy and embarrassment for the jealousy.

"I'll see you," I finally said as I gave Auggie a rub and turned to walk away.

"Wait," Leslie called out. Fern had the good grace to pretend to study the Gap windows as Leslie drew near. "What's up? Why are you acting so weird?"

I shook my head because there were no words.

"What? What's up?"

"I was surprised to see you with Fern, that's all." It sounded so childish. I hated every word that escaped my mouth.

"We're friends, Syd. We bumped into each other, that's all. What are you, jealous?" The hint of a smile played at her mouth, but her eyes were hidden behind her sunglasses.

"Should I be?" I locked my lips together too late.

"Don't be silly. Fern's family." She reached out and held my arm. "Honey, do you realize how many mood swings you've been having lately?"

Perhaps I didn't, but I was keenly aware of one taking place at that moment. Discomfort had given rise to anger so deep that I could barely breathe. How could I possibly answer her? Was she, like the butt-head Buddhist hit man—whom I had all but forgotten about—bringing my age into question? Could my lover, a woman younger than I, yes, but a woman nonetheless, really be suggesting that my reaction was hormonal and therefore not valid? Over the last several weeks, she had blamed my hormones for a host of reactions, but the hot flashes were really the only ones of merit.

I would gladly have spontaneously combusted at that very moment. Instead, I told her I needed to get going and would call her when I was back at the office. Without another word, I sprinted across the street and down into the subway. It wasn't until I hit Thirty-fourth Street that I realized I was shaking.

THIRTY-TWO

The night after John got home from the hospital, there was what started out as a simple celebration, so as not to tax him. Aunt Minnie, Max, and I put together a feast that included a watercress and arugula salad with an apricot vinaigrette, vegetarian chili with tofu, shrimp with a Cuban parsley sauce, homemade corn bread, and an assortment of pies brought in from the Little Pie Company for dessert. However, as soon as the word got out that John was home, everyone wanted to say a quick hello, and by the end of the evening, close to seventy-five people had come and gone. The pinot grigio and Corona flowed as easily as the sense of relief that John Cannady was on the road to recovery.

His fellow officers at the precinct had all chipped in and given John an X-Box so he could entertain himself as he recuperated. "Yeah, buddy, you can learn how to shoot the bad little girls the same way they learn to shoot us!" John's friend Hank Yarberg, who had been at the hospital with Peggy that first day, was clearly enjoying this reunion.

Only a small handful of friends knew all of the details behind the Cannady-Dexter odyssey, and that night, when the evening had come to a close, a few remaining intimates debated whether it was wise to let Lucy keep a dog that would only remind her of having been kidnapped. Public opinion was split about keeping the dog, but Lucy and Brutus were already inseparable, so it was really a moot point.

"Personally, I think if you keep the damned dog, Lucy will start to romanticize what the lunatic did and will never fully understand the severity of this whole episode," Aunt Minnie's boyfriend, EZ, said over cognac.

"Melinda's a sick woman," I murmured.

"All the more reason to expunge the memory," EZ insisted.

"Yes, so that when Lucy grows up, she, too, can be an ostrich, like ninety-eight percent of the world," said Minnie, taking a shot at EZ as she sat by the window so she could smoke.

"Tell me it doesn't creep you out that this girl wanted to be a boy?" EZ said to Minnie.

"I hardly think her lesbianism is the real issue here," Minnie replied, dismissing him.

Then Max jumped in. "That's not lesbianism. It's something very different. I mean, *Sydney's* a lesbian. . . ."

"Thank you for the public announcement." I nodded.

"If she gets help while she's incarcerated, which would mean placing her in a psychiatric facility, rather than simply tossing her into a cell, it might make a difference." This came from Peggy, who was sitting on the sofa next to John, holding his hand.

Apart from Peggy, John, and me, no one knew that there was a possibility that the Cannadys would continue to have a relationship with Melinda.

"That's hogwash, my dear. Pretty wishful thinking from a woman who is clearly a compassionate, bleeding—" EZ was cut off by Minnie.

"Ah, ah, ah, don't you dare add 'bleeding heart liberal,' Enoch Zarlin, or you'll find yourself without a date for a very long time."

"Careful, EZ. A man your age can't do for too long without a date." Max laughed, trying to lighten the mood.

"The bottom line is that Melinda, who was already walking a thin line between sanity and insanity, hooked up with Karl, who was easily able to wield power over her. He supplied the motive, the concept, the game plan, and the gun. If you really stop and think about it, Karl and the adoptive father are the ones to blame for all this."

"Oh, please don't try to present her as an innocent victim," interjected Enoch.

"Innocent, no, but she is a victim nonetheless," I said.

"I don't know, Syd. I think I'm with Enoch on this one," said Leslie, leaning against the doorway. "I mean, if you think about it, more people have been damaged in childhood than haven't. Whether induced by the circumstances of poverty, or war, or angry adults acting out, most children on this planet are scarred. So why should Melinda be treated differently from anyone else who has committed not one but two very serious crimes? You can't forget what *might* have happened if she hadn't been stopped. Christ, you seem to be forgetting that she took your goddaughter. She threatened to sell Lucy."

"Look, this is an imperfect world," I replied. "But it doesn't seem to me that the practice of an eye for an eye and a tooth for a tooth has made any appreciable difference in how people behave. You're right. Most children are scarred, but perhaps if compassion, instead of corporeal punishment or revenge, was enlisted when they behaved illegally or even inappropriately, this would be a different place." Even I was surprised by the passion behind my words.

"This from a woman who bags the bad guys," Max said as he got up to refill his drink.

"That's just it. I have seen so many ugly things in life, and despite that, I can tell you that an act of love has far more impact than one of rage."

"Forgive me, Sydney, but that's Pollyanna bullshit," EZ muttered, along with accompanying approval from Leslie, Marcy, and Max.

"I don't know," John interjected softly. "I've always believed that the only way the world can change for the better is if children get love in their formative years, but I don't know if compassion can make a difference *after* the fact. I keep thinking about the Matthew Shepard case and how his parents, after losing their son the way they did, decided not to ask for the death penalty but, rather, for life without parole. As far as I'm concerned, they took a high road, and I have profound respect for that. But then I read that when the killer came back from court, he was suddenly a big man in prison, a sort of cult hero, giving out autographs and becoming a role model to the younger inmates—younger than this prick, who was only twenty-two at the time. Anyway, when I read that, I thought, If I were Shepard's father, I would kill him with my bare hands. And that bothered me, because I am a compassionate, loving man, and yet there I was, experiencing a visceral reaction, advocating that violence be met with violence. I know that if Lucy had been hurt, I probably would have killed Melinda."

"I doubt it, Johnny," Minnie said, blowing a steady steam of smoke from her nostrils. "You know as well as I do that if we lose our humanity, we just lose."

"But we *are* losing, Minnie," Peggy said. "Violence and avarice have become so much a part of our culture that we don't even recognize that they've become a patina for even the more *evolved*, as it were. Even those of us sitting in this very room."

"That's not true. Sydney's not evolved," Max said.

"Nor is she greedy," I added without missing a beat.

"Television, advertising, entertainment—from film to sports—computer games, the current administration . . . it's all about the wrong message; it's all about greed and violence. And it makes me sick," Peggy said vehemently. "And as much as I would like to continue this discussion, the truth is, we are not going to solve the world's problems here this evening." She got to her feet. "John's had a very long day, and although I love each and every one of you, I am going to take my husband and put him to bed now, because I'm greedy; I want him around for a long time. Stay as long as you like, just be sure to shut off the lights when you go."

After kisses all around, John let himself be led away, rolling his eyes and promising that Peggy's mothering would have him up and dancing in no time.

"Sydney?" Peggy pulled me aside after John was in the bedroom.

"Yes?"

"You won't forget, will you?"

"I'm planning to go there first thing in the morning." I said as I touched her arm. What no one knew was that after great debate and soul-searching, John and Peggy had decided to cover the costs for Melinda's legal defense and I had promised to get detailed photographs of the bedroom dresser for the attorney to present to the psychiatrist they had hired to examine her. Neither Peggy nor John was interfering with the charges leveled against her, but they both felt a sense of personal obligation to try to help her, despite what she had done to them.

"Thanks." She paused. "Do you think I'm crazy?"

"Quite the contrary. I think you're both incredibly brave. It takes courage to be compassionate, Peg. I would, however, like to see your brother burn in hell." Karl had tried to blame everything on Melinda, insisting that he never knew that "Frank" was a woman, let alone his child, but the evidence was building against him. Fortunately, he had been unable to make bail, and his court-appointed lawyer had a reputation for being overworked. Karl hadn't pulled the trigger, but in my mind, he was far guiltier than Melinda.

Max and Marcy took Enoch and Minnie home while Leslie and I finished in the kitchen. We worked in easy silence, sweeping and wiping the counters and setting up the morning coffee.

Half an hour later, as we walked Auggie along Riverside Park for her evening relief, Leslie said, "You think I'm a witch, don't you?"

"I do? Why?" I asked as we neared the Soldiers' and Sailors' Monument at Eighty-ninth Street and Riverside Drive. Actually, there were myriad reasons to choose from, but I was determined to work through the hard stuff without enmity. "Oh, I get it. You mean the way you made my six-month collection of *New Yorker* magazines disappear? I admit I was miffed at first, but I have to say that it's nice to have that space magically reappear in my office."

She waited for Auggie to explore a particularly interesting hydrant. "No. Because of Dot."

"I don't think you're a witch, honey. I think you were concerned and, ultimately, hurt. Then again, you were the one who said we're all on a path. We gave your mom all the information we had and she chose to move forward with Harold. It's a choice. It may not be the best one, but she's an adult, just like us."

I slipped my arm through hers and drew her closer to me. "As Jerry Herman once said, 'Time heals everything.' You guys will work it out."

"I know. I just hate feeling so torn. I want Dot to be happy, but another part of me is so angry with her for not trusting us. I mean, she had more faith in that piece of shit than she did in her own kids. I think that's what I'm having such a hard time resigning myself to."

"Trust is a big issue." I let my understated platitude lie where I'd tossed it. In an attempt to sidestep it, I said, "I know what would make me feel better if I were in your shoes."

"Really? What?"

I reached into my pocket and pulled out a plastic bag. "Being the official pooper picker-upper."

"You're an idiot," she said with a smile.

"Thank you," I said as she took the bag. I followed her to the nearest trash basket. "You know, honey, life is too short not to settle differences with people you love and try to find peace inside."

"Are you talking about mom or us?" She seemed to be searching my eyes for something, but finally the dark fringe of her lashes shuttered her huge gray eyes and she turned away. "You're right," she said, her back to me.

"Sydney?"

I spun around, ready for a fight. The Buddhist hit man was walking toward us, his hands held up as if in surrender. I moved my left hand behind me to signal Leslie not to join us.

"I'm not here to cause a problem." The Voice stopped, keeping a six-foot distance between us. "We have to talk."

"What about?"

"I have some information you might find useful."

"Sydney, are you okay?" Leslie asked.

"You are," he assured me, and for some strange reason, I trusted him. Great, I didn't trust my lover when I saw her on the street with an old friend, but I trusted this man who had threatened to poke out my eyes and had called me old.

"Who are you? Who hired you?"

"Slow down. I want you to listen carefully, because I don't like repeating myself. Karl Dexter has a safe-deposit box at the Bowery Savings Bank on East Forty-second Street. It is registered under the name Ralph Jefferson. In it, you'll find, among other things, photographs that prove he was shadowing his sister and her family, as well as the specific location where he planned to dump the child."

His hard features and uneven complexion were softened in the glow of the streetlight.

"I give you this information for two reasons: because Karl lied to me and because I'm a father. He called me the day you went to see him at his office. I owed him a favor, which is why I agreed to pay a visit the next day. It doesn't matter that he told me you were looking for a woman, not a child. Suffice it to say I believed him, and like I said, I owed him one. Hours after you visited him, when the police took him in for questioning, he called me again in a panic. The man was an idiot, but I had a soft spot for him. That is, until I took a look in his safe-deposit box. The next afternoon, after you and I had talked, I got the key, went to the box, took everything out, and went to his home to deliver it to him. However, when I arrived in Jackson Heights, the police were there. Naturally, I left and took the package home, where I looked at the contents." He took a deep breath and shook his head. "I took the papers back to the bank and placed them in the box. I want nothing to do with this."

The Voice held out a potentially lethal hand and dropped a tiny red envelope into it. "Inside there is the key to the box. My guess is, you won't need it, since the police can get into it easily enough. But I don't want it, and I had a feeling I could trust you with this. Hopefully, there's enough there to send that crazy fuck away forever." He glanced at Leslie and then brought his gaze back to me. "Good luck."

"Thanks."

He turned to go and I called out, "Wait."

He stopped and cocked his head.

"The last time we met, you said you were being easy with me because of someone from the past. Who?"

His long face brightened. "Huh? Oh, that. I was just fucking with your head." He winked and returned to the shadows of Riverside Park.

On the way home, we passed other dogs being walked, most of whom Auggie granted a quick sniff, but nothing more. While I called Gil on my cell phone and gave him the particulars, she tugged at the leash as if she had a reason for rushing home.

"Do you want to invite your mom for breakfast tomorrow?" I asked Leslie in the elevator. "I won't be here, so you'll have privacy."

"Where will you be?" She unclipped Auggie's collar.

"I have to go to Brooklyn." As I said it, I couldn't shake the image of Fern looming in my mind's eye, too large to ignore, too stupid to acknowledge.

"What time?" she asked as I unlocked the front door.

"I have to pick up something in Boerum and have it uptown by ten, so I'll need to be in Brooklyn by eight o'clock."

Once Auggie had her bedtime treats and all evening rituals were completed, Leslie climbed into bed, tossed and turned for a good ten minutes, turned the light on again, picked up the phone, and dialed. I kept my eyes closed and my back to her, but she knew I was listening when she said, "Hello, Mom. It's me."

THIRTY-THREE

For this visit to Melinda's apartment, I had the key. Eventually, the lease for 3B would revert to the landlord, but I didn't know whether she'd paid her rent in advance or what plans would eventually be made for the storage of her belongings. All I knew for sure was that no one was prepared to put up bail for her, which meant that she would be in jail, or a psychiatric hospital, until her case was brought to court, which was a long way off. It was easy to envision her things set out on the street, to be picked over by neighbors and garbage collectors. The television and stereo, books, housewares, and furniture would be plucked off the curb in a matter of minutes, then the clothes. But things like her papers and photographs would probably only interest a collector of crime memorabilia, or crime writers—two of whom had already approached her. I didn't know what would happen to the chest of drawers, though I couldn't imagine it ending up as landfill. It was easier to see it in a museum of American Crafts or in Mary Sullivan's personal collection.

I was surprised to see that apart from the few signs that the police had been through the apartment, nothing much had been moved since I had last been there, which meant that the place was getting pretty rank. I opened the windows and tossed all potentially foul-smelling items into the trash, which I would deposit in the garbage bin as I left.

It was an odd sensation going through another person's home when she wasn't there. Surrounded by the things that comprised her life, I was completely absorbed with them, yet at the same time they seemed both vulnerable and inconsequential.

As I took detailed digital photos of the dresser for her defense team, I felt the physical effect of being sandwiched between love and rage and the impact that each of those emotions could have on a single life. Clearly, Melinda's soul had become a battleground, the place where she struggled between the desire to be loved and the panic that came from thinking she didn't deserve it. As it turned out, the photos on her nightstand were a pictorial history of Melinda's development into Frank, which had started at a young age. It wasn't something I wanted to leave for the curious or put in the trash, so I stuffed them all into a manila envelope, thinking if it didn't help the psychiatrist understand her, it would be one less thing lost from her own life.

Before leaving, I made a note to call Mary Sullivan. After the news hit the papers, Mary had called and asked how to contact Melinda. "The poor kid needs a friend right now, and I seem to be the only likely candidate," she'd told me.

Once out on the street again, I felt the weight of Melinda's reality lift off me, like a shroud of sadness being literally peeled away.

It was a perfect morning. There wasn't a cloud in the absolutely blue sky, and I thought that after delivering these pictures, it might be a great day to play hooky and take Auggie for a walk in the Palisades.

My first instinct was to reach for the phone to call Leslie, but I didn't. She was with her mother, trying to reconnect the tattered threads that had once been an ironclad connection. I tried to shake off the passing thought that perhaps she wasn't with Dot. Instead, I called my aunt Minnie, who was always good for a distraction.

"Hey, what are you doing?"

"Reading a list of phobias. Listen to this: Arachibutyrophobia. Know what that is?"

"I haven't a clue."

"The fear of peanut butter sticking to the roof of the mouth. Or how about this . . . geniophobia?"

"I don't know. Either the fear of denim or women named Gina."

"Wrong. It's the fear of chins." Her laughter was just what I needed to get me out of my own head.

"Nudophobia, Numerophobia. Octophobia."

"What's that? The fear of octopus?"

"No! The fear of the number eight." She was clearly loving this, and I loved that fact that my old aunt took the time to do things like read about phobias in her spare time. "Here's one, a fear of wet dreams."

"What's that called?" I asked as I crossed the bridge into the city.

"I can't pronounce it. Oneirogmophobia, something like that."

"You want to have lunch with me today?" I asked.

"Yes. Jean George has a great lunch special. Twenty bucks for three courses. Add a glass of wine and its sixty something, but who cares. Let's celebrate."

"What are we celebrating, Min?"

"Okay, I am going to shut my eyes and randomly choose a phobia we can celebrate today, okay?"

"Okay."

"Here we go . . . phasmophobia, the fear of ghosts. Oooh, I like that one. What time shall we meet?"

"Noon? I'll pick you up."

"No, it will be easier to take a taxi. There's no parking in that area. See you then, my dear."

And she was gone, leaving me with a smile plastered to my face. What with Lucy, Leslie, Peggy, Melinda/Frank, Karl, John, Harold, and Fern, it had been a roller coaster of a week, illustrating once again that there was nothing constant but change.

I spent the rest of the drive uptown trying to find something else in the universe that was constant, but there was nothing. Instead of fulminating on my Fernophobia (an unsubstantiated fear of women named Fern), I would spend the afternoon at one of the best restaurants in town, celebrating the fear of ghosts with one of my favorite people.

Ah, change.